The world ... essed everything from ... sublime to the ridiculous while watching the decades-... feud between the world's richest ... ders, the Blackstones, and the ... ... But yesterday's scene ... ops even that. Blackstones' exclusive ... supermodel, Briana Davenport – the "Face of Blackstone" – was seen on the arm of none other than supposed enemy Jarrod Hammond.

The two were spotted together at the roulette table in the Crown Casino last week, and yesterday at the Melbourne Grand Prix. "They looked to be a *lot* more than friends," said one attentive attendee. According to an inside source, Davenport's contract with Blackstones is soon to be up for renewal. Locking lips with a Hammond may not be Davenport's best move to ensure longevity with the diamond moguls. Then again, she may not care, if the consolation prize is the sexy Melbourne millionaire. One thing's for sure: at Blackstones, the flawless diamonds may be costly, but the family high jinks are priceless.

Satin & a Scandalous Affair
by Jan Colley

SYDNEY'S SCENE

In the decades-old feud between the world's richest gem dealers, the Blackstones and the Hammonds, no one and nowhere is off limits. Not even Danielle Hammond, the up-and-coming jewellery designer who thought she'd escaped family high jinks up north in the Port Douglas tropics.

The flamboyant Dani has been hired by broker Quinn Everard to design for him – the same man who some time ago nearly destroyed her fledgling career with his caustic critique of her work. What would make the colourful Ms Hammond agree to that unique assignment? And just who is Quinn's mysterious client?

The Blackstones and Hammonds, no strangers to rumours, are once again the topic of water-cooler conversation as rumours abound that the missing son of recently deceased founder Howard Blackstone may indeed have been located.

Before his death, Howard – dubbed "the man people love to hate" – left his billion-dollar diamond firm to the missing son, James, who was kidnapped over thirty years ago. Tempers are high at Blackstone's Pitt Street offices – where the diamonds are rare, but the drama is rampant!

Mistress & a Million Dollars
MAXINE SULLIVAN

Satin & a Scandalous Affair
JAN COLLEY

MILLS & BOON®

Pure reading pleasure™

*First published in Great Britain 2009
by Harlequin Mills & Boon Limited,
Eton House, 18-24 Paradise Road, Richmond, Surrey TW9 1SR*

Mistress & a Million Dollars © Maxine Sullivan 2008
Satin & a Scandalous Affair © Janet Colley 2008

ISBN: 978 0 263 87090 9

51-0209

*Printed and bound in Spain
by Litografía Rosés S.A., Barcelona*

MISTRESS &
A MILLION DOLLARS

by
Maxine Sullivan

Dear Reader,

When I sold my first book to the Desire™ line back in January 2006, the senior editor, Melissa Jeglinski, commented that the Down Under Desire authors should put a continuity series together – and the DIAMONDS DOWN UNDER series was born.

With much enthusiasm we set about coming up with story lines. I'd always wanted to write an indecent-proposal story, and this glitter and glamour series was the perfect backdrop for that. I really enjoyed writing about a hero who desires the heroine so much he is prepared to pay her a million dollars to sleep with him. Now that's desire!

I had a great time with this book, and I'm so proud to have worked with such talented writers. Writing this series bonded us not only in friendship, but also as a "family" of authors. And, yes, a family who has arguments and who want to strangle each other at times. But I wouldn't have missed out on this for anything.

I hope you enjoy our series. Personally, I think it's fabulous.

Happy reading!

Maxine

MAXINE SULLIVAN

credits her mother for her lifelong love of romance novels, so it was a natural extension for Maxine to want to write her own romances. She's very excited about seeing her work in print and is thrilled to be the second Australian to write for the Desire™ line.

Maxine lives in Melbourne, Australia, and over the years has travelled to New Zealand, the UK and the USA. In her own backyard, her husband's job ensured they saw the diversity of the countryside, including spending many years in Darwin in the tropical north, where some of her books are set. She is married to Geoff, who has proven his hero status many times over the years. They have two handsome sons and an assortment of much-loved, previously abandoned animals.

Maxine would love to hear from you and can be contacted through her website at www. maxinesullivan.com.

To Melissa Jeglinski for "everything."
To the Down Under Desire authors –
with admiration.

One

"*W*e are gathered here today in the face of this company to join together Kimberley Blackstone and Ricardo Perrini in matrimony...."

Jarrod Hammond heard the words of the female marriage celebrant, but his eyes were drawn not to the bride, but to the woman sitting opposite him in the horseshoe circle surrounding his cousin Kim and her soon-to-be husband, Ric Perrini.

Adrenaline kicked in as he leaned back in his chair and let his gaze rake over Briana Davenport, the Australian supermodel who was the face of Blackstone Diamonds. Through the massive yacht's large windows behind her, the late-afternoon sun highlighted the most glorious harbor in the world and created a picture-perfect backdrop for her beauty.

Framed by the Opera House and Sydney Harbour Bridge, and dressed in a silky, pale blue pantsuit that flowed as she moved, she was elegance and sophistication. The epitome of glamour. A crowning glory for the diamond company she symbolized. He could see why Howard Blackstone had chosen her to represent his business.

And just as expensive, Jarrod mused rather cynically, noting with satisfaction the exact moment she saw him looking at her. Her eyelids flickered just a bit before she looked away, but only someone with an internal radar for this woman would pick up on it.

Someone like him.

"If anyone can show just cause—" the celebrant continued.

Much to Jarrod's displeasure, his internal radar was constantly tuned on Briana. It had been that way from the moment he'd set eyes on her at his brother's marriage to her sister four years ago. It had been on high ever since, even though he knew Briana had a serious flaw. An *expensive* serious flaw. She liked money, and plenty of it, and went through it like it was going out of fashion, according to her now-dead sister, Marise.

Of course, being attuned to Briana didn't help when everywhere he turned she was there in front of him: up on billboards…on television…in glossy magazines. Nor was it easy knowing they lived in the same city in another part of the country. Thankfully with her jet-setting around the world as a supermodel, and him with his law practice, Melbourne was big enough for the two of them not to run into each other.

"Ric, do you take Kimberley for your lawful wedded wife, to live in the holy estate of matrimony? Will you love, honor, comfort and…"

But now, seeing Briana in the flesh again—her oh-so-delicious flesh—reminded him why he'd inveigled an invitation to the Blackstone Jewellery launch here in Sydney last Friday and flown up from Melbourne. And why he was glad he'd accepted Kim's invitation today. Being a Hammond at a Blackstone wedding was never going to be easy, but with Briana here, the day suddenly seemed full of sensual possibilities, despite the presence of millionaire Jake Vance, who once again partnered her.

"Kimberley, do you take Ric for your lawful wedded husband, to live in the holy estate of matrimony? Will you love, honor, comfort and…"

Jarrod's mouth tightened as he looked at the man sitting beside Briana. The pair had been photographed together in the Melbourne papers at the St. Valentine's Day races a few weeks ago. And again last Friday at the jewelry launch. Were the two of them lovers? Probably, he decided, not pleased by the burst of irrational jealousy he felt at the thought of her in the other man's bed.

"May this ring be blessed so that he who gives it…" the woman continued.

Dammit, was he being a glutton for punishment by going after her? Hadn't he already made his decision to bed her? A decision based on wanting to find out all he could about her sister for his brother's sake. He'd seen

Matt only two weeks ago and had been shocked at how worn and bitter he'd become. Jarrod and Matt may have been adopted, but they were closer than blood brothers, and he'd do everything in his power to make sure Matt found some inner peace—no matter what it took.

Or whom.

But he couldn't blame his brother for being bitter when his wife, Marise, had died from injuries sustained in a plane crash almost two months ago, along with Howard Blackstone and four others. It had conjured up a myriad of questions: questions that no one had any answers to, except maybe Briana Davenport.

"Wear it as a symbol of love and commitment…"

Surely Briana knew why her sister had been on Howard's plane before it crashed. And she knew if her own sister was having an affair with Howard, the enemy of the Hammond family ever since his greed parted the two family factions many years ago. She just wasn't saying.

And then there'd been the shock of Marise having been named as a beneficiary in Howard's will. A seven-sum figure and the Blackstone jewelry collection was a considerable inheritance for a young mistress. And that begged the question as to whether Blake was really Howard's son and not Matt's. Blake certainly had the same dark hair as Howard, unlike Matt's sandy-blond head. It made Jarrod sick to his stomach to think about it.

"You may now seal the promises you have made with each other with a kiss."

Dammit, the Blackstones had caused enough pain for his family. His parents would be devastated if they found out that Blake was not their grandson, but their great-nephew, instead. Not that it would make any difference to the way they felt about the child. They'd proven that by adopting him and Matt all those years ago. As for Matt and how he would feel about Blake not being his own…

"Ladies and gentlemen, I present to you Mr. and Mrs. Ricardo Perrini."

Just then, as if his angry thoughts had drawn Briana's blue eyes back to him, Jarrod held her gaze among the clapping and the cheers, and let her know with a look what he had decided. She was the woman he wanted.

She was the woman he would have.

While she was waiting to be seated for the wedding feast, Briana sipped champagne and listened with delight as the beaming and slender Jessica Cotter talked about her newly announced pregnancy. They'd spoken last Friday night at the jewelry launch, but it had been a busy night for both of them and their chat had only been brief. Now it was great to be able to catch up with each other.

"Ryan's thrilled," Jessica said, sending the man in question an adoring look across the deck where he stood talking to his just-married sister, Kim.

And the ruthless and handsome Ryan Blackstone smiled back. A warm, love-filled look that was meant for one woman and one woman only—his fiancée.

"You're one very lucky woman, Jess," Briana said with a smile, envious of Jessica's happiness but so very pleased for her.

"I know," Jessica said, grinning. Then her gaze slid to the woman standing next to Ryan, brother and sister clearly both Blackstones. "And doesn't Kim look absolutely gorgeous? That white gown is exquisite, but with her dark hair and green eyes, she looks stunning."

Briana's gaze slid over Kimberley Blackstone, now Kimberley Perrini, who wore an elegant couture wedding dress. "I've got to agree. She's stunning."

"I bet Ric thinks so, too." Jessica gave a dreamy sigh. "This must be so different from the first time they were married in Las Vegas. It just goes to prove that divorce isn't always final."

"I guess it all depends on the couple," Briana said, thinking about some of the people she knew in the modeling world. Her profession wasn't easy on a marriage. She'd seen some wonderful partnerships, as well as some horrors.

"By the way," Jessica said, interrupting her thoughts. "Did you contact Quinn Everard yet about those diamonds Marise left in your safe?"

At the thought of her dead sister, Briana's heart squeezed tight. "Yes, I phoned him the other day. I've been so busy lately that I just kept putting it off. What with work and trying to help Dad cope with Mum's death and now Marise's, it hasn't been a priority."

"That's understandable," Jessica said sympathetically. "You just make sure you take care of yourself, too."

"I will," Briana said, her eyes thanking her friend. "Anyway, Quinn said to drop the diamonds off at his office. He's away at the moment but I can leave them with his office manager. I'll do that tomorrow morning." She grimaced. "Frankly, I'll be glad to know their value so that I can decide what to do with them. Matt said he didn't want anything of Marise's, but I just can't keep them."

Jessica nodded. "Well, Quinn's the man. He's got an excellent reputation as a gem appraiser. He—" All at once her gaze focused on the men across the room and she scowled. "Oh no, I think I'm needed. Ric and Ryan look like they've had enough of each other for a while." She rolled her eyes. "Men!"

Briana chuckled as she watched Jessica hurry away, but she knew that tensions associated with members of the Blackstone family right now weren't anything to laugh about.

Knew it only too well, unfortunately.

Not that any of them held the controversial deaths of her sister and their father against her. They'd all been very considerate. Ric and Ryan had treated her with respect, and Jessica and Kim had become good friends. Not to mention the elegant Sonya Hammond and her charming daughter, Danielle. Though the latter two were not blood relations to Howard Blackstone, they were still related, and they'd shown her kindness at Howard's funeral, and welcomed her warmly today.

Of course, she couldn't think about the Blackstones without thinking about Matt Hammond. Her brother-in-law could be hardnosed but he was also a fine, upstanding man, and hadn't deserved the legacy of doubts her sister had left him and their young son, Blake. His adoptive parents, Katherine and Oliver Hammond, had been wonderful to Marise, too, but her sister hadn't really appreciated them.

As for the older adopted son…it was obvious to her that beneath Jarrod Hammond's veneer of sophistication, he fully believed she and Marise had shared the same liking for the good life that Marise had enjoyed as Matt's wife.

Only, nothing was further from the truth. Marise may have been flighty and always looking for something more, but *she* was happy with her lot in life. And for that she still felt guilty. If only she'd been closer to Marise, maybe then she'd understand why her sister had been keeping company with Howard Blackstone and why he'd left all his jewelry to Marise in his will. But no matter how she'd tried to breach the gap, they were poles apart. She didn't understand how Jarrod couldn't see that.

Just then, her eyes met the man in question across the breadth of the middle deck, and a hush seemed to descend upon everything in the room. An imaginary hush, obviously, though there was nothing imaginary about the hunger in Jarrod Hammond's eyes. The hunger had always been there, waiting…for what, she wasn't sure. He'd certainly made no move to further anything between them over the years.

Not that it would have done him any good. She wasn't getting involved with another high-powered male. Not after Patrick, her ex-business manager and lover, had invested most of her money in a "surefire" deal and had lost it.

No, she didn't need a man in her life.

And definitely not Jarrod Hammond.

Suddenly he started to walk toward her. She wanted to run as fast and as far away as she could, up the stairs and out on the top deck where the breeze off the harbor would cool her heated cheeks, but her strappy high heels seemed fixed to the floor.

And then he was standing in front of her, and she could do nothing but face him and try not to let him overwhelm her with his sheer presence.

"Hello, Briana," he murmured as he leaned in close and kissed her cheek, his firm lips lingering just a whisper too long. "We seem to be running into each other a lot lately."

She tingled. "Yes, we do," she said, then saw his eyes darken at her husky tone. Quickly she cleared her throat, trying not to show that she cared he had touched her. "Um…but I didn't expect to see you here, Jarrod."

"Really?" A cool light came into his eyes. "Why not? Kim is my cousin."

"Yes." And one he must know more than the others, seeing that Kim had worked for the Hammonds until recently.

But that was merely a reason for his presence, not an explanation. The Hammonds and the Blackstones, despite being related, had thrown some pretty wild accusations at each other's dynasties over the years. Marise had once briefly mentioned how Jarrod's father, Oliver, had accused Howard Blackstone of some pretty dastardly things, including marrying Oliver's sister for monetary gain. In retaliation, Howard had accused Oliver of arranging the kidnapping of his two-year-old son, James Blackstone. The child had never been seen again.

"Maybe I'm surprised to see *you* here," Jarrod said, cutting across her thoughts, and she knew nothing much would surprise this man. She had the feeling he'd known she'd be here today.

"Kim and I have been working together on some of the Blackstone events," she said, a touch defensively. "We've become friends."

"Good. She could do with another friend right now."

For a moment, Briana thought he was being sarcastic, but then she realized he was sincere. Something inside her softened. Kim had certainly had it tough these past few months, but coming from him—a Hammond who on his brother's behalf now had another reason to hate any Blackstone—the comment was even more surprising. Perhaps he wasn't as coldhearted as she'd thought?

"She looks beautiful, doesn't she?" Briana said, turning away from him to look at her friend, mainly so she didn't have to look at Jarrod.

"Yes, she does," he said in a seductive voice that made her spin back toward him. He was staring at *her.*

Whatever had softened inside her now turned to mush. She had to force herself not to redden, her years of modeling doing nothing to stop the faint warmth rising up her neck.

She took a sip of champagne, then, "What did you think of the ceremony?" she asked for something to say.

His knowing blue eyes held hers a moment longer before breaking contact. He shrugged. "A wedding's a wedding."

It was such a typical male reaction that she had to

smile. "Really? We're at a lavish affair on a luxury cruiser in the middle of Sydney Harbour on a perfect autumn day, and the daughter of one of Australia's richest men has just re-married her late father's right-hand man." She gave a rueful smile. "No, this wedding isn't just any wedding. This is a *Blackstone* wedding in all its glory."

The corners of his mouth curved with the beginnings of a sexy smile. "Do Blackstones pay you to promote them like this?"

She laughed. "I'd be stupid *not* to promote them, don't you think?"

He paused, his eyes hardening as they swept over her features. "And you're definitely not stupid, are you?"

Her smile disappeared. "That doesn't sound like a compliment."

Something came and went in his eyes. "I admire how far you've come in this business."

She tried not to stiffen, but she did anyway. What was he implying? "It still doesn't sound very flattering," she challenged.

His lips twisted, then he appeared to mentally back off. "So you like to be flattered, do you?"

She realized he'd backed off only because he chose to. "Didn't you know? I need to be flattered at least once every hour," she mocked, then arched a slim eyebrow. "After all, isn't that what all models are about?"

His eyes narrowed slightly, but there was a sardonic tilt to his mouth. "But you're a *super*model."

"So I need to be *super*-flattered," she returned as a waiter offered to refill her half-empty glass of champagne. She put her hand over the glass and shook her head. She didn't need more to drink. She needed her wits about her.

"I'm told I'm usually good at *super*-flattering a woman," Jarrod murmured, once the waiter moved away.

Her gaze flew back to the man beside her and panic stirred in her chest. "I'm sure you are. Usually." In a deliberate movement, she looked around for her date. Where on earth was Jake when she needed him?

And then she saw him listening with mild amusement to Danielle Hammond. The other woman's coppery curls bounced as she moved her head animatedly, her full mouth wide and smiling in a friendly fashion.

"Looks like your date is occupied," Jarrod said pointedly.

She glanced sideways at him and shrugged.

"So you're not the jealous type?"

"Not in the least." She enjoyed Jake's company but, as handsome and charming as he was, he was only a friend. And thankfully he was someone who had nothing to do with the Blackstone dynasty and all its associated problems. But she wasn't about to tell Jarrod any of that. "Danielle's such a sweetie," she added to show her non-jealousy.

"That she is," he agreed slowly, but she could hear in his voice that he was still looking at her, trying to get inside her head and figure her out.

Pretending not to notice, Briana let her gaze wander around the room, forcing herself to concentrate on the other guests. Anything but concentrate on Jarrod Hammond...or let him concentrate on her.

There were about sixty guests and most of the faces were strangers to her, but she did see Sonya Hammond talking to Garth Buick, an urbane and charming man who'd been Howard Blackstone's company secretary. They were only a few feet away and Briana could hear them talking about going sailing together. Something about the way they looked at each other—or perhaps it was the way they were trying *not* to look at each other—made Briana wonder if there was something between the two of them. If so, they were a good match. In her late forties, Sonya had a tall, willowy elegance that complemented the trim and well-toned Garth, who was just a few years older.

"Are you always so trusting?" Jarrod said, bringing her focus back on him.

She'd grimaced. "Unfortunately, no."

His glance sharpened. "What happened to rob you of your trust?"

Heavens, how was she going to get out of this one? She only had to look at that firm jaw to know he wasn't a man to give up when he wanted something.

"Nothing of interest," she said airily, but her heart was pounding in her chest.

"Oh, but I think there is," he said, confirming her suspicions.

"Let it go, Jarrod. It's nothing important." And to prove it, she scooped a canapé off a tray as a waiter passed by.

"Let me be the judge of that."

"Ahh, but I thought you were a property lawyer, not a judge."

His lips began to twitch. "And you're obstructing the course of justice, Briana."

"Or guilty of contempt," she mocked, then popped the canapé into her mouth, feeling pleased with herself.

He laughed out loud, taking her unawares. "I didn't realize you had such a smart mouth."

Because she'd never let him know it before, that's why, she mused, chewing the delicate morsel. She'd never let him get close enough.

So why was she letting him get close now? More importantly, why was he *trying* to get close now, she wondered, watching as his gaze fell to her lips and darkened, as if he were thinking about kissing her. She quickly swallowed, then took another sip of champagne.

Just then, the sound of a helicopter rent through the air as it came close and swooped the yacht. Far too close for Briana's piece of mind.

And obviously for Ric Perrini's.

"Damn the media!" Ric growled, striding across the middle deck to look out the side window of the cruiser right near Briana. "Can't they leave us in peace for one day?"

It broke the moment between her and Jarrod, for which she should have been grateful but wasn't. Instead she kept remembering that gorgeous laugh of his. It sent shivers of desire down her spine.

"I'm already on it," Kim said, coming over to her new husband and slipping her arm inside his. "The captain should be on the phone right now to the water police. They'll sort it out."

"They'd better," Ric warned.

"Anyway, we have more immediate problems. The photographer's about to have chickens if we don't let him take some pictures of us with our guests." She smiled at Briana and Jarrod. "You two will have your photo taken with us, won't you?"

Briana's fingers tightened around her glass. She knew it hadn't been Kim's intention, but even a small mention of her and Jarrod doing something together made her uncomfortable.

"Perhaps later, Kim," Jarrod said with a tight smile, then excused himself and headed to where an older couple stood looking out the back of the cruiser.

There was a flash of disappointment in Kim's eyes and Ric stiffened beside his wife, before she quickly gave his arm a squeeze. For all that Jarrod was here today, it was apparent Kim's falling out with his brother was still an issue between the Hammonds and the Blackstones.

For the Hammonds anyway.

To cover the awkward moment, Briana pasted on her best smile for the new bride. "Hey, that's all the more coverage for me then. You know how I love being in front of the camera."

Kim smiled with gratitude. "Thanks," she murmured, just as the photographer appeared.

Later, when everyone sat down to dinner, Sonya asked Briana how she managed to look so good in front of a camera when it was such hard work.

"You don't know the half of it," Briana said, smiling across the table at the other woman.

"I'd love to hear about it," Sonya said, the warmth in her eyes belying her cool reserve.

Briana obligingly chatted about some of the more obvious facets of modeling, yet she knew they'd all be surprised if she told them the truth. She'd fallen into modeling as a teenager but much preferred being behind the camera than in front of it.

Perhaps one day after she'd made enough money to recoup the money Patrick had lost, she'd further her dream. Until then it really wasn't such a hardship smiling for the camera or showcasing Blackstone jewelry. And it certainly wasn't a hardship attending a Blackstone wedding like this one.

Except for Jarrod.

She groaned inwardly. Lately he was turning up everywhere she went. At the jewelry launch the other night she'd never felt so self-conscious being on show before, but seeing him there in the audience, feeling his eyes upon her, she felt as if she was showcasing *herself,* not the Blackstone jewelry.

And now here he was at the wedding, sitting next to Vincent Blackstone, the late Howard Blackstone's older brother, deep in conversation. From time to time, though, his eyes were on *her.*

"You seem to be pretty cozy with Jarrod Hammond," Jake murmured in her ear, startling her when she must have looked at Jarrod once too often.

Trying to appear nonchalant, she glanced at Jake and

saw a very male look in his eyes that reminded her too much of Jarrod. This guy hadn't missed a thing going on around him. No doubt such ability was part of the reason he was now a rich and successful businessman.

But at least he wasn't the jealous type, she mused. "We're distant in-laws, that's all. Nothing special."

"Really?" he mocked in an arrogant way that said she wasn't fooling him.

"You know, Jake," she said, getting a little irritated being surrounded by males who thought they knew everything. "I think all the testosterone on this boat must be keeping it afloat."

A surprised look entered his eyes then he burst out laughing. For a moment she stared at him, then began to smile in return. It *was* quite funny, now she came to think about it.

"I'd have thought a beautiful woman like yourself would be used to being surrounded by testosterone," Jake teased.

"In the modeling world?" she jokingly scoffed, and received a chuckle from Jake.

"No, I guess not," he agreed with a rueful grin.

Suddenly she caught Jarrod looking at the two of them. A slither went over her skin and quickly she looked away just as the waiter brought the next course. Once the food was served, talk at the table turned to other things.

Briana deliberately didn't look at Jarrod after that, preferring instead to concentrate on the speeches and proceedings, though she was aware of him. Afterward, dark descended and they all moved to the well-lit top deck where the bride and groom began their first dance. Before too long, others had joined them, including her and Jake.

As for Jarrod, he seemed to have disappeared. She remained on edge, at first expecting him to show up at any tick of the clock, but when he didn't, she quickly pushed aside the disappointment that filled her. She wasn't going to let herself be disappointed by a man again, she reminded herself, then promptly did the opposite when she saw the lights from a small boat moving away from the cruiser, taking Jarrod back to shore.

He hadn't even said goodbye, she thought, then something on the shoreline caught her attention. Myriad lights began to flash as the small boat approached them.

The media.

Not that Jarrod would give them a second thought. No doubt he'd stride through the pack to a waiting car like he was parting the Red Sea.

After that the evening seemed flat. Briana smiled and talked, and when it came time for the yacht to return to shore, she was glad that the security people held back the media circus while they made their way into a fleet of cars.

Lights flashed in her eyes as Jake guided her into the back of a limousine, but the media's attention soon focused back on Kim and Ric, who had insisted they would only leave the boat after all their guests had alighted.

"They're a brave couple," Jake said, shaking his head as a shower of flashes seemed to light up the night sky through the back window of the car.

"Yes," Briana agreed. "And very determined to show the world a united front."

His smile disappeared. "I can understand that."

The limousine drove off but they didn't talk much while it weaved through the streets of Sydney to her apartment building. Then Jake walked her to her door.

"I had a good time," he said, moving in closer, pushing a strand of hair off her cheek.

Briana knew it was a prelude to a kiss and she moved in closer, too. Jake had kissed her before and it had always been nice, but tonight she suddenly wanted him to kiss her like he meant it. As if she was the only woman in the world he wanted.

Only, when the kiss finished, one thing was clear. Jake's kiss had been just a kiss. And by the wry glint in his eye he knew it, too.

"I think you'd better get some sleep," he said, tapping her on the end of her nose with his index finger. And then he pivoted and headed back to the elevator.

Briana watched him go with a sinking feeling in her stomach. Jake was an extremely handsome man who knew how to treat a woman right. And he knew how to kiss. It was just a pity she hadn't felt anything when his lips were on hers. Not like she would if Jarrod Hammond had kissed her.

Of that she was certain.

Two

The next morning Briana caught a taxi to Quinn Everard's office and left the diamonds with his office manager. Then, after another couple of days in Sydney, including lunching with her agent, she caught a plane back to Melbourne on the Wednesday, and drove to her father's house to check on him first. Then she'd go home to her apartment on the other side of the city. She still had to prepare for the Moomba Fashion Show this coming Labor Day weekend at the casino.

So it was mid-afternoon by the time Briana parked in the driveway of the solid brick home that her parents bought when they'd moved to Melbourne from Sydney nearly thirty years ago. They'd never been rich but had been comfortable. Her mother had even insisted on sending her and Marise to one of the top private schools here in Melbourne, after a spinster aunt had left her some money.

Now, when Ray Davenport opened the front door to her, Briana noted with concern that her father was looking tired. He'd been through so much, having kept her mother's secret of the cancer that ravaged her body, until the end, when her mother had become so ill he'd finally told their daughters she was dying.

"Want some coffee, honey?" he asked, walking ahead of her into the kitchen.

"Thanks, Dad. That would be lovely." She followed him, noting the stoop to his shoulders. "By the way, I dropped those diamonds off for an appraisal."

He looked over his shoulder with a frown. "Diamonds?"

"The ones Marise left in my safe."

His face cleared. "Oh, that's right. You found them in your safe after the plane crash, didn't you?"

"Yes." Overcome with grief, she'd nearly forgotten Marise asking for the safe combination to keep some jewelry in there.

Briana had thought nothing of giving the combination to her sister. She'd also let Marise stay in her Sydney apartment once she and her father returned to Melbourne, after Barbara Davenport had been buried next to her own parents in Waverley Cemetery. It was then that Marise seemed to go off the rails, those last few weeks before the plane crash. Their mother's death had devastated Marise, but for her sister to remain in Sydney had been unwarranted.

Especially after she'd started to be seen around town with Howard Blackstone.

Especially when she had a husband and a small son back in New Zealand waiting for her.

No wonder Matt had said he didn't give a damn about any jewelry belonging to Marise. But she knew her brother-in-law wasn't thinking straight, and that was part of the reason she'd decided to get them appraised. Perhaps if they were valuable they'd be worth keeping for Blake as a memento of his mother. Or maybe one day Matt would forgive his late wife and want the diamonds back. In the meantime, getting the diamonds valued was something *she* could do for her dead sister.

"So you're getting them appraised, you say?" her father said now, bringing her back to the moment. Again she noticed he didn't look well.

She stood in the kitchen doorway, her forehead creasing. "Dad, are you okay?"

A moment crept by.

"Dad?"

He looked up at her then, and there was a despairing look in his eyes that had her sucking in a sharp breath. "I'm a thief, Briana. I've stolen some money."

The breath caught in her lungs. "Wh-what?"

"I stole from Howard Blackstone."

She stared in astonishment. "My God! How much?"

He paused, then let out a shaky sigh. "One million dollars."

* * *

Briana was still reeling from her father's confession as she sat at the roulette table at the casino on Saturday evening. It had taken such an effort to keep her mind on the fashion show today, then again at the cocktail party this evening, but somehow she'd put a professional smile on her face. Afterward, not ready to go home to an empty apartment, she had stayed on.

It wasn't every week a daughter learned her father had stolen a million dollars. And from a "secret" account he'd been told about while working as an accountant for one of Australia's richest men thirty years ago, after Howard's previous accountant had passed on that bit of information.

Nor was the reason her father had taken the money in the first place enough to stop Ray Davenport from going to jail. Medical expenses for his wife's cancer, then a world cruise after a terminal diagnosis would garner immense sympathy, but in the end, the law would not condone embezzlement.

A lump wedged in her throat. With the newspapers continuing to report on the anonymous buy-up of Blackstone shares, she could just imagine how the media would hound her poor father, not to mention herself. They'd already gone through that after the plane crash. She didn't want to go through it again.

Besides, it wouldn't look good that her father had never forgiven Howard for firing Barbara when she'd become pregnant with Marise. Yet even after the Davenports had pulled up roots and moved from Sydney to

Melbourne, the Blackstones had ended up an intrinsic part of their lives. In the latter years, Marise had worked for Blackstone Diamonds in sales and marketing, then Briana had found herself a model and the face of Blackstone Diamonds. And then Marise had been with Howard on the flight to New Zealand, and had died in the aftermath of the crash. It was crazy, but it was as if destiny had somehow wanted the Davenports and the Blackstones to keep a connection.

And how ironic that his supermodel daughter couldn't help Ray out with money when he needed it. Her new million-dollar contract with Blackstone's was due to be renewed in three months' time, but nothing was ever certain until it was signed. Until then she had just enough to live on, thanks to her ex-business manager and lover, Patrick, who had convinced her to invest nearly all her money in an unbuilt apartment complex. It had sounded like a good investment at the time, until the developers had gone bust and she'd lost the lot.

She'd never told her parents about it, feeling like a sucker. They'd known she'd invested her money. They just hadn't known she'd lost it.

All at once someone sat down on the seat beside her, and the hairs on the back of her neck stood up. She turned toward the man who suddenly and completely filled her vision.

"Jarrod!"

"Briana," he murmured, his blue eyes trapping hers for a heart-stopping second.

She moistened her mouth even as she realized something. "You knew I'd be here, didn't you?"

One brow rose. "Did I?"

"It's too much of a coincidence otherwise," she said, letting him know she wasn't being hoodwinked.

He shrugged. "Perhaps."

Her forehead creased. "You want to see me?"

"Oh yes," he drawled, his gaze going over her long, blond wavy hair that tumbled around her head, before dipping to the creamy expanse of her neck and shoulders above the black cocktail dress, then further down and over the gathered bust held together by a diamond center clasp.

Her heart dropped to her toes but she managed a glare. "I meant that you wanted to *talk* to me?" she said, in no frame of mind to fend off his seduction.

He paused, his face turning unreadable now. "Yes."

She waited for him to speak, and when he didn't, she said, "Then talk."

"Not here." He got to his feet, his hand cupping her bare elbow, sending a warming shiver through her. "Come have a drink with me in the lounge."

She looked up at him standing so close beside her, an air of command exuding from him, threatening to engulf her. She wanted to say no, but couldn't think up a suitable excuse. "Just for a moment."

Then she stood up too and his eyes approved the short, glamorous dress. Heat curled in her stomach, before he led her away from the crowds and into one of the lounges. It was quieter in here with plenty of small tables circled by large comfortable leather chairs.

He took her to some seats in a secluded corner that was much too intimate for Briana's peace of mind, but when she saw some of the other patrons looking their way she was rather thankful no one could listen in on their conversation.

A waiter immediately came over to them, and she agreed to join Jarrod in a brandy. It would calm her nerves, she decided, watching him place their order, his self-confidence and sophistication an attraction many women would find appealing.

Dressed in dark trousers and a sports blazer with a white T-shirt underneath, he could have been a male model himself if there hadn't been such a hard edge to him. Those blue eyes clearly showed that hardness, an arrogance that would never let anyone dictate to him, let alone a camera.

"No Jake Vance today?" he said once the waiter left.

"I gave him the day off," she quipped.

The edges of that firm, sensual mouth tilted. "I doubt Jake would think of it that way."

She doubted it, too, but she didn't say so.

His smile disappeared and he fixed her with a candid gaze. "You and Jake are an item then?"

She lifted her chin. "I don't think that's any of your business."

He considered her for a moment, a pulse beating in his cheekbone. "The two of you were having a good laugh together at Kim's wedding."

For a moment she didn't know what he was talking

about. Then she remembered her comment about testosterone keeping the boat afloat and a bubble of laughter rose in her throat.

His eyes narrowed. "So there *is* something going on between you two."

She lost her amusement, not sure why he was being so insistent. "You wanted to talk," she reminded him, crossing her legs, pretending this line of questioning wasn't getting to her.

His eyes plunged to her legs in the ultrasheer silk stockings revealed by the ruffled hem, admired them, then rose back up to her face. "Are the two of you lovers?"

Her own eyes widened in dismay. "I don't believe I'm hearing this."

He held her gaze. "Tell me the truth, Briana."

Panic stirred in her chest but she kept it at bay. "Why, Jarrod? Why do you want to know about Jake and me?"

"Because if he doesn't want you, *I* do."

Her head reeled back. "What?"

"I want you to be my lover," he repeated firmly, leaving no doubt this time.

She gave him a glance of utter disbelief. "You can't be serious!"

"You deny you want me, too?"

She swallowed past her suddenly dry throat, tried to speak and had to swallow again. "I *can* deny it and I do," she lied, knowing she couldn't admit wanting him. It would give him an unfair advantage over her. One he wouldn't hesitate to use.

"Why sound so shocked? I'd have thought a woman

like yourself—" he gave a tiny pause "—would be used to such propositions."

Her blood pressure began to rise. "You mean because I'm a model?"

He inclined his dark head. "What other reason would there be?" he said silkily, as the waiter arrived with their brandy.

Her lips flattened with anger. At the wedding, Jarrod had made a similar comment about how far she'd come in the business. It hadn't sounded like a compliment back then, and neither did this comment. Had he thought she'd slept her way to the top? It sickened her to think that, yet why she cared she didn't know. It would serve him right if she called his bluff.

Why not?

"Okay, I'll sleep with you," she said, once the waiter left. "For a million dollars."

His eyes flickered then became shuttered. "That can be arranged."

Her brain stumbled. "What?"

He shot her a dry look. "Sleep with me and I'll give you a million dollars."

He'd well and truly called her bluff. "But—but you don't have that kind of money to give away."

His brows lifted. "You know that for a fact, do you?"

Oh heavens. Was she stupid or what? Apart from coming from a wealthy family, he'd made a name for himself as a property lawyer. Of course he'd have a million dollars to spare. What an idiot she was!

From somewhere she managed to scoff, "Ill-gotten gains, Jarrod?"

Contempt flashed in his eyes. "No. I'll leave that to the Blackstones."

"That's my employer you're talking about," she said coolly.

"Doesn't change a thing. The Blackstones are far from saints." He picked up the two glasses and passed one to her. "Now, about our agreement—"

She took the brandy glass from him, but an acute sense of panic raced through her again. "Keep your money. I don't want it. I—" She stopped.

She *did* need the money.

Needed it more than he could ever know.

"Having second thoughts?" he asked.

"No." She took a sip of brandy, and wished her denial carried the same strength as the alcohol now burning her throat.

"We can always do with more money," he pointed out, watching her as if knowing all along it would come back to this.

This being money.

Of course, she now realized that by even suggesting the million dollars she was playing into his belief that she was cut from the same cloth as her sister. Marise had said she'd fallen in love with Matt, but Briana suspected Matt's wealth hadn't hurt, either. And then there was Marise and Howard….

"A million dollars, Briana," he reminded her.

No, she couldn't do it. She wasn't for sale.

Then she forced her heart to steady itself. What if she looked upon it as a loan, asked a small voice inside her. A loan she would pay back once her contract with Blackstones was renewed.

A million-dollar contract.

But if it wasn't renewed? What if they got someone else to replace her as the face of Blackstone Diamonds?

What if—

No, she wouldn't think about "what if's". Nor would she think about not repaying the money to him at all. It just wasn't in her to be underhanded.

But could she make love to Jarrod Hammond?

Oh God. How much of a hardship would that really be? She was attracted to him, no doubt about it. Intensely attracted, if she were to be honest with herself. It wasn't like she would be making a huge sacrifice and giving her body to someone who was revolting and wouldn't appreciate her. Jarrod would definitely appreciate her. Oh yes. She didn't know a man who would appreciate her better.

"Briana?"

She glanced at him then. He looked cool and calm, yet she sensed he was anything but. He wanted her just as much as she wanted him. So what harm would she do in sleeping with him? It wasn't as though she would be doing anything against her will.

On the contrary...

"It's a deal," she heard herself say.

He scowled. "It is?"

"You don't have the money?" she said with a rush of

disappointment that was about more than just getting her father out of trouble.

His dark brows straightened. "I have it." Just as quickly a considering light came into his eyes. "But now that I think of it," he drawled, "a million dollars for one night *is* a bit too much money—even for the face of Blackstone's."

Her lips tightened. He'd been playing with her. "Fine. That's it then."

"No, I'd say it's worth a month of nights together, don't you?"

She stiffened in shock. "No! I can't. A month is too long."

He shrugged his broad shoulders. "That's my offer. Become my mistress for one month and I'll give you a million dollars."

She swallowed hard. "That wasn't what I agreed to, Jarrod, and you know it."

"You agreed to sleep with me. True. But we didn't mention a timeframe."

She shook her head, not understanding him. "Why can't you be satisfied with one night?"

He didn't move a muscle. "Can you?"

She winced inwardly. Could she do it for one whole month? One night was so different. Or was it? Wouldn't only one night make her feel as if she really were selling herself? Wouldn't being his mistress for a month make her feel better about it all? Or was she just kidding herself?

"Briana, you want the money. Don't deny it." He waited a moment. "And I want you."

She cleared her throat and ignored an inward shudder of heat that couldn't be attributed to the brandy. "Who said I want the money?" she asked, trying to put him off the scent of her father's trail.

"You don't? Then it must be *me* you want," he mocked, his smirk saying he'd backed her into a corner.

Mentally kicking herself, she raised her chin. "I'm not denying the money wouldn't come in handy." She saw the hard look that entered his eyes. "And I don't deny that sleeping with a man such as yourself wouldn't be a—nice experience."

He smiled sardonically. "I'm glad you think so."

"But a month does seem a bit too long."

He swirled the brandy in his glass, then looked up at her. "Take it or leave it. But let me tell you, if you leave it, there won't be another chance."

Suddenly a feminine power settled over her, giving her confidence. "You might want to rethink that, Jarrod. After all, I've got something you want—my body. And if in a month's time I say I want you, I'm pretty sure I won't have to beg."

His nod acknowledged her words. "Oh, I don't deny that. But next time there won't be any money involved, sweetheart. It'll be just you and me. I won't be offering a million dollars again."

She gritted her teeth. He was a clever devil. Somehow he sensed she wouldn't walk away from the money. What he didn't know was that she *couldn't* walk away from it. Not if she wanted to help save her father.

So what if she accepted Jarrod's extended offer? The month would go fast. She had quite a few modeling engagements around the country to give her a break from Jarrod's overwhelming presence. At least there was that.

And perhaps she could even prove to him that she *wasn't* like her sister, she thought, then immediately rebuked herself. Why would she even want to? She owed Jarrod Hammond nothing.

She placed her glass of brandy on the coffee table in front of her. "I'll give you until the end of the month. That's three weeks. Take it or leave it," she said, putting the ball back into his court.

A moment crept by.

Static crackled the air between them.

Then he drained his glass and put it down next to hers. "I'll book a room," he said, about to get to his feet.

Her eyes widened. "What? Here?"

He stopped with a frown. "I thought it might be easier for our first night together."

"For whom?"

"You." He watched her in silence for a moment. "If you like, we can go back to my apartment…or to yours."

That was the last thing she wanted. "No," she said quickly. "A room here will be fine."

"Good." He stood up. "Wait here. I'll send you a note to say what suite I'll be in." He glanced around at the other patrons, then back at her. "I'm sure you don't want your reputation to suffer if somebody sees us going up together."

"Not to mention yours," she managed to say, still reeling from what tonight's outcome would be.

His eyes darkened. "I don't give a damn about my reputation, Briana. It might be wise to remember that." He strode off.

Three

It was silly to feel so nervous, Briana told herself as she tapped lightly on the door to the room fifteen minutes later. Heavens, she'd paraded in front of prime ministers and heads of state, done photo shoots in the middle of huge crowds, stood practically naked backstage at fashion shows, yet nothing made her feel as exposed as she did right now.

And was it any wonder, she decided when Jarrod opened the door to the deluxe suite and she met the full power of those intense blue eyes. Her stomach did a slow somersault.

And just as slowly, he reached out and curled his hand around her wrist, drawing her into the room before closing the door behind them. There he stood looking down at her, his hand still holding her, his palm warmly touching her skin, his thumb resting against the tender inside of her wrist where her pulse raced. She could feel him through every living cell in her body.

And then his gaze dropped to her mouth. He was going to kiss her. She could even feel herself lean just the barest hint toward him. Suddenly she wanted those lips on hers...wanted that body against hers.

"Have you eaten?"

His words snapped her out of her trance. Dismayed at how easily she would have succumbed, she stepped back, letting his hand drop away from her. "Just some finger food at the cocktail party," she said, walking casually into the suite. A wall of floor-to-ceiling glass drew her attention to the city lights below, but Briana only gave the view a quick glance. The world was out there but tonight that's where it would stay.

"You look disappointed a moment ago."

Her heart slammed against her ribs as she glanced across at him. "I did?" She shrugged. "I thought—"

"That I wouldn't waste any time getting you into bed?" A seductive glint entered his eyes. "Briana, being in your company, looking at you, isn't wasting time. Far from it." A smile touched his lips. "The ravishing comes later."

Her breath quickened. He made it sound so... ravishing! "Yes—well—"

"Unless you'd like me to start now instead of ordering you some food?" he drawled.

She sent him a wry look. "No thanks. I'd prefer soup."

His lips twitched. And then his gaze swept over her and awareness danced between them again, and for a moment she thought he really was going to come over to her and ravish her on the spot. And she wanted him to. Dear Lord, she did.

He broke eye contact and strode toward the phone. "I'll order room service," he said, his voice sounding gruff.

Knowing she had affected him, her heart skipped a beat. "I'll just go and freshen up."

He indicated across the width of the room. "The bedroom's that way."

The bedroom.

Carrying her small purse, she took her time to walk across the room, while fighting every instinct to break into a run and lock the door behind her like some frightened virgin. Wouldn't that go down well, she mused with a dash of humor.

The problem was that's exactly how she felt. This was her first time with Jarrod and she was feeling overwhelmed. Despite knowing him for years, despite now acknowledging to herself that she had wanted him for years, there was a difference in the *doing*. A huge difference. She doubted she could ever have prepared herself for this.

Needless to say, seducing women was par for the course for him. He would have done all this before. He certainly seemed to know his way about the suite. He'd probably even met some other women here, just like he'd met her tonight. Had he brought them up here, too?

No, she wasn't going to think about that. She had enough to worry about tonight, she decided as she entered the lavish bedroom, her eyes immediately fastening on the huge bed and her heartbeat skidding to a screeching stop. She and Jarrod would make love on that bed tonight. The thought made her go weak at the knees.

She hurried into the equally giant bathroom and freshened her lipstick. Then she combed through her wavy tresses that bounced along her shoulders as she moved, though why she bothered she wasn't sure. Jarrod would only mess her hair up, just like he would mess with her dress and...

Help!

She took some deep breaths. Okay, so she could stay in here and act like a coward, or she could go out there and face the music. She'd made a deal with the devil, but that deal still stood. And unfortunately so did the devil.

She didn't stay in there long. There was no reason to hide from him or their situation, though she had a few things to say to him first.

"I hope I can count on you not to tell anyone about this," she said, once back in the main area, her chin held high.

He scowled as he stepped away from the bar, carrying two glasses of wine. "Why would I? What we do is our own business."

"As long as we're clear on that."

He handed her a glass and gestured for her to sit on the sofa. "I'm a grown man, not some high-school kid. I don't need to prove anything by telling the world."

She sank down on the soft leather lounge and hoped she could believe him. Patrick had been different, a fact she'd only found out after she'd ended their affair. Apparently he'd often boasted about bedding the face of

Blackstone's. She wished Jarrod was the same type, then she might have the strength to leave right now, but she instinctively knew he wasn't.

He sat down on the chair opposite. "But first, tell me why."

Her throat almost closed up, knowing instantly what he meant. "Er…why?"

His eyes said she wasn't deceiving him. "Why you're willing to sleep with me now and not in the last four years."

She took a sip of her wine before answering. "You never asked before."

And she knew the reason for it. He considered her the same as Marise and hadn't wanted a bar of her. She knew that, and had felt protected by it. Until today.

"Oh, I wanted to ask. But you knew that, didn't you? There's always been an attraction between us."

Her mouth went dry. "You're imagining things."

"The only thing I'm imagining is you in bed with me. And soon I won't need my imagination for that."

Her breath suspended for a full five seconds.

His eyes held hers captive. "Why now, Briana?"

She slowly released her breath and pasted on a cynical smile. "How can I refuse a million dollars *and* the chance to have sex with a man like you?"

He sent her a measured look. "Don't try and pick a fight by insulting me. You're here of your own free will. If you don't want to go through with it, then say so now." A heartbeat passed. "I want you with every breath I take, but I won't force you."

Her heart bumped against her ribs. Oh, how she

wished she could blame him for all this. But he was right. She'd made the choice to be here tonight, if only for her father's sake.

"It won't be force," she agreed, then saw him visibly relax, but he kept his eyes trained on her.

"Tonight is the beginning of our three weeks together, Briana. Nothing more. Are you clear about that?"

Her body immediately tensed. "Very clear. And by the way, *you* were the one who wanted the full month together," she reminded him. Oh, how she'd love to tell him where to shove his money.

"I'm not talking about a month. I'm talking about anything beyond that. I'm not after a long-term relationship."

She gave a derisive snort. "Long-term relationship? With you? I'd rather put my head in an oven."

His hard sensual mouth lifted at the corners. "Now, that would be such a waste."

"Not from where I'm sitting."

He gave a light chuckle as someone knocked lightly on the door and called out, "Room service."

Jarrod pushed himself to his feet and went to let the waiter in. Briana got a good look at the cut of his tailored trousers and blazer from behind. Superb. And so was the masculine body beneath it, she grudgingly admitted, even as she realized something else.

"Wait!" she hissed just as he went to open the door. She jumped up and almost ran across the room to the bedroom and out of sight. She didn't want anyone seeing her there.

A couple of minutes later, Jarrod called to her, "You can come out now."

Feeling slightly foolish, she straightened her shoulders and calmly walked back into the living area, constantly aware of his eyes on her every movement, and trying to keep her own eyes off him. He'd taken off the blazer, and the white T-shirt underneath exposed the muscles of his upper torso.

"Ashamed to be seen with me?" he mocked, holding out a chair for her at the small dining table.

She shrugged. "Don't take it personally. I'd do the same with any man."

His eyes hardened. "Is that so?"

She ignored the implication in his eyes and sat on the offered chair. "Don't you know? The media would love to catch me in a compromising situation such as this."

He walked around the table and sat opposite her. "I'd have thought you'd revel in media attention," he said, showing his low opinion of her.

She flinched inwardly but on the outside, she arched a brow. "You really think I would welcome bad publicity?"

"No, I guess not," he admitted, and she felt the tightness inside her unwind a little. "No doubt bad publicity wouldn't look too good for the face of Blackstone's," he said, lifting the lid off his plate of food.

Briana felt the words sting.

Then he looked up and caught her staring at him. "Aren't you going to eat?"

She shook her head.

He watched her with an observant eye. "Are you okay?"

Suddenly it all got the better of her. "Okay?" she choked, throwing her napkin aside. "I'm about to make love with a stranger, Jarrod. Is it any wonder I'm on edge?"

"I'm not a stranger, Briana," he corrected calmly.

"For all intents and purposes, you are." Unable to sit still a moment longer, and knowing she couldn't eat now anyway, she walked over to the windows. "Can we please get this over and done with?"

Silence hung in the air behind her.

"Don't sound so eager," he drawled, but a moment later she heard movement. "Let's have some privacy, shall we?"

Tension rattled inside her as the suite flooded in darkness, leaving only a faint glow from the city lights beyond the glass. She still didn't turn around. She needed to focus on those city lights, to remember she was here for a purpose.

"Will you respect me in the morning, Jarrod?" She heard herself mutter the cliché, but needed to say it all the same.

"Yes," he said quietly, close behind her, so close his breath stirred strands of her hair. "But will *you* respect you in the morning?"

She thought about that, surprised by his astuteness. His question had dispelled any hint she was selling herself, and she was grateful to him for that. "Yes," she murmured.

And then his hands cupped her bare shoulders, the thin straps of her dress were little protection against him. "I'll make this special for you, Briana."

She could see his reflection as if they were standing in

front of a mirror, the gleam in his eyes seeming to pierce the glass to reach her, seeming to suspend them in time.

Her throat thickened. "I know."

All at once he slid his hand under her golden-blond hair, held it up as if loving the feel of it, then letting it fall like sparkling champagne over her shoulders.

"You're stunning," he murmured, admiration in his voice as he pushed some strands aside to kiss her nape in a gesture that was simply and deliciously sensuous. "A natural beauty."

For a split second she tried to stay in control...tried but soon weakened when his kisses continued to caress her skin. She lowered her lashes, silently shocked at how easy she was succumbing to his touch.

Yet it wasn't just this moment between them. Jarrod was right about there having always been an attraction between them. And that attraction had been unrelenting in its pursuit of them. Tonight, right now, was the cul-mination of it all.

She couldn't help herself. She tilted her head to the side to allow him easier access—and she gave in. There was no going back now. Nor did she want to. She wanted to be in his arms.

Slowly he undid the zipper at the back of her dress, his lips whispers of sensation as they followed the low-ering zipper, making their way down her spine, kissing her where no man had ever kissed before. It was a se-duction of the senses that made her head spin.

At the base of her spine he let go of the zipper, and her dress plummeted to the floor and pooled around her ankles. She held her breath, frozen in this instant, watching in the glass as he straightened behind her, all the while admiring her lacy black bra, matching high-cut panties and thigh-high silk stockings.

"My very own model." His hands splayed over her hips as he moved closer, letting her feel his arousal.

A moan escaped her but she managed to say, "Supermodel," and was proud of herself for still having some sort of fight left in her.

He gave a husky chuckle, then lowered his head. He placed his lips against her shoulder and began to nibble at even more pleasure points she never knew she had. When his hands slid around to capture her lace-covered breasts and his fingers lightly squeezed her nipples with the sweetest torment, she moaned with wanting him.

"Too much?" he muttered.

"Yes."

"Good."

He scooped her up and carried her into the bedroom, spreading her across the thick bedspread as if she were a pleasure to be savored. She lay there in the lamplight and stared up at him. His eyes glittered as he took in her half-naked state, her breasts eagerly straining against the lace, the V-shape of her high-cut panties a sensual delight.

His gaze soaked her up, then landed on her face. "Do you realize I've never kissed you?" he muttered roughly, his eyes focusing on her mouth.

She inadvertently moistened her lips. "Same here."

Neither of them smiled. The moment was too intense. He pulled the T-shirt over his head, his chest bronzed and sprinkled with hair. He kicked off his shoes and slid onto the bed next to her. And then he claimed her mouth in a kiss that was so passionate it made her head spin. This first touch of his firm lips against her softer ones was more than she had ever expected, more than she'd ever wanted from a man—until now.

And then his tongue parted her lips and stole into her mouth, stole the breath from her, demanding she give him everything of herself. When she capitulated, his groan of appreciation sent a thrill through her as she clung to him like there was no tomorrow.

Right now there *was* no tomorrow. There was only him and her, and the wonderful sensations he was stirring inside her. He undid her bra and eased back, the lace falling away, and she quivered when his fingertips brushed her bare breasts.

"Aah, something else that needs kissing," he murmured as he lowered his head and took a nipple in his mouth, playing with it with his tongue, then sucking in the sweetest of tortures.

Needing to touch him, to be a partner in this, her hands cupped the back of his head and held him to her. She loved spreading her fingers through the short hair, loved it even better when she slipped her hands down to his sculpted shoulders, then the length of his back to the waistband of his trousers.

He shuddered and muttered low in his throat, "You're distracting me." Then he took a deep breath and got to his knees beside her. "Now, what else needs my attention?" he teased, though his eyes were dark with desire as his palm glided down over her stomach, farther down where he dallied and stroked her through her panties, until heat washed over her and made her limbs tremble.

And then his gaze dropped to those trembling limbs, covered by the sheer silk stockings. "I love these things on you," he rasped, slipping his finger under the band of one stocking, and ever so slowly peeling it down her smooth leg. His lips followed the trail until she breathed his name through parted lips.

He repeated the process with the other leg, and when she breathed his name again, his lips trailed back up to her thighs, up the center of her panties where he paused to inhale her.

He turned his head and looked up at her. "Are you sure?"

Tender warmth entered her heart. He was giving her another chance to back out, another chance to say no to all this. As if she could now.

"Yes, I'm sure," she said on a whisper, and that was all the encouragement he needed.

He rolled off the bed and shed the rest of his clothes, and he was suddenly, magnificently, naked. She stared at his unashamed erection, the hardness of him, the powerful male perfection, and she knew that she had to have him inside her. She put out her hand to reach for him, then stopped.

Instead, she lifted her bottom off the bed, pushing her panties down and off herself. Her eyes connected with his as she held them in the air with one finger before dropping them on the floor like a flag of surrender. It was a surrender she willingly made tonight. There was no tomorrow after all.

Something smoldered in the depths of his eyes, and a pulse leaped along his jaw, making her hold her breath. A moment later, he didn't say a word as he reached for the condom from the bedside table and sheathed himself, before coming back to her, kissing her deeply, the full length of his body pressing her down against the mattress.

She kissed him back, loving the feel of his hair-roughened chest against her own tender breasts, the heat of his arousal as he melded into her femininity, filling her completely. She felt like she had never made love before. Not like this.

And then he stopped kissing her, and his eyes captured hers with a look that was undeniably male. It was a triumphant look that said he was here, he had conquered and now he would take.

She thrilled to the silent communication, allowing him his moment of masculinity. And then he began to move his body inside her with long, slow strokes that had her own body raising to meet him with a feminine power of her own. Together they built pleasure upon pleasure, until slow was no longer enough, and fast and deep became a necessity, an essential part of their love-making. Of them.

And together they came as one.

If any woman in the world had been worth a million dollars, it was the woman next to him, Jarrod reflected the next morning as he lay facing Briana sleeping on the pillow next to him. They'd made love three times throughout the night. Three times and he still hadn't had enough of her.

She was dazzling, this golden glamour girl with her velvet eyelashes fanning her smooth cheeks, and her blond hair tousled so sexily over her naked shoulders. The sweet scent of her gorgeous body drifted up beneath the sheet and reeled him in, making the blood pulse in his temples, rush through his body.

Suddenly he wanted her a fourth time.

And a fifth.

And he would have her, too.

Just not right now, he thought regretfully as he glanced at the clock and saw the time. Dammit. He had a meeting with a client in an hour. A very important one, or he would cancel it. But the guy was going overseas later today, and needed a Sunday morning appointment.

Sighing with regret, he slid his hand off Briana's slim hip. It was probably for the best anyway. Despite his body's urges, he needed a moment to himself. Why, he wasn't sure, except that having Briana in his arms had been fulfilling in a way he'd never felt before. And that just didn't make sense. Why did he have to feel this way about a woman beautiful enough and sexy enough to eat?

Yet it was more than a physical sexiness. It was something in her. Something that drew him to her. Drew many men, no doubt, he thought as cynicism gnawed at his gut. How many lovers had seen her like this? Probably too many to count. She may have put on an act about accepting the money, but she'd still accepted his offer.

She was definitely a gold-digger, even if something wasn't quite right here. His lawyer's instincts told him there was more to her taking the money than she was letting on. But what?

His dark brows knitted together. Perhaps he just wanted to believe she had a motive that wasn't attached to the money. More fool him. In his experience, beautiful women couldn't be trusted. They'd always wanted something, always had an angle. The only exception was his adopted mother, Katherine Hammond. She was lovely inside and out.

But his birth mother, an ice-cold beauty whose looks had started to wear thin, was out for all she could get. She'd given him up for adoption to remain footloose and fancy-free. She'd told him so the first time she'd come looking for a handout. The times he'd seen her since hadn't changed his mind.

She and Briana would get on well.

Or would they, he wondered, his eyes resting on Briana, her sheer beauty making him doubt himself. But he had to remember she was the sister of his dead sister-in-law. She and Marise were the same breed of women. Out for all they could get. Marise had proved it with his brother. Briana had just proven it with him.

He slipped out of bed and reached for his checkbook, wrote out the million-dollar check and put it on the pillow he'd just vacated. Then he left Sleeping Beauty in the bedroom, closing the door behind him to go into the main suite to make a phone call. Soon he'd head home to shower and change before his meeting.

But as he hung up the phone, he heard a noise in the bedroom. He strode over and opened the door, but she must not have heard him. She was sitting up in bed, having wrapped the sheet around herself. In her hands was the check and she was looking down at it as if she was defeated rather than pleased.

Something twisted inside his gut, reminding him that there was more to this than met the eye. "Isn't that what you wanted, Briana?"

Her head shot up, her wide-eyed beauty latching on to him. "I thought you'd left," she accused, heat rushing into her cheeks.

Her reaction wasn't what he'd expected from such a woman of the world. For a moment she almost looked...guileless.

"You mean, you were *hoping* I'd left," he said, leaning against the doorjamb, fascinated by every aspect of her. What was going on in that mind of hers?

She angled a chin that was more defiant than delicate right now. "So you don't feel you got value for the money, Jarrod?"

"You know I did. And it's not over yet. We have three weeks of—getting to know each other."

Her lips briefly stretched in a fake smile, then not. "How nice."

"Yes, just like your 'nice' experience last night," he drawled, reminding her of her words last night down in the casino lounge. *Nice* didn't describe the half of it. "At least, I assume it was as 'nice' for you as it was for me."

"Searching for compliments, Jarrod?"

All at once he'd had enough. As much as he liked verbally sparring with her, he had other things to do this morning. "What do you have planned for the rest of the long-weekend?"

She blinked, then wariness clouded her eyes. "Why?"

"I want you to spend it with me."

"So soon?" she said with obvious dismay.

His mouth twisted. "Your enthusiasm is refreshing. Is that a problem?"

She took a ragged breath. "I guess not."

His mouth flattened in a grim line. Anyone would think he'd asked her to give up all her earthly possessions. "Do you have any further engagements this weekend?"

She shook her head. "No, just some things to do in the lead-up to the Grand Prix next weekend."

Yes, the papers were already advertising her attendance at the Melbourne Grand Prix. "Look, I've got an appointment with a client, but I'll be back in a couple of hours to take you to lunch. And tomorrow we can go to the Moomba Festival together."

"Oh, but—"

"I've asked them to send you up some new clothes to gad about in now," he said, preempting her.

Anger flared in her eyes. "I don't want a new set of clothes to gad about in."

"Then wear none," he mocked.

Her mouth thinned. "I prefer my own clothes, thank you."

He glanced at his watch then back at her. Time was running out. "Just relax, order some breakfast and take another nap. You didn't get much sleep last night. I'll be back at noon."

"And if I don't want to spend any more time with you?"

"Then I'll know you're not a woman of your word." He turned and walked out of the hotel room.

Four

After Jarrod left the suite, Briana wasn't sure how long she sat in the king-size bed, cursing him, cursing herself for being attracted to such a man. He'd made love to her last night as if she'd been meant to be in his arms all along. He'd made her feel special and complete, taken her to heights she'd never imagined. She could still feel the remnants of his lovemaking; her breasts were still tender from his touch, her mouth still swollen from his kisses, her lower body still sensitive from his possession.

And she *had* been possessed, there was no doubt about it. Possessed by him. Possessed by her desire for him.

The latter had been a shock.

She couldn't remember even coming close to this with Patrick. No, Patrick had taken what he'd wanted, when he'd wanted in bed, but had never really given her the same fulfillment. Because she'd been in love with him, she hadn't let herself think about it. Her love had covered up a multitude of his flaws...until her rose-colored glasses had been well and truly ripped off her.

And now Jarrod Hammond was making her feel special again, not because she'd fallen in love with him, but because he treated her as the woman he wanted.

She didn't fool herself that it was more than sex—for either of them. He'd wanted to possess her body and he had. She'd wanted him to make love to her, and that was the reason she was feeling fulfilled. Nothing more. It was only about sex. Good sex, admittedly.

All paid for and delivered, she reminded herself, making a half-choked sound as she looked down at the check in her hands. She still couldn't believe she'd given her body to a man for a million dollars. Her father would be horrified. *She* was horrified.

Yet, to be honest, Jarrod hadn't made her feel as if she'd sold her body to him. And that was totally crazy. Any other man would have made her feel cheap.

What was she going to tell her father about the money she'd suddenly acquired? She'd found it lying around in an old bank account? No, too far-fetched. Only Howard Blackstone had kept money in old, "secret" accounts, she mused cynically.

Then the answer came to her. The check was one of Jarrod's, so she would tell her father she'd asked Jarrod for a loan to buy more property. Yes, that was it! Her father probably wouldn't think anything out of the ordinary, not with Jarrod being a Hammond, and with Marise being married to Jarrod's brother.

Of course, loan or not, she still had to pay the money back. She just hoped to high heaven that Blackstone Diamonds wanted to continue their contract with her.

And if she couldn't pay it back? No, she wouldn't think about being beholden to Jarrod any longer than necessary. As it was, he had started to boss her around already, telling her to stay in bed and take a nap, buying her clothes, telling her to wait in the room until he got back, expecting she'd go to lunch with him.

Did that mean he expected her to do everything he asked? Would he expect her to be at his beck and call for the next three weeks?

She was no man's plaything. Not even for a million dollars, she told herself as she pushed aside a sense of trepidation and asked herself what to do next. Oh, she'd keep her word to spend the next three weeks with him, and she'd no doubt enjoy some of it. But she wasn't about to wait around this hotel room for him to return. If he wanted to take her to lunch, then she'd leave him a note and go home to her apartment until he called. She certainly wasn't chasing him. If necessary, she'd meet him at the restaurant.

And she would still be a woman of her word, she decided, throwing back the sheet and pushing her naked body out of bed.

Of course, as soon as her doorbell buzzed, Briana knew who it would be. Despite having a doorman who was harder to get past than a crocodile, somehow Jarrod had managed it.

And now he stood there, looking like a man should look—handsome, confident, charismatic—sending her pulse racing into overdrive. She had no idea how much she'd been wanting to see him until this moment. Correction, how much her *body* had wanted to see him.

"You left your new clothes behind," he drawled, empty-handed.

"I don't need you to buy me clothes," she said coolly as she turned into her apartment, only to find herself twirled back toward him.

Without warning, he kissed her. For heart-stopping seconds she tried to hold something of herself back, but he deepened the kiss. When a faint groan escaped from his throat, she slid into meltdown. Her lips parted.

Just as suddenly he let her go. "Not so cool, eh?" he murmured.

She forced her head to clear. "Talking about yourself?" she challenged.

"Talking about *both* of us."

The nerves in her stomach tightened and she quickly turned into the living room. "How much did you pay the doorman to let you in?"

"He happens to be the father of a friend."

She picked up her purse from the sofa and shot him a look of disbelief. "My, that's quite a coincidence."

He held her gaze. "Yes, it is."

She realized he was serious. Either way, she needed to have some discreet words with the doorman.

"Don't try and get him fired," Jarrod warned.

"Who said anything about getting him fired?" she said in astonishment.

"Oh, I don't know. There's a certain look of revenge in your eyes."

A smirk coated her lips. "That isn't for the doorman."

He gave a husky chuckle, taking her unawares. She wished he'd stop doing that. It was one thing knowing he was enigmatic, quite another to see his more human side. It was best she keep her distance.

She mentally straightened her shoulders. "I'm ready."

His gaze traveled down over her outfit. "I can see why you prefer your own clothes."

She glanced down at her sleeveless, slimline knit dress in vivid marigold, the material lightly rouched at the waist and harmonizing with her hips. It was sexy and flattering and she felt good in it, especially when she combined it with delicate high-heeled sandals in the same color. And heavens, she needed every bit of confidence she could find right now.

She looked back up at Jarrod. "Actually this was a gift from someone."

A cynical look entered his eyes. "A male, no doubt?"

Ah, so they were back to that again. He thought she had conned every man she'd ever met out of something or other.

"Who else?" she retorted, walking toward him. One of the designers had given it to her after a fashion shoot, but she'd let Jarrod think what he liked. It's what he *wanted* to think anyway.

Yet he frowned as she preceded him out of the apartment, and he was still frowning when she closed her door behind them. She hid a small burst of satisfaction. Good. Let him be the unsettled one for a change, even if she had no idea why. It would be too much to ask that he might think he was actually wrong about her.

Her inner poise restored, she headed toward the elevator. "Where are we having lunch?"

"Southbank."

She inclined her head. "Lovely." Lunch at a riverside restaurant would at least surround them with a multitude of people and would take an hour or two out of their day. She dare not think beyond that.

Only, once he'd parked his BMW Coupe in an underground car park in the city center and they rode up the elevator, she realized he was taking her to one of the top hotel restaurants, rather than one of the many places alongside the Yarra River.

Pity it wasn't as crowded as she wanted, she mused as the waiter walked them through luxurious surroundings and seated them at a table for two overlooking the river.

The picturesque city views beyond the glass gave a feeling of spaciousness that would have been delightful if she'd been with anyone else. In Jarrod's company, not even watching the slow-moving riverboats and the strolling couples along the promenade below could put her at ease. The world was still out there but it was hard to notice when she was seated intimately with a man who was now her lover and who intended to remain her lover for three more weeks.

"So," he said, leaning back in his chair once the waiter had departed after taking their order, "tell me about Briana Davenport."

"Read my bio," she quipped, leaning back in her chair, too, pretending to be relaxed.

A corner of his mouth twitched upward. "I want to know about Briana Davenport, the person. Not Briana, the model."

She shrugged her shoulders. "Same thing."

"No, different." He tilted his head, considering her with a slight frown. "I'm just not sure how yet."

"Don't tax yourself thinking about it."

His eyes suddenly narrowed. "So you think I'm only interested in you for your looks?"

She kept her gaze steady. "You mean you aren't?"

A muscle tightened at the edge of his jaw. "No."

Oddly enough, she believed him. But it probably wasn't a good thing to delve too deeply. It would mean having to consider why he was sleeping with her.

"It's a bit late asking me about myself, don't you think?"

He offered her a smile. "I knew enough to sleep with you."

"Hey, don't say that too loud," she whispered, straightening and looking around but seeing there was no danger of anyone's hearing. Thank goodness, she thought, her gaze returning to Jarrod's.

A smile reached his eyes, then was banked. "Okay, let's start again. What do I know about Briana Davenport?" He gave her a silent appraisal. "Hmm. You don't snore."

"I'm pleased."

"You like to snuggle up against a man."

"A natural reaction."

"And you like to be kissed all over."

"Shhh," she hissed.

"It's all true."

"So is the million dollars."

The amusement left his eyes and his gaze hardened, but just as quickly he arched a brow at her. "You don't want to know about me?"

She looked at him long and hard. "I know all there is to know."

"Really?"

She assumed a thoughtful expression. "You have no hesitation in taking what you want."

"True."

"You'll go to any means to get it."

"True."

"You're suspicious of beautiful women."

"True."

"Oh, I forgot. They have to be beautiful *and* greedy."

"Now you're getting there," he said in a dry tone, just as the waiter brought over their first course.

But Jarrod didn't seem fazed by her comment, and after that they ate in silence for a while. She used the time to recover from the constant barrage of awareness Jarrod's presence caused. In her job she was used to being constantly "on," but this was different. Being with Jarrod was being *turned* on.

They had just finished their appetizer when the waiter brought over a bottle of wine.

Jarrod frowned. "I didn't order this."

"No, sir, you didn't. It's compliments of the gentleman over there." The waiter's gaze went across the room to the gray-haired man sitting at a small table by himself, watching them. "For Briana," the waiter added as the older man raised his glass at her.

"Send it back," Jarrod snapped.

"No!" Briana exclaimed, horrified. She speared Jarrod a dark look then smiled at the waiter. "Please pour me a glass," she told him as she got to her feet. "I'll be back in a moment."

"Briana," Jarrod said through gritted teeth.

"Pour him one, too," she instructed the waiter, turning away but not before she saw the glint of humor in the waiter's eyes.

Laughter bubbling within her, her steps were light as she walked across the room with a natural smile on her lips. She couldn't help but feel good that she was winning this battle against Jarrod.

Then she thanked the older man and spent a few minutes talking to him. He turned out to be a fan of hers and was a thorough gentleman.

When she returned to the table, Jarrod's eyes burned through her. "Made an arrangement to meet later?" he snarled.

She shot him a dark glance. This was going too far. "No, but I can go back and ask him, if you like."

"How much did he offer you? One million or two?"

She sucked in a sharp breath. "Don't be ridiculous."

"Isn't that why you went to thank him?"

He sounded jealous, and the thought sent a weird thrill through her. Then she realized this wasn't about jealousy. This was about belonging to Jarrod Hammond, as temporary as that was.

"He was just being nice," she said firmly. "He's a gentleman."

"He wants to take you to bed."

"So does most of the male population, I imagine, including yourself."

A second ticked by, and a smug look crossed his face. "Ah, but *I* did, you see," he drawled, his voice silky-smooth now.

Her mouth tightened. "I hope you marked it on that belt of yours with all those other notches."

Sexy amusement flickered in his eyes. "You know something, Briana? I really like fighting with you."

She ignored that, even as she privately acknowledged enjoying a verbal victory with this man every now and then. "By the way, it's part of my job as the face of Blackstone's to maintain good public relations. I wouldn't want to offend him."

"As long as they are only *public* relations."

"If they weren't, it's none of your business."

"Don't bet on it, sweetheart."

So, she'd been right to be worried about his thinking he could boss her about. Her chin tilted in defiance. "You don't own me, despite the million-dollar check."

His eyes grew cool. "No, but I do own three weeks

of your time. And don't forget you're the one who suggested the million dollars. And you're the one who took the money. I would have just been happy to go to bed with you."

"Yes, and I'm the one who'll pay the price," she said, suddenly feeling sickened by it all. "I think I'd like to leave."

Jarrod's gaze swung across the room. "Won't your number-one fan over there be offended if you don't drink his wine?"

"Oh, you're so right." She picked up the glass and drank it in one go. Thankfully it was only half-full. "There." She put her empty glass back down on the table.

Jarrod's brow rose. "You can handle drinking it that fast, I presume?"

"It was only half a glass." She went to get to her feet but all at once he leaned across the table and put his hand over hers, his touch heating her skin.

"Unless you want our little tiff in tomorrow's papers, you'd better stay here and finish your lunch."

Her forehead creased. "What do you—"

"Here we are, madam," the waiter said, startling her as he slid a plate on the table in front of her. Not that she had much of an appetite by this time. Jarrod seemed to rob her of that once again.

The waiter walked around to Jarrod and did the same. "If there's anything else you would like—"

"No," Jarrod cut across him. "We're fine."

"Very good, sir." The younger man left them alone. Jarrod waited a moment before speaking. "I saw your fan talking to some guests at the table over there. They've been checking us out, so I wouldn't be surprised if he said something about the bottle of wine. If you get up and storm out it'll be in tomorrow's paper."

"Maybe you shouldn't have acted like a jealous husband, then," she said without thinking.

He actually looked surprised. "Is that what I sounded like?"

"Either that or a jerk," she said as the rush of wine made her feel a little light-headed.

He grinned. "I think that wine's gone straight to your head."

"No."

"Yes," he insisted.

"Okay, just a little," she acknowledged, finding it easier to give in this time. "But I'm used to it."

"Really?" he mocked.

"I don't have a drinking problem, if that's what you're implying." But somehow she couldn't seem to summon up much anger. She was beginning to feel relaxed and mellow. And, oh my, Jarrod Hammond really was a hunk. And that slow smile…combined with his expert hands…

"I think we'd better finish lunch," he said, breaking into her thoughts, "then I'll take you home."

Would he make love to her?

"Come on, eat. It'll soak up some of that wine. The media would have a field day if they heard the face of Blackstone's was drunk *off* her face."

That brought her out of her trance. He was right. It

could jeopardize her contract renewal. And then she wouldn't have the money to repay Jarrod....

She took a steadying breath, picked up her fork and started eating. Not long after, Jarrod began speaking of general things and she was glad to answer. Polite conversation she was used to. Personal, she was not.

She refused dessert but as they drank their coffee, he sat there looking at her. "How do you feel now?"

"Back to normal. The food helped."

"Good." His eyes took on a sudden sensual warmth that made her heart start hammering. "Now that you're no longer tipsy, I'm going to take you back to my apartment."

Her mouth turned dry. "Why?"

"I want to make love to you. I want you in my bed. Today. Tonight. Right now."

She gave a soft gasp. "Don't say things like that, Jarrod."

"Does it offend you?"

Unfortunately, no.

"It...unsettles me," she admitted, not knowing why she was even admitting that to him.

His gaze took on a piercing look. "I thought you'd be used to men saying they wanted you in their bed."

"Then you'd be wrong."

He gave her a sharp look, as if he had trouble believing that. Then he signaled to the waiter to bring over the check, and before too long they were walking back through the restaurant, through the diminishing crowd of people. The older gentleman had gone, and so had the other people, and that made her wonder if Jarrod had just made that up to keep her here.

But why keep her here when he wanted to take her to his home and make love to her?

And he proved that point as soon as they stepped inside his downtown apartment. She had a glimpse of luxurious surroundings before he swept her up in his arms and carried her into his bedroom.

"I almost hate to take this dress off you," he said in a gravelly voice, slipping it over her head anyway. "It's so very sexy." His gaze slid down over her bra and panties. "*You're* very sexy."

And then he pulled her toward him and his lips found hers, his kiss flooding her with want and need and must haves. Before too long she was aware of a mattress giving way beneath her, of his hands cupping her breasts, touching her secret parts. Then he entered her in one swift movement. When he started to move inside her, hard muscle against soft satin, desire exploded inside her. Finally…finally…he consumed her.

It was dark when she woke and she had to gather her bearings. Her job took her all over the place, so she was used to waking up in strange beds. Alone.

"It's eight-fifteen," a deep male voice rumbled in her ear.

Jarrod!

"At night?" She should move, instead of lying there in the curve of his shoulder, her face pressed against his warm skin.

"I suppose we could be having an eclipse," he joked in a husky voice, his sense of humor surprising her. It wasn't something that came to mind with this man.

She stayed where she was. She couldn't seem to find the energy to move. "Why didn't you wake me?"

"I've been asleep, too. Neither of us got much sleep last night, remember?"

Everything came flooding back. The casino. The million dollars. Being possessed by this man.

Suddenly panicked, she lifted her head. "I'd better get back to my apartment."

"Why?"

She looked up at him in the dim light, trying to focus, trying to think, but it was hard when "God's gift to women" was beneath her. "Um—so I can go to—"

"Bed? You're already in bed. With me."

She moistened her lips. "I need to shower and get something to eat."

"No problem. I'll order in pizza. We'll sit on the balcony and watch the Moomba fireworks light up the sky." All at once, he put her away from him and rolled out of bed. Naked. And then he pulled her up on her feet. Naked.

"What are you doing?"

He bent and scooped her up in his arms. Naked. "We're going to take a shower first."

"Together?"

His brow rose as he carried her into the bathroom. "You have a problem with that?" he said, his blue eyes sure she wouldn't object.

And for once she didn't. "No."

He gave her a look of mild surprise. "Sweet acquiescence?"

She nodded. "Maybe."

His eyes dropped to her mouth. "I think I like it."

Her heartbeat accelerated. "Don't get too used to it."

"That's good. Because I kind of like that snappy Briana Davenport, too, remember." He stood her inside the glass cubicle and picked up the soap. "And now, let's see what type of fireworks we can make for ourselves tonight."

She opened her mouth to jokingly point out that water would put out any fireworks, but his kiss stole her words away. Before too long she didn't care anyway. She went up in flames first, then he joined her, and it proved one thing. They were combustible together, wet or not.

Afterward, he left her on the bed and walked out of the room with a towel wrapped around his hips, saying he'd be back shortly. Satiated but trying not to show it too much, Briana pulled the edge of the comforter over her nakedness. It was silly to even consider hiding her body, but she was still tingling from his touch. She had been putty in his hands. And that wasn't good. Not good at all.

He was back in a few moments, carrying a woman's robe. He came over to the bed and held it open for her, but she stared at the oyster-colored silk as if it carried the bubonic plague.

"Don't worry. It's new."

"Order in a supply, did you?" she said, relieved not to be offered something worn by one of his previous lovers. Then she saw the label still attached to the sleeve.

She glanced up at him. "This is one of the pieces you bought at the casino."

"Yes."

She almost said something about his getting his money's worth, but she didn't want to bring that up. Not right now. Not after he'd made such wonderful love to her. Besides, her brain was tired from fighting.

She let her mouth ease into a smile. "I hope you don't plan on me wearing them all."

A surprised glint of amusement appeared in his eyes. "That was my intention."

"Good luck," she quipped, throwing the cover aside in an attempt to be blasé. Then she got up and slipped into the robe. "You're going to need it, mister."

A moment's silence met her ears, and she looked back at Jarrod behind her, only to find his eyes dark with desire.

He turned her in his arms to face him. "Lady, having you in that robe is all the luck I need," he murmured huskily, his gaze raking down her bare skin exposed by the open gown, making slow warmth heat her cheeks.

"Um…what about the pizza?"

"They deliver late."

He kissed her then and it turned her inside out, and soon he had slipped the robe back off her shoulders, slowly, slowly making love to her once more.

As Briana watched him enter her, she knew one thing. It was wonderful to be wanted by a man who wanted *her*. Not just Briana, the model.

Five

The sound of muffled voices out in the living room woke Briana the next morning, but it was the angry undertone in Jarrod's voice that made her sit up and listen. She hadn't quite heard that disdainful tone before. She'd been the recipient of his derision, but his voice held so much contempt she felt sorry for the other person.

"This is the last time, Anita," he was saying now, in a firm tone that brooked no argument.

"How can you say that, Jarrod? I'm your mother," a woman's voice said tearfully, making Briana gasp.

"You are *not* my mother. My mother is back in New Zealand looking after my sick father."

"And who gave you the opportunity to be a Hammond?" Anita said, her tone coldly unemotional now. "If it hadn't been for me, you would never have been given that silver spoon in your mouth."

He made a harsh sound. "Yes, I suppose that's the only decent thing you ever gave me."

"There you are, then. You should be grateful."

"Anita, don't pretend you gave me up for adoption for *my* sake. It was for *you,* and *you* alone."

Briana was out of bed by this time and slipping into the silk robe, curious in spite of herself. She had to see what Jarrod's real mother looked like.

"That may be so," Anita was saying as Briana tiptoed up to the bedroom doorway. "But I need money, Jarrod, otherwise I'll lose the house."

"That's not my concern," he snapped, as Briana carefully peeked around the doorframe and saw a petite, well-dressed blonde facing her hostile son. But even from here, Briana could see the hardness in her face. It was written clearly in her eyes and in the tight way she held her mouth. This woman was out for all she could get.

"You can spare ten thousand dollars for a loan, Jarrod. You probably make that much money every time you go to sleep."

"I work hard for my money. I invested it well."

"We're not all good money managers, son."

"Don't call me that," he growled, then swore and strode over to his briefcase and took out his checkbook. "This is it, Anita. This is all you're getting." He quickly wrote out the check, then shoved it at her. "Now here. Take it. And don't ever come back."

The woman greedily snatched the check, read the

amount, and her eyes widened with glee. She folded the paper and put it in her handbag. "I won't come back. I promise." A minute later, she left without a word of thanks, or regret, and Briana's heart squeezed with hurt for Jarrod. He didn't deserve a mother like that. No one did.

"You can come out now, Briana."

She stepped away from the door with as much aplomb as she could. "How did you know I was there?" she asked, moving into the living room.

"I heard the swish of your walk."

"Oh, you did not," she chided, slightly embarrassed. He'd been much too busy with Anita.

"I did." His eyes slid over her with lazy sensuality. "Like now."

The arm of the sofa was close by, so she casually sat herself down on it, her knees weak. Then she took a breath and concentrated on the woman who had angered him so much. "She'll come back, you know."

All at once, he turned toward the patio door, but not before she'd seen the bleakness in his eyes. "Yes, I know."

"Will you give her more money?"

His shoulders stiffened but he didn't turn around. "No. She's gotten enough out of me over the years."

She soaked up this information as she considered the tense line of his back beneath the gray polo shirt and black trousers. His clothes may be casual but their quality wasn't. Neither was the tumultuous feelings he must hold inside him.

"How long have you known her?" she asked, not sure he would share any information with her.

He remained where he was. Then, "Anita first came looking for money in my early twenties."

Her heart softened with sympathy. How terrible that his mother had come looking for money, and not her son. "Does she come often?"

"She turns up every couple of years and asks for a 'loan,'" he said, and this time he did spare her a look over his shoulder, his eyes filled with cynicism.

Briana stood up and went beside him. "You don't owe her anything," she said quietly.

"I know."

She put her hand on his arm. "But I guess it's hard to cut ties, no matter what she's done to you."

He glanced at her, put his hand over hers. "She never hesitated to give me up, you know," he said, surprising her with the admission. "She told me so the first time I met her. She said she'd been young and single, and a baby would have tied her down, and she'd had no intention of giving up her freedom."

Briana winced at the other woman's insensitivity. She hated thinking how he must have felt when he discovered she had so easily given him away. Up until then he had probably given his mother an excuse, some leeway, as to why she'd given him up. But to face the reality that she just hadn't wanted a baby, hadn't wanted *him,* and worse, that she hadn't cared, must have been a dreadful shock.

"She's just selfish, Jarrod. Lots of single mothers keep their babies, even back then."

He dropped his hand and turned to face her. "Exactly. If she'd given me up for *me,* then I could have forgiven her. But it was all for her." His jaw clenched. "I was better off without her."

"Absolutely." She paused, not sure whether to ask or not. "What about your real father?"

He shrugged. "Apparently he died years ago."

She arched a brow. "You were never curious about him?"

"No. Should I have been?" He grimaced. "Look, I was never curious about my birth parents. Never. I had a terrific upbringing and so did Matt. As far as I'm concerned, Katherine and Oliver Hammond are my real parents and Matt is my real brother."

Her throat almost closed up for a moment. "Good for you," she said huskily, and meant it. She was beginning to see a new side to the Hammond family that was no longer tarred by Marise's somewhat sarcastic comments. Not that she hadn't liked the Hammonds when she'd met them at Marise's wedding and the few times since. Only, now she could see a different dimension to them, and she liked what she saw.

She gave a slight smile. "It may sound crazy, but when I first heard how Howard believed his kidnapped son was alive, I thought for a moment it might have been you."

Jarrod snorted. "There's a thought. Son to Anita Stirling or Howard Blackstone? What a choice!" He shook his head. "No, I'm afraid I'm not the missing heir to the Blackstone fortune. Thank God!"

Briana had to agree with him. He'd been adopted by the Hammonds, raised by the Hammonds—he was a Hammond. To find out he actually belonged to his family's enemy would have been hard to take. And now that she knew how cruelly his mother had abandoned him, the blow would be doubly hard.

Not that he wouldn't rise above it, she knew, admiration stirring inside her with a new understanding of this man.

He put his hand under her chin, and for one heart-stopping moment held her gaze. Then he leaned forward and kissed her softly on the lips.

"Thank you," he said, lifting his head.

"For?"

"Listening. Understanding."

Her stomach fluttered like a butterfly's wings. "I'm told I have a good ear for listening."

He lifted a finger and ran it around her ear. "They're beautiful ears. Perfect." He placed his lips against it, then gently tugged at her lobe with this teeth.

She groaned as his lips began making their way down her throat. "Um—weren't we going to the—"

Where were they going?

Oh yes.

"—Moomba Festival?" she finished.

"After."

"After?" she murmured.

"After we make love."

Regardless of the way Jarrod made love to her—with a passion that hadn't diminished despite the numerous times he'd taken her in the last thirty-six hours—Briana didn't deceive herself that anything had changed.

And obviously he'd thought the same. He certainly seemed in a hurry to dress and leave the room afterward, saying he had some work to do before they went to the festival. That was probably so, but she suspected he needed some time to himself. It wasn't every day a man like him let a woman see his vulnerable side.

Still, she was relieved he had put up that wall of reserve again. It made her remember that the only reason they were together right now was the money.

So why fool herself that what she knew about him now made any difference? His dislike of the woman he thought she was hadn't changed. He still put her in the same category as Marise—and as his mother.

Having met the older woman, Briana felt doubly insulted. She got out of bed, showered and dressed in one of the outfits Jarrod had bought in the casino. It was either that or put on yesterday's clothes.

Then she left the bedroom and poured herself a much-needed cup of coffee. She was standing with her back against the black granite counter and sipping the hot liquid when Jarrod spoke from the doorway.

"You look great."

She glanced up into his approving gaze. "Thanks," she said somewhat sourly.

"I mean it," he said, obviously sensing her withdrawal.

"I know."

"And?"

"What do you want me to say, Jarrod? That I've been waiting all my life for you to come along and tell me how wonderful I look?"

His forehead creased in a deep scowl. "What's the matter with you?"

She took a deep breath and told herself to take things easy. Okay, so nothing had changed, but then had she really wanted it to? Besides, if he wanted to consider her a money-hungry gold-digger, then nothing she said or did would change his mind.

She pasted on a sickly sweet smile. "How can there be anything wrong when everything is so right?"

He shot her a wry look. "Yes, I can see that," he mocked, but there was also a guarded look in his eyes, as if he suspected she was feeling hurt because he'd shut her out after they'd made love.

Well, she wasn't.

She placed her cup on the sink and tried to sound casual as she said, "I know it's out of our way, but can we go to my apartment first? I'd like to get my camera so I can take some pictures of the festival."

His eyes gave a flicker of surprise. "I have a camera you can use."

"No, that's fine. I'd prefer to use my own camera. It's a very expensive one."

"And you think mine isn't?"

She conceded the point. "A camera's a rather—personal thing."

He scrutinized her response. "I never thought of it that way." Then studied her further. "You like taking pictures, do you?"

All at once she felt uncomfortable. "It's a change from being on the other side of the lens."

He stared hard for a moment longer. "Give me five minutes, then I'll be ready to go," he said, and turned and walked into his study.

An hour later, they'd found a good vantage point along Swanston Street. The Moomba Festival was Australia's biggest community festival and a Melbourne tradition for over fifty years, with firework shows, outdoor movies, the Moomba parade and lots of water-related activities on the Yarra River.

The parade was the highlight of the Moomba Festival and Melbourne families turned out in droves, creating a sea of color and excitement.

The celebrations continued in Alexandra Gardens and along the riverfront, with live entertainment, roving performers and water sports. Briana strolled next to Jarrod, clicking her camera whenever she saw something of interest. She particularly liked taking pictures of people's faces when they were unaware of it. She loved to capture the wondrous expression of a child watching a magician, or the parents watching that child with such love on their faces.

"Don't you get sick of people looking at you?" Jarrod asked after she'd taken a picture of a group of people who'd kicked off their shoes and were having dancing lessons.

She looked at him, startled. "Do they? I hadn't noticed."

"Everyone's recognizing you."

"Maybe it's the camera. Maybe they think I'm someone important."

"You *are* someone important."

She laughed that aside. "Only to my father."

He looked at her a moment or two, a rare, soft light entering his eyes.

Her heart skipped a beat. "What's the matter?"

"You are."

"Why?"

He gave a slight smile. "Maybe one day I'll tell you."

Just then someone jostled them and the moment was broken. She quickly glanced down and pretended to check a setting on the camera, his comment reminding her there never was going to be a "one day" for them.

When she looked up again, she trained her camera on some children having their faces painted. The thought that she and Jarrod were going their separate ways at the end of the month brought an unwelcome lump to her throat. Yet she didn't want to feel even the slightest bit miserable about that. So why did she?

"Do you like being a model?" Jarrod asked as they continued their stroll in the sunshine.

She stumbled a little and he put his hand out to steady her. "That's an odd question." She could feel his warm, firm touch through her sleeve. "Why do you ask?"

"You seem to have quite a talent behind the camera."

She was surprised by his perception. "Thank you. I enjoy it."

"Perhaps it'll turn into more than a hobby."

"Perhaps," she agreed in a noncommittal voice, and moved to take another photograph, making Jarrod drop his hand from her arm. She felt awkward, being unused to sharing her dream with anyone. Not even Patrick had noticed her talent for taking pictures. He'd been too busy complaining she had been ignoring him.

Just then she spied a vendor selling hot dogs, and her stomach growled, reminding her she hadn't eaten. "Hey, how about we get some hot dogs for lunch?"

"Pizza last night, hot dogs today. Sure you don't want to go to a restaurant?"

"No, this is fine." She glanced around. "Let's grab some food and go sit on that bench down there on the riverbank."

"Good idea."

A few minutes later, Briana placed her camera on the bench between her and Jarrod to keep it safe, and then she began eating her hot dog.

"You look like you're enjoying that," Jarrod remarked.

She nodded. "I am."

His eyebrow rose a fraction. "So you don't watch your weight?"

"Of course I do, but sometimes I like to break out." She prided herself on the fact that she wasn't anorexic thin like some of the other models. "Still, in the last two days I've eaten enough junk food to last me six months."

His gaze swept over her. "You've got the perfect figure."

She wondered why she didn't care about any other man's compliment, but Jarrod's stirred awareness inside her.

"Then maybe I should be the body of Blackstone's," she joked. "Perhaps I'll even get them to include that in my next contract."

A curious look came into his eyes. "So they're

offering you another contract, then?" he asked in a measured tone.

"I expect so." Her forehead creased. "You sound surprised. Why?"

There was a short pause. "I thought with all the controversy lately, the Blackstones might—"

"Drop me like a hot potato?" she cut across him, stiffening.

He inclined his head. "Something like that."

She suppressed a shiver, refusing to think right now about *not* being offered a new contract. So far no one had held Marise's antics against her. "You may not have noticed, but I was at Kim Blackstone's wedding. I'd like to think that was a good sign."

"Oh, I noticed," he drawled, a sexy timbre to his voice. "And yes, definitely a good sign."

Still, she needed to reiterate something. "Jarrod, as much as you don't like the Blackstones, they *are* professionals."

The lines of his face turned instantly rigid. "Howard Blackstone was never professional," he rasped.

That may be so but, "He was always good to me," she felt obliged to point out.

"And Marise?" he sneered. "Was he good to her, too?"

She sucked in a sharp breath. "What are you implying?"

"What everyone else is implying, Briana. That they were lovers."

"You have no proof."

His gaze sliced over her. "No, but a woman usually

doesn't leave her husband and child to spend time with another man just to be friends."

"Don't," she whispered, feeling a stab of fresh pain. She looked toward the river and away from Jarrod.

God, she hated to think about her own sister doing something like that, but she suspected he was right. She had tackled Marise about being seen with Howard, but had received a smug comment that she didn't know what she was talking about.

Perhaps if they'd been closer as sisters, Marise would have come to her when she and Matt were having problems. Only, they weren't close, and Briana had always felt guilty about that, yet realistically she knew she couldn't do anything about it. Marise had been her own worst enemy. She'd held people at a distance, then pulled them close when she wanted something from them. She knew her sister's faults as much as anyone.

Of course, it still didn't stop her from thinking that if she had been there for her sister, perhaps Marise might not have been with Howard on that plane…might not have died. It was a sobering thought.

"Was she having an affair with him, Briana?"

She looked back at Jarrod, held his gaze, definitely not appreciating the demand in his tone. "How do I know?"

A hint of anger entered his eyes. "You were her sister."

"Her sister. Not her keeper." A knot lodged firmly in her throat. "Look, Marise was my sister and I loved her dearly. And whatever she did, she did for a reason. I have no doubt about that."

Seconds ticked by. "She doesn't deserve your loyalty. She certainly wasn't loyal to my brother. Or to her son."

Briana bit her lip. She knew he was right but she couldn't say it out loud. She just couldn't betray her sister's memory in this way. She owed Marise a sister's loyalty and understanding. Somehow.

"How *is* Matt?" she asked quietly, trying to remain composed. "And Blake? Is he okay?" She hadn't seen Matt since Howard's funeral so she had no idea how her little nephew was doing. The poor little guy must be missing his mother terribly.

"As well as can be expected." Jarrod sent her a hard look, as if everything that had happened was *her* fault. "Rachel Kincaid is looking after him."

She tried to push his silent accusation aside. "Rachel Kincaid?"

"She's a nanny. Her mother is my parents' house-keeper."

She nodded. "Oh, yes. I remember her name now." She'd never met Rachel, but if Matt thought she was good enough to look after little Blake, then that was good enough for her.

A shutter came down over Jarrod's face. "The only decent thing to come out of all this was Blake."

Everything inside her squeezed tight with anguish. It was all such a mess. If only she could go back and somehow help change things. "I agree."

"Your sister left a legacy of heartache, Briana," he said in disgust, then tossed his half-eaten hot dog into the garbage bin a few feet away.

She winced inwardly, knowing it wasn't the food that disgusted him. "I know she did." Her own appetite totally lost now, she stood up and threw her own partially eaten hot dog in the bin before picking up her camera. She didn't bother to take the lens cap off, having lost her hunger for taking any more pictures today, as well.

After that, they walked around for another hour or so, watching the water-skiers and the bands playing music, but the day was flat now. She was quite relieved when Jarrod suggested he take her home, then oddly disappointed when he walked her to her door but only took a few steps inside her apartment.

"You're not staying?" she said before she could stop herself.

"No."

So that was that.

Weekend over.

She squared her shoulders and met his gaze. "This isn't going to work, Jarrod."

He shot her a level glance. "Yes, it is."

"But—"

"We had a deal, Briana. You'll be my mistress until the end of the month. But you'll be happy to know you're getting a small reprieve. I'm off to Singapore tomorrow for a conference."

"Singapore?" Relief warred with disappointment once more, and she told herself not to be silly. Just because he would be away shouldn't mean a thing. And because the following week she had to go to Brisbane, she should be happier about their having less time together.

So why wasn't she?

"What are your plans for next weekend?" he said, as if she had a choice in the matter.

She frowned. "I'm going to the Grand Prix on Sunday. I'm invited to lunch at the Blackstone corporate box."

He nodded to himself. "Okay, that'll work out well then. My plane lands just after lunch and I'm meeting some business acquaintances at one of the corporate boxes. I want you to join me as soon as you've finished with the Blackstones."

Surprise kicked in. "You don't mind being seen with me at a public function?"

He shrugged. "We'll be in a corporate box together, that's all."

"It could cause speculation in the papers," she warned.

"We'll worry about that when and if it happens."

She tilted her head, not exactly sure why they should bring attention to themselves.

"I'll call you on your mobile phone when I arrive at Albert Park," he said, cutting through her thoughts. "Make sure you take a taxi there because I intend taking you home."

All at once his arrogance got to her. "Is that another way of saying we'll be having sex afterward?" she snapped, deliberately sounding crude and as offensive as him.

His dark look said he didn't appreciate her comment. "I don't need to take you home for sex."

"No, you only need a checkbook."

"Shut up about the bloody money, will you?" he growled.

Her mouth dropped open in surprise, yet she'd seen a glint in his eyes that made her wonder who was more shocked by his reaction.

Then he appeared to bounce right back to his usual arrogant self. He gestured toward the telephone on the side table. "Answer your messages."

With difficulty, she drew her gaze away from his face, seeing the red light flashing on her answering machine. "They can wait."

He arched a brow. "Hiding something?"

She thought of her father and could feel herself blush a little. "No, of course not."

He looked at her sharply. "This deal of ours works both ways, Briana. Don't play me for a fool."

"I don't 'play' people, Jarrod," she told him, chin in the air.

"Is that so?" he said, not looking convinced, reminding her that once again memories of Marise rose between them. And it showed Briana that sex and mutual attraction were really all she and Jarrod had going for them.

She stepped aside but he pulled her into his arms. "No kiss goodbye?" he murmured silkily.

Not giving her a chance to reply, his mouth claimed hers in a hard, brief kiss that seemed to punish rather than enjoy. She pushed at his chest, and the pressure of his mouth eased...and then eased some more...and suddenly they were in the middle of a long, languorous kiss that did delicious things inside her blood, pulsing it through every pore of her skin, leaving his mark.

Eventually he put her away from him. "I look forward to having you in my bed again."

Then he headed for her door and closed it behind him, leaving her standing there for a moment, still tasting him in her mouth. Oh heavens. She looked forward to being back in his bed, too.

Thankfully the winking light on her answering machine drew her attention, and she pulled herself together and hurried to listen to the message. Nothing from her father, but Jake Vance had been in town for a couple of hours today and thought they might have lunch if she called him back before he left for Sydney again.

She discovered that Jake had also left the same message on her mobile phone, and she sighed with a hint of regret. She'd accidentally left her mobile on the sofa when she'd come rushing in earlier to get her camera. It would have been so much easier spending time with any man other than Jarrod. But she was committed to Jarrod now. Totally and irrevocably.

Until the end of the month anyway.

Six

Briana had attended the Grand Prix last year, so had previously witnessed the sensation of the world's fastest men racing at incredibly high speeds around the track. It was a four-day action-packed extravaganza of on-and-off-track activities, culminating in the main race on Sunday.

She knew the layout of the corporate boxes above the pit. Thankfully fumes weren't a problem but ear plugs were supplied for use during the races. Invitations were at a premium, so there was always a good turnout of high-profile guests.

Kim and Ric were in the box to greet her.

"Briana, hello," Kim greeted with a quick hug. "I was so looking forward to seeing you."

Briana was moved that Kim thought her worthy of a

friendly hug. "You, too." She offered Ric her hand. "Hello, Ric."

He took it. "She's talked of nothing else all week," he said with obvious affection for his new wife.

"I'm sure," Briana said with a wry smile. "How was the honeymoon? You went up to Leura, didn't you?"

Kim gave a happy sigh. "The mountains are just beautiful at this time of year. It was such a perfect time for us."

"But far too short," Ric added.

Kim smiled in appreciation. "Yes, far too short." Then her smile slipped a little, and her eyes held a hint of worry. "Unfortunately we couldn't take any longer."

Briana knew Kim must be thinking about the fallout from her father's death, and the many rumors in the business community, including the mysterious buy-up of the company shares.

Ric looped his arm around Kim's waist and pulled her in tight next to him. A look of support passed between husband and wife, confirming they would be okay no matter what happened to Blackstone's. They deserved their happiness.

Just then, Ryan Blackstone and Jessica Cotter came through the door. Pregnant with his twins, Jessica looked happy and healthy, with a still small baby bump.

Briana felt a lump in her throat. She was so pleased it had worked out for both couples. She just wished....

No, if she wished for the same thing for herself, then she'd have to find a man who was her soul mate. It had happened for her parents but she didn't really believe that would happen for her.

When most of the guests had arrived, Jessica patted the chair next to hers. "Come and sit down, Briana." She waited as Briana sat on the chair next to her. "Now," she said, lowering her voice. "Ryan and I are getting married next month, so you'd better be able to make it to the wedding, my friend." She named the date.

Delighted, Briana gave Jessica a quick hug, pleased that she would be back from her overseas assignment by then. "I wouldn't miss it for the world, Jess."

Jessica beamed. "Great. It's all going to be hush-hush, but I'll let you know the details later." She waited while the waiter passed behind her chair, then, "So what's happening with the diamonds? Have you heard back from Quinn yet? You dropped them off at his office after the wedding like you said, didn't you?"

Briana nodded. "Yes, I left them with his office manager. But I haven't heard anything so Quinn must still be away. He said it would be a few weeks." She'd had so much going on that she hadn't given the diamonds any thought. Being Jarrod's lover had kept her fully occupied.

And then some.

Even this past week she'd found herself thinking what he was doing at the conference in Singapore. He hadn't called, but she hadn't really expected him to.

Or had she?

Okay, so she had. She understood being busy, but just a quick phone call to say hello would have been thoughtful. After all, didn't being a temporary mistress afford her some consideration?

Obviously not.

"Is everything okay?" Jessica suddenly cut across her thoughts. "You look a little bit—oh, I don't know—tense."

Tense? That was an understatement. Trust Jessica to see through her.

"You're seeing someone, aren't you?" Jessica said, excitement in her voice.

"Kind of."

Jessica stared at her, then just as quickly pulled a face. "You're not back with Patrick, are you?"

Briana snorted. "Wash your mouth out with soap, Jessica Cotter."

"Thank heavens! That guy was such a sleaze."

Briana felt more than a flicker of surprise. "Why didn't you say something when I was going out with him?"

"Sweetie, you had stars in your eyes. Nothing I said would've mattered."

Briana cringed inwardly. That was probably true.

"So who's making you so tense?"

Briana thought about whether to tell Jessica or not. It was probably going to be in the papers soon enough anyway, once she met with...

"Jarrod," she admitted.

"Hammond?" Jessica squeaked.

"Yes. I'm meeting him this afternoon."

"Here?" At Briana's nod, she sent her a shrewd grin. "That's so great. He's such a hottie. If anyone deserves happiness you do."

"Happiness? Who's talking happiness? I'm meeting the guy for a drink," she fibbed, stretching the truth a little. "It's no big deal."

Jessica wagged a finger at her. "That's what I said when I first went out with Ryan."

Briana opened her mouth to speak, but one of the Blackstone clients interrupted them and she was glad to get off the subject.

She thought it was all forgotten, until Jessica came up to her after lunch and whispered, "He hasn't called yet?"

Briana's mind whirled in surprise. "How did you know he was going to call me?"

"Easy. You keep checking your mobile phone."

"Oh." She hadn't realized she was so obvious.

As if their conversation had conjured him up, Briana's phone rang. Her heart jerked inside her chest as she took the call.

"You answered," Jarrod said in a husky murmur that almost made her forget to take her next breath.

"You expected I wouldn't?" she murmured, keeping her voice low.

"Yes."

"Good." A ripple of anticipation shot through her. "I'm glad I keep you on your toes."

"Actually, I prefer to be lying down. With you."

She caught Jessica looking at her knowingly, and that brought her down to earth in a hurry. "Where are you?" she said, making her tone a shade cooler. If he knew she'd missed him, there'd be no end to his demands.

There was a slight pause. "Just getting out of my car," he said, his own tone cooler now. "Come down the stairs and meet me."

Cooler *and* arrogant, she decided. "Why don't you come up here and get me?"

"Is that wise?"

She realized why. He didn't want to meet up with Kim and Ryan again so soon. They may be cousins but there was still a huge gap between them and him.

"I'm only thinking of you," he added quietly.

He had a point. Why put herself under Blackstone scrutiny and put her contract renewal into jeopardy?

"Maybe this isn't such a good idea," Jarrod said out of the blue, surprising her. He wasn't a man who second-guessed himself, and having him do that now on her behalf made her heartstrings catch.

"Yes, it is," she murmured. "Come and get me, Jarrod."

And suddenly she knew she was doing the right thing. For Jarrod, not herself. For his family's sake he needed to touch base with the Blackstones whenever he could. He'd already attended the jewelry launch and the wedding, so he must at least want to try and breach the huge gulf between the Hammonds and the Blackstones.

She knew that Kim would not hold her involvement with Jarrod against her, short-lived as it would be. She just prayed that Ric and Ryan wouldn't either.

"I'll be there in five minutes," he said, an odd tone to his voice, and ended the call.

Briana turned off her phone and put it inside the pocket of her jacket.

"He's coming here?" Jessica said from behind Briana, startling her again.

Briana spun around. "Yes. I hope no one minds."

Jessica eased into an encouraging smile. "Of course they won't mind. He's family."

Briana ruefully shook her head. "Jess, you know as well as I do that there's family, and then there's *family.*"

Jessica acknowledged the comment with a nod. "Yes, but I think it's time everyone stopped thinking about what Howard wanted and got on with their lives and with what *they* want."

"I think you're right," Briana agreed, as one of the clients came up to talk to her. For the next five minutes Briana chatted with her and Jessica, even as she kept her eye on the door.

And then the waiting was over, and Jarrod walked in the door like he'd never had a moment of doubt. He headed straight for her, making her heart skip a beat. He looked so handsome. So much a lover. And he was hers.

For now.

But before he could reach her, Kim called out his name in a surprised tone. "Jarrod?" She hurried over and kissed him on the cheek. "How lovely to see you here."

"Kim," Jarrod said, acknowledging her, and Briana swore she saw a trace of affection in his eyes for his cousin. She reminded herself that Kim had worked for Matt back in New Zealand, and Jarrod would have gotten to know her over the years. And just because Kim and Matt were now no longer talking…

"What are you doing here? Not that I mind. I just wasn't expecting you," Kim said as Ric and Ryan moved toward the pair, both men frowning.

Jessica went to move, but Briana beat her to it. "He's

come to collect *me*," she said, stepping forward, just stopping herself from slipping her arm through his. But her chin did angle with a touch of defiance. "Jarrod asked me to accompany him to one of the other corporate boxes and I said yes."

There was a shocked silence.

Kim recovered first with a warm smile. "How nice. But please don't run off just yet. Stay for a drink with us."

Briana watched Jarrod look from Ryan to Ric and back, his shoulders tensing. The two men were standing either side of Kim like a pair of guards. For a moment she thought Jarrod was going to refuse.

"I'd be happy to," he said, his gaze telling the other men he wasn't backing away. That he intended to stay as long as he wanted.

A moment crept by, and it flashed through Briana's mind that perhaps they should leave after all. Jarrod had proven his point.

But before she could say anything, Ric said, "I'll get you a whiskey." He strode away to the bar area and everyone watched him go like he had taken their tongues with him.

Kim asked Jarrod how his parents were doing, and Jessica asked another question, and before too long Ric was back with a whiskey, and talk turned to general things, if a little awkwardly.

Briana stood there and joined in when she could, but she was aware of the speculation in everyone's eyes as they glanced back and forth from her to Jarrod. Did they know she and Jarrod were lovers? Jessica and Kim probably suspected it, but she was certain Ric and Ryan knew. She could see it in their eyes. It was that all-male, all-knowing look that held a new and growing respect for Jarrod for bedding her.

And Jarrod noticed, she was sure. She could tell by the pleased expression on his face. Soon he'd be strutting around like a rooster in a barnyard.

Thankfully Jarrod finished his drink and they took their leave. While Briana was glad to see a slight improvement in the relationship between the men, she didn't like it being at her expense.

As they were heading along the corridor toward the other corporate box, Jarrod drew her into another passageway off on the side where it was quiet.

"What are you—" she began.

He covered her mouth with his for the longest moment, and her legs weakened. She had to grip his forearms to hold herself up.

Eventually he pulled back. "I missed kissing you," he murmured, turning her heart over in response.

She noted he didn't say he missed *her.* He missed *kissing* her. But that's all a man like Jarrod would allow.

"That must be a new feeling for you."

He chuckled in a low throaty sound. "It is actually." Then his gaze lowered over her very feminine, grape-colored suit. "By the way, I love your outfit."

All at once the pleasure on his face reminded her of that rooster look back there. "They know we're lovers, Jarrod."

He frowned. "Who?"

"Ric and Ryan."

His face cleared. "So?"

"You let them think it to boost your ego," she accused.

"No, I didn't."

"You did. You—" He kissed her again, and this time his kiss was even longer and deeper, as if he was trying to stop all thought.

He succeeded.

She sighed deeply with delight.

But when he finally ended the kiss, he didn't wait for her to respond. He took her by the elbow. "Come on. Let's get this afternoon out of the way. I want to take you home and make love to you."

Before she could say anything else, let alone protest, he led her along the corridor until they reached one of the corporate boxes. A Grand Prix staff member immediately opened the door, but not before Briana saw Jarrod's company name on the nameplate. Her head cleared from his kiss.

"You didn't tell me this was *your* box," she said in a low voice as they stepped inside.

He spared her a glance. "Didn't I mention that?"

"No." But then, why should he? If temporary mistresses didn't warrant phone calls from Singapore, then she probably didn't warrant knowing this.

He led her over to a group of men and women about to watch the race. As he began to introduce her, one of the men stood up. "No need to introduce this lovely lady, Jarrod. We all know who Briana is." He smiled at her. "You're certainly a sight for sore eyes, young lady."

Briana put on her model's smile. She didn't always enjoy meeting new people but she never let it show. Most people were genuinely nice.

And then she *did* begin to enjoy herself. And as she saw how the others held Jarrod in high regard, something inside her warmed to him, and before long the incident back at the Blackstone corporate box was mentally filed away. He was a good escort and included her in the conversation, never leaving her side. For a while she let down her guard and forgot all about the family issues between them.

She even caught him watching her with a lazy smile that made her toes curl, and she suddenly felt even more amiable toward him. "I have something to confess. Remember when I said I wasn't taking any of the clothes you bought me at the casino?"

An alert look entered his eyes. "Yes."

"I lied. I took one of the outfits and wore it when I was leaving. I didn't want anyone seeing me wearing the same dress from the night before."

"Obviously you feel safe telling me this while we're in a crowd," he drawled.

"Of course," she said with a shrug and a smile. "But I plan on giving it back to you."

"Keep it."

"No."

"Will you stop being so damn stubborn?" he said in mild exasperation. "The boutique won't take it back, and I certainly have no use for it."

He was right. "Well, when you put it like that…" she

said with a wink, then turned to reply to a question from the gentleman seated on the other side of her.

Jarrod felt the blood rush to his groin at that wink. She'd never been playful before and it had caught him by surprise. He was more than a little charmed, in fact.

Of course he'd always been charmed by her whether she smiled at him or not, he decided as he watched Briana work her magic on his guests during the afternoon. She laughed at exactly the right moments, listened when she needed to, told some modeling anecdotes, and genuinely seemed to be enjoying herself. Not only was she beautiful and intelligent, but he could see that her work ethic was beyond question. She appeared to be a woman with high morals. She wasn't flirting with the other men, or making the women feel less in her presence. Yet he couldn't deny she had slept with him for money.

So why did she appear to have a conscience about that, considering the type of person she supposedly was, according to her sister? That made him wonder now if Marise had been playing games. The other woman had been excellent at stirring up trouble over the years. Certainly she'd played games with Matt, so why not with *him?* More importantly, why had he believed her?

Looking back, all those suggestions about Briana liking money had made sense at the time, but he'd seen no hint of Briana overspending, or of her having a good time now. The Briana he'd been with these past few weeks just wasn't the same person he'd expected from Marise's comments.

Hell, Marise wouldn't have put her Blackstone contract in jeopardy for him as Briana had today. And he sure as hell wouldn't have discussed his adoption with someone like Marise, nor would he have missed Marise like he'd missed Briana in Singapore this past week. It was the reason he hadn't called. He hadn't liked the effect Briana was having on him and he had been determined to ignore it—and her. Now he wished he hadn't. He'd been the poorer for not hearing her sexy voice.

Late afternoon, Jarrod decided to hand over the event to his second-in-charge. They said their goodbyes and were just reaching his BMW when he heard another man call Briana's name. Thinking it was one of her fans he was surprised when a tall, well-dressed man walked up to them and kissed Briana on the cheek.

"Patrick!" she said, and Jarrod saw her face reflect dismay before she quickly schooled her features.

"You're looking gorgeous as ever," this Patrick said, his gaze sliding over her in a way that ate her up.

She glanced at Jarrod as if she knew he wouldn't be pleased, then back at the other man. "What are you doing here?"

"Drinking lots of champagne and enjoying the sights," Patrick said. "And you're one of them." He pulled her toward him and kissed her again. "It's good to see you."

Jarrod watched her step back as fast as she could, and decided it was time to stake his claim. He moved in closer and put his arm around her waist. "Aren't you going to introduce us, Briana?"

Her mouth tightened, though whether because of him or this Patrick he wasn't sure. "Jarrod, this is Patrick. He *used* to be my business manager," she said pointedly.

Definitely meant for Patrick, Jarrod mused. But he could feel her tenseness against him, so it must not have been a friendly parting, on Briana's part at least.

Patrick's slyly amused gaze noted his hand on her hip. "Oh, but we were much more than that, weren't we, Bree?"

Something fierce slammed into Jarrod's gut when he heard this guy call her the nickname. It confirmed what he'd already suspected.

"Were we?" she said coolly.

Patrick quietly chuckled as he looked at Jarrod. "Women! They never forget a thing."

Jarrod's hand must have tightened on her hip because she winced. He relaxed his hold but that didn't stop the feeling that this other guy was a jerk. For the first time in years he wanted to hit another man.

Patrick didn't seem to notice anything out of the ordinary. "I'm really sorry to hear about your mother. And Marise, too."

She inclined her head but her eyes remained cold. "Thank you."

"Look, I don't suppose you want to meet up later for a drink," he said to Briana, and Jarrod had no doubt *he* wasn't included in the invitation.

"No thanks, Patrick. I'm busy."

Patrick looked disappointed but there was a cold gleam in his eyes. "Well, if you change your mind, you know how to find me."

Jarrod's jaw clenched. These two had a past and he didn't like it. Not one bit. Nor did he like the implication that Briana could easily call this idiot and slip into bed with him.

"Goodbye, Patrick," Briana said, then walked to the car a few feet away.

Jarrod shot the other man a hard look then followed her. He didn't say anything as he unlocked the car door, then held it open for Briana. By the time he came around the other side, Patrick was no longer in sight.

He wanted to say something to her about it but noted she had a withdrawn look that said she didn't want to talk. He allowed her that. He could wait.

Once inside his apartment, he could wait no longer. "How long were you and Patrick together? As lovers, that is."

Wariness clouded her blue eyes, but her chin lifted. "A year."

"He's the one, isn't he?" he said, sounding calmer than he felt. "He's the one who stole your trust."

"He stole more than my trust," she said with a touch of bitterness, then seemed to freeze.

"Go on."

She hesitated only briefly. "He invested all my hard-earned savings and lost the lot."

Jarrod swore. "How?" Then he listened as she explained what the other man had done. He swore again.

"The guy looks like a con-artist to me. I could check it out for you. I *am* a property lawyer, after all."

"No!" she blurted, then seemed to pull herself together. "Look, I thoroughly checked the paperwork before I handed over anything to him and it was all aboveboard. I realize now he just gets involved in schemes that sometimes work out, sometimes don't. My one didn't."

He suddenly didn't like the way she was defending the other man so readily. "You still have feelings for him?"

A derisive sound emerged from her throat. "To tell you the truth, I don't know what I ever saw in Patrick."

Relief washed through him, but, "Then why defend him?"

"I wasn't. I—" She stopped, and started again. "Look, what Patrick and I had is dead and gone." Her mouth tightened. "And that's all I'm going to say on the matter."

Something wasn't quite right, but he felt that "something" was to do more with Briana than Patrick. He was sure of it. And it occurred to him that perhaps this was the reason she had slept with him.

"So you recouped your losses by taking my million dollars?"

Her eyelids flickered. "Yes. It was the only way I could get some money."

He saw she had hesitated. And that meant she wasn't telling him the truth. At least, not the *whole* truth.

"Why did you take the million dollars, Briana?" he asked silkily.

Her gaze darted past his shoulder, then back again. "You already have your answer, Jarrod."

"Do I?" He recognized evasion when he saw it. He was a lawyer for God's sake. He knew how to respond to a question without actually giving an answer. And she was doing it well.

Too well.

He started to demand she tell him everything, only he looked at the stubborn angle of her chin and knew she had gone as far as she would go right now. He would bide his time.

Yet suddenly time was the one thing that was running out for them. He pulled her close and started to make love to her, a tenseness in him that for the moment had less to do with knowing Patrick had been her lover, and more to do with letting Briana go.

Briana spent the weekend with Jarrod then had a couple of days at her apartment to prepare for her Brisbane trip on the Wednesday. After all, staying in top shape and looking good kept a model busy.

Still, she couldn't shake the unsettled feeling she'd had since seeing Patrick at the Grand Prix. She had hated running into him. He brought back too many unpleasant memories.

But it had been Jarrod's reaction to Patrick that worried her more than the meeting itself. Could he have been jealous? The thought made her feel light-headed, as if the oxygen had just been sucked from the room.

On the other hand, perhaps he just didn't like another

man wanting what he had, especially if it was an ex-lover. Yes, that sounded more like it, she mused, as she stepped out of the shower and heard the phone ringing.

"I'm taking you to the airport," Jarrod said before she could speak.

She frowned. She didn't have to leave for two hours. "But you'll be at work."

"I'm taking you."

"Why? Don't you think I can find it myself?" she quipped, but she felt uneasy. This wasn't just about him being his usual, arrogant self. This was about him having what Patrick wanted.

"Did it occur to you that I just might like to spend a bit more time with you?"

"Actually, no."

There was a small pause. "Your loss," he said and hung up the phone.

Briana winced. Had she misread him after all? She wasn't sure, but she knew he was right about it being her loss. Any woman would think her mad for missing the opportunity to spend more time with Jarrod Hammond.

But she didn't call him back.

And she didn't call him while she was away either. Nor did he attempt to call her.

The three days went quickly, and Briana was more than a little anxious to see how things were between them once she was back in Melbourne.

Her mind was fully on Jarrod when early evening on Good Friday she stepped off the plane at Tullamarine Airport in Melbourne and got the shock of her life.

Patrick was waiting for her as she wheeled her small suitcase through the lounge gate.

Her mouth dropped open. "Patrick! What are *you* doing here?"

He kissed her cheek, a cold smile lifting the corners of his mouth. "Striking while the iron's hot."

Apprehension rushed through her. "What do you mean?"

"We need to talk."

Her misgivings increased. "Now?"

"It would be in your best interests if you did."

A feeling of uneasiness went through her. "Patrick, whatever my interests are they don't concern you any longer." She went to step past him. "Now, if you'll excuse me."

He put his hand on her arm. "Your father may not agree," he warned, his "Mr. Charming" persona wearing thin.

"Wh—what?" He couldn't possibly know. He couldn't. Just couldn't.

"That got your attention, didn't it?" he said, looking pleased with himself. "Come on. Let's talk over a drink."

"But—" She was still reeling. Still trying to take all this in.

"This way," he said, guiding her forward, his hand on her elbow.

Briana was stunned, her mind going over all the possibilities. If he had said anything else, she would have told him to get lost. But mentioning her father was disturbing.

He took her to a bar along the walkway, then sat her

down near one of the large windows where she could watch the planes take off. She wished she was on one of them right now. She had a feeling she wasn't going to like what he had to say.

"How was your flight?" he asked, once he'd bought their drinks.

She glowered at him. "Cut to the chase, Patrick. What do you want?"

A moment passed, his stare drilling into her. "You're going to Asia soon."

Her forehead creased in a frown. "Yes. So?"

"I want to be reinstated as your business manager. I'm coming with you."

She made a derisive noise. "No chance."

"Is that so?" he said, a lethal calmness in his eyes that worried her.

She shook her head, trying to make him see reason. "I don't understand, Patrick. *Why* do you want to be my business manager again? It didn't work out the first time."

He paused, as if deciding how much to say. "Things haven't been the same since we parted. I need to renew some high prestige connections, and two weeks with you in Hong Kong, Taiwan and China should do it."

"Maybe you should have thought of that before you lost all my money in a bad investment," she choked, not in the least sorry for him. Yet she blamed herself, too. She shouldn't have taken his advice and gotten a second opinion.

"It was a good investment, Briana. It just went wrong." Just as quickly, he pasted on a sly smile. "But then, it's easy to get tangled up in something bigger than ourselves at times, don't you think?"

What was he implying? "Look, I don't know what you're hinting at, but just say what you have to say so I can go home."

"Okay then." He waited for effect. "I *know* what your father's been doing."

She tried not to flinch. "And that is?"

"Stealing money from Howard Blackstone."

Her heart dropped to her feet, but she forced herself not to react. Whatever he knew, he may not be certain. "I don't know what you're talking about."

"Don't play games," he said cynically. "Remember last year when your parents went on that world cruise? Remember how you suggested I stay at their house for a week when my apartment flooded?"

"Yes." Surprising how even then she hadn't wanted Patrick moving in with her, not even for a week. She had the feeling she wouldn't get rid of him, and her parents' house had been a blessing. Or so she'd thought at the time.

"I was using your father's laptop one night because mine was having problems—I think some water had got into it," Patrick said in an aside that made her want to snap at him to get on with it. "And I found something interesting. There was some bank information on it that at the time I didn't realize meant much. It's only now that I've put two and two together."

"Really? That's amazing. But I don't know how you can come to the conclusion my father stole from Howard Blackstone."

"Give me a moment to explain," he said as if he was talking to a two-year-old. Then he deliberately took time to sip his drink before answering. "Okay. It was only after I saw you the other day at the Grand Prix I was thinking about that world cruise and how your parents could pay for it. Your father had retired from his job and your mother was dying at the time, only none of us knew it."

There wasn't even a hint of sympathy in his voice, Briana noticed.

"You had no money to spare, either," he continued. "It was all tied up in your investment. And Marise was over in New Zealand, your parents rarely saw her, and I'm sure if she had loaned them the money I would have heard about it."

His touch of cynicism for Marise was justified, Briana admitted. "So?"

"Well, then I got to wondering how your father paid for everything—the cruise, the medical treatments. And it all fell into place. Your father used to be Howard Blackstone's accountant. All those figures and dates and an account called 'Black Rock' got me doing some investigating. And what I discovered was *very* interesting."

Her hand tightened around her wineglass. "You're making this up."

"Fine. Then let's go the police and I'll get them to check things out. I'm sure they'd be more than interested in anything to do with Howard Blackstone and his death in that plane crash."

Her heart slammed against her ribs. "My father had nothing to do with the plane crash!"

"No, but I'm sure they'd have to investigate everything I tell them anyway."

He was right. Even the suggestion of her father being involved in the crash would be enough to have the police checking out everything to do with their lives.

Defeated, she slumped back against the chair. "So you want two weeks as my business manager?"

His eyes flared with triumph. "In writing." He took a piece of paper out of his jacket pocket and slid it across the table like a snake. "Sign this."

She opened the paper and began reading with a numbness that was comforting. "You've certainly thought of everything."

"Everything except you becoming my lover again," he said in a deceptively relaxed voice. "I don't think we need write that down, do we?"

She shoved the paper at him. "No way. That's not part of the deal. I won't sleep with you, Patrick." Why, just the thought of it turned her stomach. After Jarrod….

He fixed her with a stare. Then, "Okay, we won't become lovers," he relented, and pushed the paper back for her to sign. "But I don't want anyone else knowing that. To the world, we're lovers again. It's the only way I'm going to renew my contacts."

Relief washed through her. There was no way she could have given in to that demand. She had slept with

Jarrod because she'd wanted to. That wouldn't be the case with Patrick.

"What happens after the two weeks and they realize we're no longer an item?" she asked.

"By then I'll have signed up Lily Raimond. She's going to be the next big superstar." His lips twisted. "Move over, Briana."

"Gladly."

He considered her. "You never did realize what power you had at your fingertips."

She ignored that as she picked up the pen and signed. "You stick to your end of the bargain and so will I. Otherwise, my father or not, I'll tell the police about your blackmail—and the rape." She watched his face blanch and felt a measure of power. "Because that's what it will be if you touch me, Patrick."

He folded the paper and put it in his jacket pocket. "I don't remember you being so reluctant to be in my arms before," he scoffed but she could see fear in his eyes.

She stood up. "Think again."

Seven

Briana wasn't sure how long she sat in her car at the airport car park. One minute the sun was setting, the next it was dark and the overhead lights were on. She needed some time to think and sort things out. There was no getting around Patrick over this, of that she was certain.

How on earth had he figured it all out? It wasn't like the account had been one of Howard's regular ones. It was a "secret" account, for heaven's sake. An obscure account in the bowels of some banking institution somewhere in the world, which no one had known about except her father, Howard's previous accountant and Howard himself. And the last two men were now dead.

But Patrick was experienced at walking that fine line between legal and illegal, and like a dog who'd sniffed out a buried bone, he had unearthed the one crime committed from her father's lapse in judgment.

Now she had to phone her agent, who would declare her absolutely crazy to even *think* about reinstating Patrick as business manager, let alone doing it.

And then there was Jarrod.

Oh God.

Yet what business was it of Jarrod's anyway, she asked herself a touch defiantly. He only wanted her for the rest of the month, and after that she was free to do what she liked. Even if she wasn't going to be Patrick's lover, it shouldn't matter to Jarrod what she did with the rest of her life.

So why was she worried? She'd end her relationship with Jarrod, go away on assignment with Patrick, and after that it would be rare that she ran into Jarrod again.

And if at some time he heard she was back with her ex-business manager, well, Jarrod hadn't wanted her anyway.

She felt sick at heart at the thought of it all, but despite everything she suddenly wanted to see Jarrod. Wanted to be in his arms, feel his reassuring presence, even if that reassurance was all in her mind.

But as soon as she pressed his buzzer, she knew she'd made a mistake in coming here. The last time they'd spoken, he'd hung up on her for not letting him take her to the airport. And heavens, what if he had decided to come and get her today? If he'd seen her with Patrick and somehow found out about her going away with Patrick, then that meant the end for them now instead of ten days time. Suddenly those ten days were so extra precious…

She turned back toward the elevator just as he opened his door. "Hey, you're not going anywhere," he said, pulling her into his apartment and into his arms. He kicked the door shut behind them and kissed her, and once again she melted into him.

Then he slowly broke off the kiss. "I think I missed you."

Her heart thudded at his words. He wasn't saying he missed *kissing* her, like he'd said last time. This time he missed *her*. Oh Lord. What did that mean? Did he actually have feelings for her?

She prayed not. Jarrod was not for her. Especially now, not with Patrick blackmailing her. Things would be just too complicated.

She swallowed her anxiety and managed to tease him with, "You only think?"

"If I said I missed you for sure, you'd do that female thing and assume you have a hold over me."

He had it wrong. It would be the other way around. "Actually, I wouldn't."

His intense blue eyes riveted on her face. "You really wouldn't, would you?"

"No."

He didn't give her a chance to reply. He began kissing her again and she kissed him back, and suddenly she felt desperate for him. She so badly needed his touch right now. When all this ended she wanted to remember being in his arms.

Afterward, Jarrod came back from the bathroom and sat on the edge of the bed. "You okay?"

She looked away, then back. She couldn't let him find out about Patrick. "I'm fine. Just a bit tired, I guess."

His eyes seemed to probe her own. "Your job's pretty time-consuming, isn't it? Not to mention sheer hard work."

She almost felt dizzy at his words. It wasn't just his acknowledgement of the many hours she put into her job. It was the growing respect in his eyes. She hadn't felt that from him before.

"Yes, Jarrod, it is," she said, knowing that if she had achieved one thing in their time together, it was this.

His gaze held hers for a moment, then, as if he had better things to do, his face went blank and he pushed himself off the bed. "I'll make us something to eat," he muttered.

Briana watched him leave the room and sighed. He may have new respect for her now, but that respect obviously didn't extend to asking if she actually *wanted* to eat.

And right now she wasn't sure she could.

Briana felt refreshed when she woke the next morning, lying spoon-fashion in front of Jarrod, his hand resting on her thigh. She glanced at the clock and saw it was almost ten and suddenly felt guilty for lying in so late. She had things to do today, including visiting her father and preparing for a fashion show next week and—

It all came rushing back with a vengeance then.

She was being blackmailed.

God, how was she going to find the strength of will to get through this? She wasn't sure she even could. No matter how much she tried, her modeling career, her future monies, would always be tied to Patrick now. He would make sure of that.

Next to her, Jarrod rolled onto his back and for a moment she froze. Last night when she'd arrived, he'd kissed her and they'd ended up making love, but she didn't want that to happen this morning. She needed to get moving.

Thankfully, he continued sleeping, and she slid out of bed and pulled on the oyster-silk robe. He'd brought up her suitcase from her car late last night, so she'd shower in the other bathroom so as not to wake him, then dress and leave him to sleep in peace.

Right before she left, she peeked in on Jarrod again. He was still sleeping, the sheet low on his taut hips, his naked chest muscular and arrowed with hair, a dark shadow of hair on his jaw making him look manly, short rumpled hair on his head very sexy. God, he was incredibly handsome.

Then she saw the dark circles under his eyes, and she felt bad for sneaking out like this. As much as she wanted to run, the least she could do was make him breakfast before she left.

Five minutes later, she'd just finished dishing a fluffy omelet onto a plate when she heard a noise behind her. She spun around.

"So…" Jarrod snarled, behind her in the doorway, making her jump, "it's over between you and Patrick, is it?"

One look at his face and at the newspaper in his hand which he must have collected from outside his door and her heart began to thud. Had they found out about her father? Had Patrick told anyway?

He strode toward her and held the newspaper up in her face. "You call *this* being over?"

She placed the frying pan back on the stove and snatched the paper from Jarrod. Then she glanced at the page and groaned inwardly even as relief surged through her. The papers hadn't found out about her father's embezzlement. This was a picture of her and Patrick at the airport bar yesterday. The caption read "Is Briana Doing *Business* With Her Ex Again?"

"Jarrod, this isn't what you think. I—"

"Am playing me for a fool," he said through gritted teeth.

"No!"

"You can't deny it, Briana. You were even wearing the same outfit." He stabbed her picture with his finger to prove his point.

"Jarrod, look, I'm not trying to deny it," she said, struggling to maintain an even tone. "Patrick *was* there at the airport, but he only came to meet me because—"

"He met you!"

"Yes, he was there when I came off the plane. He wanted to discuss something."

"I can imagine," he said, his voice dripping sarcasm.

She ignored that. She had to stay cool, but she had to think quickly. "It's about an assignment at the end of the month. We're both connected to it and needed to discuss it, and I had to sign some paperwork." It was her turn to stab at the picture. "See, I've even got his pen in my hand. And see, that's the paperwork on the table in front of me."

His mouth clamped in a thin line. "Why didn't you mention this last night?"

She handed the paper back to him and squared her shoulders. "I've done nothing wrong. And despite what you think, I don't have to report to you."

"And that's all it was?"

She met his gaze. "Yes," she lied.

"And there's nothing you want to tell me?"

There was plenty, but her hands were tied. "No," she said, concealing her inner turmoil. "Look, do you think if I was having an affair, I would be sitting in a bar in public with my ex-business manager?"

"Perhaps it's what you did after that—" he suggested, evidently not totally convinced of her innocence.

"I came straight here after that. You can check the time my flight landed." She paused. "So you see, Jarrod, *you're* my alibi."

He scowled at her but didn't say anything.

She arched a brow. "So what's the verdict?"

"I'm reserving judgment for the time being."

All at once this was about more than convincing him nothing was going on between her and Patrick. This was about Jarrod believing she wasn't like Marise. About him trusting her, even as a transient in his life. It may not matter to him, but it mattered to her.

"That's not good enough, Jarrod," she said, standing her ground. "You either think I'm guilty or not guilty."

He held her gaze for the longest moment, then expelled a slow breath. "Okay, not guilty."

Something inside her leaped with joy. If he hadn't believed her they could have gone no further in their relationship. She would be out that door without a backward glance, million dollars still owing or not.

He tilted his head. "I just don't understand how you can have dealings with someone who did the wrong thing by you."

"And like you don't deal with people in your world that you dislike?" she gently scoffed.

He stood there for a moment, then nodded. "You're right. My world is full of people I dislike. It comes with being a lawyer." A glint of wry humor entered his eyes. "I'm usually only involved when someone is getting screwed around."

"There you are then. Having dealings with Patrick is just business, Jarrod. He may have lost my money, but he didn't steal it."

He held her gaze a moment more, then, "Fine."

It was time for a diversion. She looked down at the omelet on the plate. "Your breakfast is cold now."

"So I see. Where's yours?"

She shrugged. "I'm not hungry. I was just cooking this for you before going to see my dad."

His eyes went over her tight jeans, thin knit top hugging her breasts, up to her ponytail but he didn't say anything, though she saw an appreciative light come in them. "You go then. I'll heat this up. Thanks."

"You're welcome." She noted he wasn't stopping her,

and that was just as well. Despite them sorting it out she could still feel things were a bit uneasy between them.

"Are you doing anything tomorrow?" he suddenly said.

"No." That meant she must not be seeing him tonight. It was crazy to feel disappointed but it was probably for the best. It was Saturday night anyway, and she'd had a vague plan to invite her father over for dinner.

"Let's go for a drive down the coast and spend the day at the beach. We can enjoy the last of the warm weather."

She blinked in surprise. "As long as you don't expect me to go swimming," she teased, trying not to show how upset she really felt about everything. "The water's far too cold now."

"No, we'll have a picnic." He gave a bit of a smile that seemed forced to Briana. "I'll be disappointed not to see you in a swimming costume."

She could feel her cheeks grow hot and said the first stupid thing that came to mind. "But you've seen me without my clothes."

Oh heavens!

Desire flared in his eyes and nothing seemed forced now. "That I have." He lifted her chin and placed a soft kiss on her lips. "You are so damn beautiful," he murmured, like he'd never get enough of staring at her. "You really don't know how beautiful, do you?"

She gave a self-conscious shrug. "I look in the mirror every day."

He shook his head. "It's hard to believe a woman so beautiful is so totally unaware of herself."

"Well, you know what they say about beauty."

"Skin deep? No, I'm talking about *you,* Briana. Not the model."

Happiness bubbled up inside her, but she kept it hidden. Everything was going to be okay between them. "Well, right now Briana 'the daughter' had better go and see Ray 'the father' so that I can invite him to dinner tonight."

A humorous gleam came into his eyes. "I'll pick you up at noon tomorrow."

Happy, she stepped around him and hurried out of the apartment. That bubbly feeling stayed with her until she walked into the kitchen of her old home and her father told her he was having trouble putting the money back in Howard's account.

Then the bubble burst.

Her heart sank.

"What do you mean, Dad? How can you take the money out but not put it back?"

He tried to look unconcerned, but she knew he was worried. "Some of the accounts are under scrutiny since Howard's death. And I'm just being extra careful." He hugged her. "Now don't you worry, honey. I'll put the money back and then I'm going to get a job to help you pay Jarrod back his loan. It's time I returned to work anyway."

She frowned at him. "Dad, it's okay. I'll be signing my new contract with Blackstone's soon," she said with more confidence than she felt.

"But that's *your* money. You shouldn't have to use it to help me."

"It isn't just for you, Dad. It's for Mum, too."

His eyes softened with tenderness and love. "You're a good girl, Briana." Then pain crossed his face. "I just don't know where we went wrong with Marise. I know your mother felt she needed more attention than you did, but I didn't always agree. We had many a fight over it, you know."

She gaped in shock. "You did?"

He nodded. "I think your mother's attitude helped make Marise the way she was." He gave a shaky sigh. "God help me, but I shouldn't be speaking of the dead this way."

She put her hand on his shoulder and squeezed comfortingly. "Dad, it's okay. I know Mum loved me."

"Yes, she did, honey. Very much," he said in a choked voice, then shuddered and took a deep breath.

Briana waited for him to regain his composure. "You know," she said gently, "we have to put all this behind us now. We can't change the past and we can't beat ourselves up about it." Easier said than done, she knew.

He offered her a hint of a smile. "You're right, honey."

"Of course I am." She pasted on a bright smile. "Now, how about you come around my apartment this evening for a nice dinner? Just you and me."

"That would be great." He paused. "But I don't want to be a bother. I know you have lots of friends and—"

Suddenly she saw the question in his eyes. "Dad, I know you must have seen the newspaper photo of Patrick and me. And no, we're not back together. I was only meeting him because he has something to do with an assignment I'm on at the end of the month."

The worry in his eyes cleared. "Good. I was never real fond of him." He hesitated. "I like Jarrod, though."

They'd never spoken of Jarrod, but there'd probably been a picture or two of her with him at the Grand Prix. She'd seen a couple of journalists clicking their cameras in their direction, and that had made her even more thankful she'd let the Blackstones know she was seeing him. At least there were no surprises.

"I've been going out with Jake Vance, too," she pointed out wryly.

"I know," he said, just as wryly, his comment reminding her she was news no matter whom she dated. "But there's just something about you and Jarrod Hammond."

Yes, and it was called sexual attraction.

"I guess we've bonded over Marise and Matt. Now, what time are you coming over tonight?"

His smile said he realized she was changing the subject. "I'll be there at six."

Jarrod had stood on the balcony and watched Briana's car drive away. Hell, the last few days while she'd been in Brisbane, he'd checked out this Patrick and found the investment made with Briana's money had all been legal, unfortunately. In the end, Jarrod had put it all to the back of his mind.

And then he'd opened the newspaper to the picture of her and Patrick together. He'd felt like someone had punched him in the gut. She'd made a deal with *him* and he expected her to honor that, not go off and jump in the sack with an ex-lover. Even now the thought of it made him see red. She was *his* for the moment.

So he'd had a few bad moments about believing her when she said nothing physical was going on between her and Patrick. But dammit, he was still confused as to why she would do business with her ex-business manager. Did she want to or didn't she have a choice?

His jaw clenched. No, he wasn't going to doubt her. He'd said he believed her and he did. And to be fair, she was right about one thing. There were plenty of people in his world he disliked, but he still did business with them regardless. Why would the modeling world be any different, he asked himself as he went to take a shower, passing by the rumpled sheets on the bed that suddenly made him want her back here.

So why had he let her leave?

Why not spend the rest of the day with her?

And the night as well?

He grimaced. Because the shock of that picture in the paper had made him feel exposed in more ways than one. It had made him admit to himself that for most of the week while she'd been in Brisbane, he'd been unable to concentrate fully on his job. And he hadn't liked it. He'd needed to clear his head, away from the influence of Briana Davenport. She'd had far too much influence over his feelings lately. More than any other woman he'd ever known. And that was detrimental to a fleeting relationship.

Just after lunch the telephone rang. It was Danielle Hammond, bringing thoughts of family to the forefront of his mind, which was just as well. He'd been trying to concentrate on a client's case, but Briana kept coming to mind.

"I thought I'd give you a call, Jarrod," Danielle said warmly but quickly, as if she half-expected him to hang up on her. "Mum and I are here in Melbourne for some Easter shopping and I thought it might be a good opportunity to have dinner together at the casino tomorrow night."

Jarrod's brows drew into a frown. He'd planned on spending the evening with Briana after taking her to the beach, and he didn't really want to share her with anyone. Still, Danielle was his cousin, and he liked her and Sonya more every time he met them.

"Mum said she'd been disappointed that she hadn't really spoken to you much at Kim's wedding, or at the jewelry launch," Danielle continued. "She really wants to get to know you."

"Does she?"

"We're family, Jarrod," she pointed out, and Jarrod realized she had taken his comment the wrong way.

Dammit, Howard Blackstone had a lot of things to answer for in breaking up the families like this all those years ago. None of it should ever have gotten to the stage where family had been set against family. Hammond against Hammond.

"Dinner will be fine."

"Great!" Danielle said. "And hey, can we keep it a secret from my mum? I'd like to surprise her. She'll be so happy."

Jarrod had to smile at her enthusiasm. "If that's what you want."

"It is. Oh, and Jarrod—" She hesitated, then, "If you'd like to bring Briana, we don't mind."

His smile disappeared. Obviously they'd been reading the newspapers and knew Briana had accompanied him to the Grand Prix. No doubt Kim or Jessica Cotter would have mentioned it, too.

"Of course," Danielle continued, "if she's with someone else—"

"She isn't," he said firmly, knowing she meant Patrick. "Briana will be with me."

"Wonderful. We'll see you tomorrow night."

Jarrod said goodbye, but as he ended the call he realized Danielle may not have meant Patrick at all. She could have meant Jake Vance.

Either way, both men were going to miss out.

Briana enjoyed having dinner with her father that night, but by the time Sunday morning rolled around she couldn't help but wonder how things stood between her and Jarrod now. After their confrontation yesterday, would Jarrod have second thoughts about believing her over Patrick?

But when she opened the door to him at noon, her fears were laid to rest. He presented her with a huge Easter egg.

"Ooh, I love chocolate," she gushed, feeling a giddy sense of pleasure, not just for the gift, but because it seemed like a peace offering. That meant things could get back to normal for them for their remaining time together.

"Some women prefer diamonds," he said, watching her.

Her excitement faded. Yes, they were back to normal all right. She angled her chin. "Not me."

His gaze became guarded. "I'm beginning to realize that," he muttered, then just as fast said, "Are you ready to go?"

For a split second she thought she'd misheard his first comment, but then realized she hadn't. He really was beginning to believe that she wasn't a money-hungry female on the prowl for a good time.

Silly tears of relief pricked at her eyes. "I'll just get my things," she said, spinning away and pretending to check through her beach bag. Did this mean he didn't think she was like Marise any longer? Was it bad of her to be grateful if that were the case? "I wasn't sure what to bring," she nattered on.

"Just yourself."

She blinked to get control of herself, picked up her sun hat and bag, then looked up with a smile. "Ready."

His gaze slid over her body in Bermuda shorts and a tank top. "*More* than ready," he said huskily, making her shiver with awareness.

She went to take a step toward him then stopped, her eyes drawn to what *he* was wearing. Her stomach did a flip.

"What are you looking at?" he asked, something lazily seductive in his voice.

"You. I can't believe you're wearing jeans." She'd never seen him dressed quite so relaxed before.

He broke into a smile. "I'm just a man."

She returned his smile. "Yeah sure."

After that, an inane sense of joy wrapped around her heart. She knew it couldn't last—happiness never did—but today she was determined to hold onto the feeling as long as she could.

The drive down the Surf Coast was pleasant in the autumn sunshine. They talked in a desultory fashion about the breathtaking view and the warm weather and things in general, until Jarrod asked how her father was doing.

Briana felt herself get defensive, even while she tried not to show it. "He's doing okay."

"Did he enjoy dinner last night? You said you were going to invite him."

"Yes. It was nice."

"Speaking of dinner, Danielle and Sonya Hammond are in town. They've invited us to dinner with them tonight."

She was caught unawares. "Us?"

He shot her a quick look. "Do you have a problem with that?"

"Um—no. I just didn't know you were that close." Danielle and Sonya had lived with Howard Blackstone all these years, so she tended to think of them as Blackstones despite their Hammond surname.

"We're not. That's what Danielle wants to rectify."

Her brow rose. "And you're happy with that?"

He gave a careless shrug and kept his eyes on the road ahead. "They've done nothing to me."

She liked his attitude. "Well then, I'd love to have dinner with you all."

"Good. It's at the casino."

"Oh." She could feel herself grow hot. Perhaps she'd been too hasty in accepting the invitation? The last time she and Jarrod had been at the casino they'd ended up in bed together.

He slanted her a knowing glance, but thankfully they arrived at the crescent-shaped sandy beach with a small pier at one end. The whole coastline was covered in glorious beaches like this, and they decided to go for a walk to the most deserted point before coming back to eat the lunch Jarrod had brought with him.

Being at the beach was such an integral part of the Australian way of life, Briana mused as they walked along the path cutting through the tufts of grass to the sand. She loved Aussie beaches... The smell of the ocean and sand... The sun evaporating the stresses of daily life...

Until Jarrod went to hold her hand, and she snatched it back. "No."

His brow rose. "No?"

"I don't hold hands."

He gave a short laugh. "What do you mean you don't hold hands?"

She moved her shoulders in a shrug. "It's so..."

"Romantic?" he mocked.

"If you like." She hesitated. "My first boyfriend always wanted to hold my hand."

His glance sharpened. "Nothing wrong with that."

"There is when it's *all* the time." She'd been young and wildly in love, but after six months they'd outgrown each other. Or perhaps *she'd* outgrown Derek, she admitted, remembering how his constant handholding had begun to make her feel somehow tied to him. A whole new world was opening up for her as a model, but he'd wanted her to stay the same. At nineteen that was the last thing she wanted.

"How many lovers have you had, Briana?"

She stopped dead. She knew she didn't have to answer but she did. "Three."

He had stopped, too. "Including me?"

She nodded. "Yes, including you."

He studied her face with an enigmatic gaze. "You're not very sexually experienced, are you?"

She stared at him, her heart seeming to open like a flower under the sun. This was another indication that he was beginning to see her as the person she was. "No, I'm not, Jarrod."

His eyes held her captive. "Was your other lover serious?"

He already knew about Patrick, so she knew he meant Derek. "At the time, yes."

"What happened?"

"I was young and so was he. It didn't work out."

Looking back, she realized how very young she'd been, and how ill-prepared for emotional commitment. It had been many years before she'd let herself fall in love again—and with Patrick this time. She winced inwardly. Both affairs had merely proven that love wasn't for her.

Jarrod nodded his head, and in silent agreement they started walking again. "You may not believe this," he said after they'd taken a few steps along the soft sand. "But I'm not a virgin, either."

She had to smile. "I'm totally shocked."

"Yeah, you look it," he teased, then they continued walking in silence for a few more yards, a rare sense of harmony between them. A light breeze from the ocean and the lapping of the gentle waves added to the mood.

A little further on, Jarrod said, "I should have said this long before now, but I'm sorry you lost your mother and sister."

For a moment her throat locked up. "Thank you," she managed. It meant a lot to her for him to say that. Then she cleared her throat. "I just wish things hadn't gone so wrong between her and Matt."

Seconds of silence ticked by and she felt a twinge of disappointment. Had she tested his goodwill to the limit? Was he going to bring up that wall of reserve again?

"I had no idea she had left him," he suddenly admitted. "Not until the plane crash."

Her mind reeled in confusion. "But she and Howard were in the papers for weeks before their deaths."

"And I was in New York working day and night on a case. I barely stopped to eat, let alone read the newspapers."

"But didn't anyone tell you?" she said, walking alongside him.

He slanted a brow at her. "Who?"

"Matt?"

He shook his head with regret. "No. He keeps things to himself."

He wasn't the only one, she mused, glancing at Jarrod's profile as they strolled along the sand. To the outside world they must look like a couple merely enjoying their surroundings. Instead they were opening up to each other in a way they hadn't done before—without recriminations. It was a major breakthrough in their relationship. Perhaps after their affair ended, they could be friends?

Perhaps not.

"Marise wasn't an easy person to love," she admitted. "But I loved her all the same."

He pinned her with another sideways glance. "Of course you did."

She gave a shaky sigh. "She didn't deserve to die."

"No, she didn't."

Briana stopped in her tracks as a sudden overwhelming sense of loss swept over her. How Marise had died would always haunt her. That was the worst part. Knowing that her sister had been floating in a life vest by herself with severe injuries. How dreadfully scared Marise must have felt, realizing she was going to die. She would have given a good fight, but not even when a passing ship had picked her up, had she been able to survive. Briana's only comfort was at least Marise had not died alone. Someone from the ship had been with her. She knew that for a fact.

Jarrod stepped in front of her and with compassion in his eyes, brushed some strands of hair off her cheek. "This is why we should live life to the fullest."

"Yes." For once she wanted to lean into him, against

him, take strength from him. She reached out and placed her hands on his hips, stepping closer, seeing his spurt of surprise and knew this wasn't about sex. This was about comfort, about giving and receiving. And that was something neither of them had tried before.

All at once someone screamed, making them both jump. It only took a split second to take in the situation. A small boy with yellow floaties on his arms had been dragged out into deeper water, his mother was on the shore screaming for help, a small baby in her arms.

"Oh God," Briana muttered, forgetting Jarrod as she immediately started to run toward the water. Others were running, too. She could hear the thud of footsteps in the sand. She wasn't sure what she was going to do. She was a good swimmer but not strong enough to swim that far out. But she couldn't let the little boy drown.

Without warning a man brushed past her as he ran into the shallows, splashing through the water. He was bare-chested but had jeans on. He had dark hair.

Jarrod!

Briana reached the mother just as Jarrod dove into deeper water and began swimming through the small waves. A couple of others were milling around the woman, someone taking the baby out of her arms, someone else offering reassurance.

Briana could only stand and watch as Jarrod sliced through the water, her heart in her mouth. She prayed he reached the child before he was dragged out even further. He was getting closer.

And then sheer fright tore through her. Would Jarrod

have the strength to swim back, let alone with a small child in tow? She didn't think so. It was too far.

She began to shake as time stood still. Yet she was aware of the sounds around her. Of the cold water lapping over her wet sneakers. Of the breeze getting stronger. Of the sun going behind a cloud, making the deeper water look even more menacing.

And she began to pray. If anything happened to Jarrod... If he drowned out there doing this heroic thing... If the ocean took him like it had Marise... She wouldn't be able to bear it.

Please God, don't take the man I love.

Her heart seemed to rise in her chest then tumble headfirst into an emotion she'd been fighting ever since she'd met Jarrod Hammond. She *loved* him. He was what love was all about.

Just at that moment Jarrod reached the boy, and a cheer went up, startling her. And then her prayers were answered when a small boat left the pier at the other end of the bay and headed for them. Another cheer went up, and this time Briana's heart cheered, too.

She still held her breath until Jarrod and the boy were in the boat and then safely ashore. There ensued a ton of commotion as the mother cried and hugged her son, then profusely thanked Jarrod with a kiss and a hug. Someone placed a towel around Jarrod's shoulders, and someone else shook his hand.

Through it all, Briana just stood there, not moving, her eyes going over him like she'd been given the greatest gift on earth.

And she had.

All at once he noticed her standing a few feet away. He walked toward her in his sodden jeans. "Are you okay?" he asked.

No, she would never be the same again.

Her gaze went over his dear, dear features. "Are *you* okay?"

He nodded. "Just a bit wet."

She remembered how she'd felt watching him out there in the ocean. "You could have drowned," she whispered.

"Yeah, well, don't make a fuss," he dismissed in a gruff voice, and turned away to collect his polo shirt and sneakers where he'd dropped them in such a hurry.

It was as if someone had snapped their fingers in front of her and awoken her from a trance. A powerful, overwhelming and crushing sensation went through her. Yes, she loved him, but the last thing she could do was tell him. Nothing had changed on his part. He'd warned her at the beginning not to expect anything more than a temporary relationship. She wouldn't go back on her word.

Besides, she had to be realistic. There were too many other things between them. Marise…Matt…her father… Oh Lord, if she told him about her father's embezzlement what would he do? As a lawyer, would he be obligated to tell the police if he knew a wrongdoing had been committed? She couldn't even tell him that Patrick was blackmailing her for fear of it all coming out in the open.

After the commotion died down, Briana suggested they leave. Though the journey back was quiet, she was inwardly screaming to get some time to herself. Jarrod needed to get out of his wet things and take a shower, only she didn't want to join him. Not when her love for him was pumping through her body…through her heart. Not when she somehow had to keep up all pretences until she could leave next week. Oh God, it was going to be a long, long week. Yet in some ways not long enough.

She was rather distant when they arrived back at her apartment building. "Please don't come up. You need to go home and change."

He stared hard, his forehead creased in a frown. "What's the matter? You've been quiet ever since I helped save the boy."

She couldn't let him dismiss his actions so easily. "You didn't just *help,* Jarrod. You saved his life."

"I couldn't let him drown."

Love swelled inside her. "I know you couldn't." She leaned over and kissed him softly on the lips. "You're a fine man, Jarrod Hammond," she murmured, pulling back. Her heart wobbled with love and a warning quickly filled her. "I just need to be alone for a little while."

His gaze softened with surprising tenderness. "It's because of Marise, isn't it? Seeing me out there in the water reminded you of how she died."

She nodded, gratefully grabbing at the suggestion, though it was true anyway.

"I understand," he said, and skimmed his lips over hers. "Do you still want to come to dinner tonight?"

The casino! She'd forgotten about that for a moment. It was going to be hard returning to the scene of their first time together, knowing she loved him. But she'd still go to support Jarrod, whether he wanted that support or not. She could do it. After all, if he had drowned today....

"Yes," she whispered, then got out of the car, hearing his comment about picking her up at seven. She nodded and said she'd be ready. She just hoped that emotionally, she would be.

Eight

"Hello, Sonya," Jarrod said as they reached the table in the middle of the luxurious casino restaurant, and Briana watched as Sonya lifted her elegant head from the menu, her eyes widening.

In her late forties, Sonya always reminded Briana of a stunning and graceful queen. Queen Sonya. Yes, she certainly seemed to be the queen of the Blackstone family, and deservedly so. The woman had lived at Howard's mansion since her sister's suicide nearly thirty years ago, raising Kim and Ryan along with her own daughter, Danielle. Remembering that, Briana immediately felt a bond with her. Sonya had lost a sister, just like she had.

"Jarrod! Oh my God! What are you doing here? What a coincidence," Sonya said with delighted surprise.

Jarrod kissed her cheek. "No coincidence," he said

as a small smile tugged the corners of his firm mouth. Then he kissed Danielle's cheek. "Danielle planned it."

Sonya swung toward her daughter. "Danielle!"

"I thought it would be a nice surprise, Mum," Danielle said with a wide smile, her golden eyes shining with pleasure, her charm a part of her beauty.

"Oh, it is. It is. It's a lovely surprise," Sonya agreed, her gaze on Jarrod, who looked handsome and debonair in a dark suit. Then Sonya's gaze fell on Briana. "And, Briana, how nice to see you again," she said warmly, and Briana wondered how she'd ever thought this woman was coolly reserved.

"It's nice to see you, too, Sonya." Briana then smiled at Danielle, whose copper-colored curls seemed to want to burst out from their bun. "You, too, Danielle."

"Please. Call me Dani."

Sonya rolled her eyes. "I give my daughter such a beautiful name and she chops it in half." She waved a hand at the two empty chairs on the other side of the table. "Please. Sit down."

Briana thanked Jarrod as he held out her chair for her.

"Well, this *is* nice," Sonya said, glowing with enjoyment. "It's just so good to have you here, Jarrod. We didn't get to talk much at the jewelry launch a few weeks ago, nor at Kim's wedding. I was hoping to catch you afterward but what with all the media swarming around afterward, I decided to go straight home."

"I left a bit early anyway," Jarrod said, confirming Briana's suspicions.

"Wise man." Sonya took a moment to smile at

Briana. "And you looked so gorgeous at the jewelry launch, Briana. I was wishing that was me up there."

"Easily," Briana said, not fawning, merely stating the truth. "But thank you. It all went very well."

The evening went well, too…until Briana's gaze caught Jarrod's by accident and everything came tumbling back. Until now she hadn't let herself think about being here, but returning to "the scene of the crime", the sounds of the casino, the scents of perfume and aftershave, of food, the gleam in Jarrod's eyes, reminded her what they had done together here in one of the casino suites—all for the sake of a million dollars.

And now she loved him.

And he could have died today.

Quickly she lowered her lashes, breaking the invisible thread between them. He may be getting a kick out of revisiting all this, but she wasn't. She would never be able to come into this place again without thinking of the man she loved. She doubted she'd ever be able to go to the beach now without thinking of him either. He would always be a part of her now. And a part of her memories.

Sonya's question broke into her thoughts. "How is your father, Jarrod?" she said casually, but they all knew her interest was more than casual about her brother— the brother she hadn't spoken to for almost thirty years.

For the first time tonight, Jarrod's face became shuttered. "As well as can be expected," he said smoothly, without any hint of the anguish that had passed between their families.

"I was praying Oliver would be up and about by now."

"So were we. But the stroke has taken its toll, I'm afraid."

"Yes, I know. I spoke to Katherine a few months ago," Sonya said, obviously surprising the others. "She's not as hopeful of a full recovery as she was before." She blinked rapidly, as if to stop sudden tears. "It *has* been five years after all."

"These things can take longer than we expect, Sonya," he said, making Briana wonder if in addition to his father's health he meant family issues, as well.

Briana could only think how much stood between these two families. Sonya and Dani were Hammonds yet they'd been shunned by Sonya's brother, Oliver, who was Jarrod's father. Families needed to work things out. How she wished she had her mother back to talk to. And Marise. She'd make it work with her sister if she had another chance, she told herself, despair cutting the air from her lungs.

"Yes, they do take time," the older woman agreed softly, a hopeful looking crossing her face.

An awkward silence ensued but fortunately their first course arrived.

"I must say," Dani began as she picked up her fork, "you have some great shopping here in Melbourne. We were going to come down last weekend, only Mum didn't want to fight the crowds from the Grand Prix."

Sonya shuddered. "I love Melbourne, but car racing is not my thing. Mind you, Kim and Ric were here. Ryan and Jessica, too. They were hosting a corporate box." She paused as she glanced casually at Jarrod. "They said they saw you, Jarrod."

"Briefly."

A moment crept by.

"I was there, too," Briana said to ease the silence. "It was great catching up with them all. Jessica is blooming in her pregnancy."

Sonya sighed. "I'm so grateful they're happy." She glanced across at her daughter with a loving smile. "Children are such a blessing."

Dani pointed a fork at her. "That's not what you said when I told you I was going back to Port Douglas."

Sonya smiled at Jarrod and Briana. "On the other hand—"

"Mother!" Dani laughingly joked.

"As I said, a blessing—" She paused. "In disguise."

Everyone laughed, and then continued eating.

"So, Dani," Jarrod said when there was a lull in conversation. "You like Port Douglas, do you?"

Her eyes lit up. "I love it."

Briana was impressed by Dani's considerable talent. "How is your shop going up there? I loved those pieces you designed for the jewelry launch."

Dani looked thoroughly delighted. "Thank you. I've got so many clients out of that. I've almost paid back Howard's estate the money he loaned me to start the business."

"You design jewelry?" Jarrod said, obviously not knowing. "You must be very good if Howard lent you money."

Dani's chin lifted in the air. "No, Howard Blackstone is *not* my father," she said, a feistiness entering her tone.

"Danielle!" Sonya said, scolding her daughter.

Dani immediately grimaced. "I'm sorry. I'm just so used to everyone thinking Howard is my father that I wanted to set the record straight." She looked across the table at Jarrod. "It's important to me that you know the truth, Jarrod. I mean, I'm grateful to Howard and I was fond of him—but I'm a Hammond, as well."

Jarrod looked directly at his cousin. "Dani, I never did believe any of that crap in the newspaper."

Sonya cleared her throat. "Thank you, Jarrod. This means a lot to me." She reached out and squeezed Dani's hand. "To us."

"Yes," Dani added, her eyes a little watery. "Thank you."

Briana could have kissed Jarrod. She knew how much his family hated Howard Blackstone, how much he disliked the man himself, yet he was able to stand back from that now and realize these two people weren't to blame. Her love for him deepened.

"I once did a magazine shoot in Port Douglas, Dani," Briana said, giving them a moment to recover. "It's beautiful, and you certainly get some pretty famous people up there. I saw a couple of movie stars from the States."

Dani waved her hand in a dismissive gesture. "That's nothing compared to all the hoopla with the Governor-General coming up there on ANZAC Day for a commemoration. You should see those preparations."

Suddenly there was a clang of cutlery and everyone

looked at Sonya, who had dropped her fork on her plate. She'd turned as white as a sheet and had a faint sheen of perspiration on her upper lip.

"Mum?" Dani said, quickly leaning toward her mother. "What's the matter?"

Sonya went to say something, swallowed, then began again. "Um—I'm fine, darling. I just came over cold and clammy all of a sudden." She dabbed at her top lip with a napkin but she still looked white.

"But I wasn't feeling the best before we came," she added, surprising Briana because she'd thought Sonya was a picture of health. Then she looked at Jarrod. "I hope you don't mind, but I think I may need to go and lie down."

"Of course I don't mind." Jarrod got to his feet. "I'll take you to your room."

Sonya waved him back in his seat. "No. Dani and I will manage."

"Come on, Mum. Let's get you up to our suite. I want to get the doctor to look you over." As Dani started to lead her away she promised Jarrod she'd call.

After they left, Briana looked at Jarrod worriedly. "I hope it's nothing too serious."

He'd been frowning, but his forehead cleared. "It's probably just a stomach bug."

"But it did come out of the blue, didn't it?" Briana said, still concerned. "It was like she had a shock, though I guess a stomach bug has the same symptoms." She dismissed her own thought. "Oh well. No matter. As long as she recovers."

"Hmm. I wonder if Sonya planned this," Jarrod said

later. "It's a novel way of getting out of paying the bill, don't you think?"

"Oh, she wouldn't—" Briana began, then saw the twinkle in his eye. "I'm sure you can afford it."

"I guess it's better than the million dollars I spent here last time," he said, more teasing than not.

But she didn't find it funny. She felt hurt. "That's not very gentlemanly of you to bring that up."

His amusement disappeared. "Hey, it's not like you didn't take the money."

Oh, how she wished she could tell him the truth. Things might be different for them. But she had her father to think about first. Herself second. She could never enjoy any happiness with Jarrod at her father's expense. If indeed there was any happiness to be had.

He tilted his head and considered her. "Would you have slept with me without the money, Briana?"

"No."

"Sure?" he asked silkily.

Her heart trembled. "I don't deny I was attracted to you, but no, I wouldn't have taken it further without the money." She would never have let herself be put in the position to sleep with him.

His mouth tightened. "Some things can't be ignored, Briana. And our attraction was one of them. I think you would have."

"Then we'll have to agree to disagree," she said sweetly, but her heart was sinking in her chest. If he knew she loved him... If he knew he held her heart in his hands...

"How about I give you another million dollars to come up to a suite with me?"

The thought staggered her. "Don't be silly."

His eyebrow rose. "So you don't want the money? That doesn't add up. You took a million dollars the first time but you won't take another million now."

"Perhaps I'm not as greedy as you think," she said, encouraging him to think that way about her. After everything, if he thought good about her, then she'd be happy.

For a moment he studied her intently. "Perhaps not."

She ignored a flash of relief. "Jarrod, it's been a long day. Would you mind taking me home? I'm starting to get a headache." She saw his instant concern. "No, nothing like Sonya just had." Her own headache was tension, she was sure. From loving a man who didn't love her, nor would he ever *want* to love her.

Once back at her building she turned to him in the car. "Do you mind if you don't come up tonight?" This was the second time today she'd said the same thing.

The streetlight showed his glance sharpen. "I mind, but if that's the way you feel I won't push myself on you."

"Thank you."

"But I insist on walking you to your door." And he did. Once there, he kissed her goodnight, but it was a brief kiss. "I'll call you later in the week."

"Okay." She breathed easier. She'd asked for time to herself and he was giving her more than enough.

"Miss me," he said, and headed back to the elevator.

It wasn't a suggestion.

She would take it to heart.

* * *

The next morning when her doorbell rang, Briana's pulse started racing. Jarrod! He wasn't waiting to phone her. He wanted to see her now. Today. It made her heart flutter even as she told herself not to care.

But when she opened the door, it was to find a stranger there. A very handsome and impeccably dressed stranger.

"Briana, hello. I'm Quinn Everard."

Her forehead cleared. She easily recognized the smooth, strong voice that would put more than a little spring in a woman's step. Not her step, of course. Jarrod was the only man to make her heart leap.

"Can I come in?"

"What? I'm sorry. Yes, please do come in." She stepped back to let him pass.

"I apologize for dropping by like this," he said as he stepped into her apartment.

She suddenly realized something. "Sorry if I sound confused, but I'm not sure how you got past the doorman."

"There was no one at the front desk, so I just followed another lady into the building."

"Oh—well, I'm glad I'm not being stalked." She smiled to take the sting out of her words, but this time she did intend to speak to the building manager about this. As a high-profile person, she was a prime target for anyone with a grudge or a fixation. The various letters sent to her agent over the years assured her of that.

He gave a slow smile that reminded her of Jarrod. "I hope I don't look the type to cause trouble."

"Not at all. Have a seat. Would you like a cup of coffee?"

"No, thanks." He sat down on the edge of the sofa, resting his elbows on his thighs. "I'm here to tell you about the diamonds you wanted valued."

"You didn't need to come all this way. You could have—"

"Have you ever heard of the Blackstone Rose necklace?" he cut across her.

She lowered herself down on the sofa opposite him. "The Blackstone Rose necklace?" she asked, thinking. Then her face cleared. "Oh yes. There was a vague reference to it in the papers recently."

"That's right. It was a necklace that went missing nearly thirty years ago. It belonged to Ursula Blackstone, Howard's wife, who died just after the necklace went missing."

"She committed suicide, didn't she?" Her brow crinkled. "But what has this to do with the diamonds Marise put in my safe?"

Seconds crept by. An excited light came into his eyes, an aura about him that held her full attention now. "Marise's diamonds belonged to the Blackstone Rose necklace."

Briana's head reeled. "What? But I don't understand. How could Marise have diamonds belonging to a necklace missing almost thirty years?"

"That's what I'd like to know."

What he was suggesting took a moment to sink in.

Then she inhaled sharply. "You don't think I had anything to do with this, do you?"

"Relax, Briana. I don't think you're involved," he assured her. "But I *am* hoping you might inadvertently know something. That's why I wanted to talk to you face-to-face."

She expelled a breath. "I'm happy to tell you what I can, but I just don't know that much."

He slowly nodded, then gave her an encouraging smile. "How about I start at the beginning and we'll see if anything rings a bell?"

She cleared her throat. "Fine."

"Okay. The story goes that in 1970 Ursula's father, Jeb Hammond, was fossicking in the Outback when he found a massive pink diamond that was a rare and extremely valuable find. Jeb called it the Heart of the Outback." He paused to let this sink in. "A few years later he gifted it to Ursula on the birth of his first grandson, then Howard had it turned into the Blackstone Rose necklace."

Her forehead creased as fragments of past information flashed through her mind. "That was the grandson who was kidnapped, wasn't it?"

Quinn's mouth flattened in a grim line. "Yes. James was two years old when he was abducted. But Howard always believed his son was alive, and now it looks like he may have been right."

"Yes, so I'd heard." She remembered thinking how Jarrod may have been the missing heir, and his derision when she'd mentioned it to him.

"Ursula never recovered from losing her son. As you

know, she had two more children, Kimberley and Ryan, but she suffered badly from post-natal depression after Ryan's birth. Eventually she walked into the ocean and committed suicide."

Briana sighed. "Such a tragedy," she murmured.

"But I digress," Quinn said. "The necklace. It was at Ursula's thirtieth birthday that it disappeared from around her neck. Apparently she was quite drunk and fell into the swimming pool. Some of the guests helped her to her room, but by this time the necklace was missing and Howard accused her brother, Oliver, of stealing it." Quinn's eyes hardened. "Of course, Howard also accused Oliver of arranging the kidnapping of James, a claim Oliver vehemently denied, and the brothers-in-law never spoke to each other again. Not that I blame Oliver," he said, a bitter twist to his lips that made her ask a question before she could stop herself.

"You didn't like Howard?"

His jaw clenched. "Howard Blackstone was vindictive and manipulative and very good at using people and destroying them." His face closed up even more. "It's personal."

She took the hint. "So, the necklace was never found?"

"No. And the insurance company refused to pay out because of a loophole in the policy wording."

"And there were never any leads?" she asked.

He shook his head. "Despite exhaustive investigations, no one was ever charged with the theft. Howard continued to blame Oliver."

Briana felt so sorry for Jarrod's father. Oliver had

more than enough justification to cut ties with Howard, though she didn't believe Oliver should have cut Sonya out of his life. A sister was for life.

And speaking of sisters… "Where does Marise come into all this?"

"I don't know," he said. "Perhaps you could start by telling me what she said about the diamonds when she put them in your safe."

"She didn't say much at all, I'm afraid."

"Tell me anyway."

Briana thought back. It hurt to picture the scene but it had to be done. "We were in Sydney for my mother's funeral and—" She stopped, then cleared her throat. "Marise, my father and I were staying at my Sydney apartment, which is paid for by Blackstone's as I do a lot of engagements in Sydney. I remember Marise asking if she could have the combination to my wall safe so she could keep some jewelry in there. Naturally I gave it to her." She took a shuddering breath. "Then after our mother's funeral, I came back here to Melbourne with my father. I was grieving, and trying to keep an eye on him, but I was also trying to fulfill my pre-Christmas engagements. It's all just a blur now."

"I understand," he said, his voice sympathetic.

"Then I started hearing about Marise and Howard and—" She swallowed hard. "I honestly don't know what to believe about them. All I know is that just before I went to Howard's funeral I remembered the jewelry in the safe. I checked and there were the diamonds, so I phoned Matt to tell him I had some jewelry belonging to Marise, but he didn't want to know." She winced, then, "So I mentioned it to Jessica and she gave me your name." She lifted her shoulders in a faint shrug. "Sorry, I'm not much help."

"That's okay. You're doing fine." His eyes took on an alert look. "Did you tell Matt they were pink diamonds?"

She thought back. "No. I just said jewelry. Why?"

He shrugged. "No reason. Was there anything else in the safe?"

"Only a few bits and pieces of my own jewelry." Something occurred to her and her eyes widened. "Oh God, could Howard have given them to her, do you think?"

Quinn scowled. "I don't know, Briana. It would mean Howard either had the necklace all along, or came into it again without telling anyone. And why give it to Marise? Unless—" His eyes flickered away then back to her.

"Unless she was his mistress," Briana said what he'd been too polite to say. "I'm afraid I can't answer that question. I just don't know why Marise was with Howard. I'm not sure we'll ever find out."

"You're probably right."

Her brow furrowed. "What happens with the diamonds now?"

"They should go to the Blackstone lawyers."

She nodded. "Of course. Would you be able to give them to the lawyers on my behalf?"

"Absolutely." He stood up. "I'm returning to Sydney this afternoon and I'll hand deliver them myself as soon as I can."

"Thank you," she said with relief. "Just do whatever

you have to do to make sure they are returned to their rightful owner."

"I will."

She didn't want the responsibility of such valuable items in her care now. God, when she thought about what she'd unwittingly had in her possession... And Matt, he'd be kicking himself for not taking them back. Not that he would have kept them once he found out they belonged to the Blackstones.

Quinn left not long after that, and Briana sat on the sofa again, thinking. How on earth had Marise come by the diamonds? And what had she been planning on doing with them? Not to mention, who had stolen the necklace in the first place?

At the thought, she felt a sudden chill. Would everyone think *she* was involved somehow? After all, it had been her sister with the diamonds, and they'd been in her safe.

What sort of person would Jarrod think she was? She'd taken a million dollars off him, and now she had the stones in her possession. She knew his opinion of her had risen lately, but now, would this set it back? More than likely, she thought with despair.

Oh Marise, she whispered to herself, what have you done?

The only good thing in all this was that the diamonds would now be returned to their rightful owner. More than likely Kim, as the eldest. And Kim would believe her, she was sure. She just hoped this didn't put her contract into question with the other powers-that-be at Blackstone's.

Nine

Time was running out, and Briana was sick at heart for the rest of the day. She felt guilty for keeping the news of the diamonds from Jarrod, yet next week her relationship with him would be over and she'd be on her way to Hong Kong anyway. With Patrick. So why bother telling Jarrod about the diamonds? Why spoil their last week together? Every moment together was precious. She couldn't think beyond that.

The only good news was when her father called and said he'd managed to put the money back in Howard's account. The relief she felt was tremendous. Her father was still guilty of embezzlement but at least now no one could accuse him of keeping the money for himself.

So for her, it was all worthwhile. Sleeping with

Jarrod, spending time in his company. Oh yes, very worthwhile. If heartbreaking now.

Over the next few days, Briana tried to forget about the diamonds while she concentrated on preparing for her overseas assignment. Jarrod had called once or twice, but he was busy with a heavy case. She understood but she missed him. And it made time tick even more loudly in her ears.

And then two days later he took her out to dinner. It was a warm March evening and daylight saving time didn't finish until the end of the month, so it should have been pleasant eating and watching the sun set over the city. Briana spent most of her time trying to act normal, but the pink diamonds from the necklace were at the back of her mind. At the front was the thought of heading to Hong Kong next week and leaving Jarrod.

They ended up back at her apartment where she went into his arms and let him make love to her. Yet no matter that she badly wanted to show him how much she loved him, she still had to restrain herself, knowing that if she gave him her all, she might well fall apart right there and then.

Afterward, she lay in the crook of his arm, a slither of moonlight falling over them. If she could just commit this moment to memory… His masculine scent… The smoothness of his skin… The springy feel of chest hair beneath her palm…

"Is everything okay?" he said, his deep voice rumbling in her ear, cutting across her thoughts.

She mentally pulled herself together. "Why wouldn't it be?"

"You tell me."

She hardly dared breathe. "I don't know what you mean."

"You were distracted tonight."

She lifted one bare shoulder in a shrug. "I've got a lot on my mind."

"Like?"

She hesitated. "I'm leaving for Hong Kong next week," she pointed out, wanting to remind him that this would all end soon. She didn't fool herself that the end of their relationship would impact him like it did her, but it would've been nice to know he'd feel a little sad about them going their separate ways.

He tensed. "So that's next week then?" he said casually, as if he hadn't realized, though she knew he must. Jarrod never forgot a thing.

"Yes. The month will be up then."

A lengthy silence followed, then all at once he gently moved her off him and pushed himself out of bed. "I'd better go home. I have an early appointment."

So much for her thinking he might care, she thought with despair as he dressed in the dark. His movements weren't hurried, yet she had the feeling he couldn't wait to get away from her. He probably couldn't wait to get rid of her for good now.

Then he kissed her and left.

It was a long time before she fell asleep after that.

The last person she wanted to see the next day at a

fashion parade was Patrick. The Chadstone Shopping Center might be one of the biggest in the southern hemisphere but it wasn't big enough to get away from this man.

"So, sweetheart," he said, standing in the doorway with a smirk as he watched her change into another outfit. "You're all ready for our trip next week I hope?"

"Yes," she all but growled at him.

He lifted an eyebrow. "Going to give lover boy the flick this weekend, are you?"

"That's none of your business."

"Yes, it is. I don't want him coming after you and spoiling things on the shoot for me." His eyes narrowed. "You make it clear to him that it's over, right?"

She considered him with distaste. "I don't know what I ever saw in you, Patrick."

His lips twisted in a cynical smile. "Do you think I care?"

"No. You care about no one but yourself."

"I'm glad you realize that."

She watched him turn and walk away like he didn't have a care in the world. It was all an act. He cared what people thought of him, but only for his own advantage.

And she knew one thing. If Patrick had known about the pink diamonds, he would have sold them on the black market, and he wouldn't have cared less. Of that she was certain.

Jarrod didn't see Briana again until Saturday. Until then he'd stayed away through choice. He was trying to wean himself off her. She'd begun to play a significant part in his life, and he wasn't happy about it. This was only supposed to be a fling with a beautiful model. He should have worked her out of his system by now. So why hadn't he?

Dammit, he couldn't deny the way his gut had knotted the other night in bed when she'd mentioned leaving. The thought of her going away for two weeks made him ache to hold her in his arms, but it was more than that. It was knowing once she left it would be the end for them.

Hell, he had to have some integrity. He'd offered her money, she'd taken it, they'd made an agreement. And now that agreement was coming to an end. He'd go his way and she'd go hers. Intimate strangers.

And then on Saturday morning his brother called him, and everything Jarrod had previously believed about Briana rose up and punched him the gut, making that knot unravel pretty damn quickly.

"I hope you're sitting down for this, Jarrod," Matt said, an excited note in his voice that immediately caught Jarrod's attention. "Quinn Everard has found four of the five pink diamonds from the Blackstone Rose necklace."

"You're kidding," Jarrod said, leaning back against the kitchen counter. He'd grown up hearing all about the missing necklace and all the heartache it had caused. "Dad must be thrilled."

"He is. It's given him a real boost." There was a slight hesitation. "There's something else. Briana had them."

Jarrod straightened. "What!"

"Quinn said Briana asked him to value them."

Jarrod swore. "Go on."

"Apparently Marise asked if she could keep some jewelry in Briana's wall safe in her Sydney apartment, so Briana gave her the combination. It wasn't until just before Howard's funeral that Briana remembered, and that's when she found the diamonds." Matt paused. "She told me, you know. She said she had some jewelry of Marise's and I told her to keep the damn lot." He cursed at himself. "How the hell was I supposed to know they were diamonds belonging to the necklace?"

Jarrod tried to take it all in. "But what was Marise doing with them? And why the hell didn't Briana at least mention them to me?"

"Who knew why Marise did anything," Matt said bitterly, reminding Jarrod that good news or not about the diamonds, this was going to stir up Matt's ill-feelings again for his late wife. Then, "I hear you've been seeing Briana."

"Yes," Jarrod said tightly.

"Quinn said she had no idea what the diamonds were," Matt pointed out, obviously still having a soft spot for Briana, despite her being Marise's sister.

Jarrod's jaw clenched and his hand tightened around the telephone. "She still should have mentioned them."

Matt didn't speak for a few seconds. "Here's something else that's strange. I heard a recent rumor on the underground grapevine. It was about the Davenports. Apparently, long ago the Davenport name was mentioned in connection to the missing necklace." He paused significantly. "*Before* Marise and Briana were born."

A second shock wave rocked through Jarrod. He tried to take it all in. "How substantial is the rumor?"

"The diamonds pretty much confirm it."

Jarrod expelled a breath. "This is too damn incredible."

Matt waited a moment before asking, "What are you going to do?"

He stiffened. "Speak to Briana," he said, his voice holding an ominous quality.

"Let me know what develops. I've asked Quinn to look for the fifth diamond, but if she knows anything at all, I want to hear about it." His unspoken words said "for Oliver Hammond's sake."

Jarrod hung up the phone and stood there letting it all sink in. He felt gutted. Briana had kept all this from him. It made him wonder what the hell else she was hiding.

Briana started frowning as soon as she heard the buzzer sound on Saturday morning. When she answered, it was to find Jarrod standing there. "You're early for our lunch date."

"I know," he snarled at her as he stepped past her into the living room.

He looked...odd. "What's going on?"

His gaze seared her. "Perhaps I should be asking *you* that."

Her misgivings increased by the moment as she slowly closed the door and turned to face him. The distance was more than the length of the room between them. "What do you mean?"

"The diamonds, Briana."

Her frown deepened. "Diamonds?"

"Pink ones," he drawled with deceptive mildness. "From the Blackstone Rose necklace."

Her forehead cleared, and just as quickly her heart sank. "But how do you—"

"Matt told me."

"Matt?" She shook her head, trying to make sense of what Jarrod was saying.

"The diamonds belong to him now."

Shock ran through her. "But how? Why?" Dear God, she didn't understand what this was all about. And Jarrod obviously blamed her already without a fair hearing.

"Marise was left the Blackstone jewelry collection, remember? On her death, it all went to her husband." He paused. "Matt."

"But I thought the Blackstone Rose diamonds would belong to the Blackstones."

"Howard obviously thought differently. He bequeathed *all* the jewelry to Marise."

"But surely not the Blackstone Rose?" She'd known about the jewelry going to Marise of course, but this was different. This was the Blackstone Rose necklace, for heaven's sake. Howard couldn't have known it was going to resurface, and even if he had, why leave it to Marise in his will?

She let out a shaky breath. "I still don't understand."

"Join the club," he said scathingly.

She ignored that, not sure if it was meant for her or himself. Probably both. "Is Matt going to give it back to the Blackstones?"

Jarrod snorted with derision. "I doubt it. My father will be very pleased to have the diamonds back where they belong—with the Hammond family. It should never have gone to Howard in the first place. The only reason Howard married Ursula was to get his hands on the Heart of the Outback diamond."

"You can't know that."

"I know Howard."

She tilted her head at him. "I didn't realize you were quite so…involved with the family feud between the Blackstones and the Hammonds."

"I'm a Hammond. I'm involved," he snapped.

She realized she'd touched a nerve about his adoption.

He pinned her with his eyes. "Why didn't you tell me about the diamonds, Briana?"

Suddenly she felt a chill. This was it. "I didn't think they were important."

"Oh come on! You must have known Marise had put them in the safe and what they were."

"At the time I knew she put some jewelry in the safe. That's all." Her eyes searched his, and hurt ripped at her insides. "You don't believe me, do you?"

"No," he freely admitted. "Not when there's a Davenport connection to the stolen necklace all those years ago."

Her stomach lurched. "What?"

"Matt learned on the underground grapevine today that the Davenport name was linked to the missing necklace almost thirty years ago."

She shook her head. "No way. Besides, neither Marise nor I were even born then."

"No, but your parents were."

His words hung in the air. She swallowed a lump in her throat. "You can't believe—"

"That your parents stole the necklace, left Howard's employ, moved to Melbourne where they sold one of the diamonds, and in later years told you and Marise all about it? Does it sound so far-fetched, considering the circumstances?"

She stared aghast. "I don't believe I'm hearing this."

"Your parents were pretty cushy with Howard at one time."

Panic flared. She didn't want Jarrod linking her father and Howard. "So?"

One dark eyebrow rose upward. "So you do know about their past association with Howard?"

"If you mean, do I know that Howard fired my mother when she got pregnant with Marise, then yes, I know." Briana still couldn't understand it but she remembered her mother saying those had been the times back then. Howard wouldn't get away with it these days.

"How did Marise come by the diamonds then?" he shot at her. "And why didn't you tell me about them?"

She didn't appreciate his interrogation. "I don't know why Marise had them. And I've already told you I didn't know what the diamonds were. If I did, why would I get them appraised and risk being discovered? Why would I have told Quinn to give them back to their rightful owner?"

"To protect your family."

She stiffened. "What do you mean?"

"You know your parents stole the necklace. You know Marise, as the eldest daughter, had been given the remaining diamonds. And you thought pretending ignorance was the best way of clearing their names."

His words distressed her. How could he think all that? "You've got it all wrong, Jarrod. Very wrong."

"I want to speak to your father."

She sucked in a sharp breath. "Wh-what?"

"I said I want to speak to Ray. I want to hear what he has to say about all this."

Anxiety twisted inside her. "But you can't—I won't—"

"Feeling guilty?" he growled.

"No." Yes, because of the money.

He stared hard. "Then you won't have a problem if I speak to him."

Somehow she had to get through to him. "Look, he's been through so much. His lost his wife and one of his daughters and now you're accusing him of God knows what. Leave him alone. Please, Jarrod."

His face remained rigid. "I'm going to speak to him no matter what you say."

Begging hadn't worked, so she forced herself to look at him with steely-eyed determination. "I'll never forgive you if you do."

He didn't even flinch. "I'll never forgive myself if I don't."

She realized he was deadly serious. He wasn't going

to be swayed. He would talk to her father with or without her. And if her father wasn't prepared…

With a supreme effort, she squared her shoulders and gave in. "I'll come with you."

Ten

"Ray, we need to talk," Jarrod said as soon as her father opened his front door.

"It's okay, Dad," Briana blurted so he would know it wasn't about the money. Despite it, she saw the flicker of apprehension in her father's eyes and prayed that Jarrod would think it was merely confusion.

Her father stepped back. "You'd better come in," he said with a calmness he must not be feeling. Then once they were all in the living room and Jarrod refused the invitation to sit down with a shake of his head, Ray stood, too. "So, what is it we need to talk about, Jarrod?"

"It's about those diamonds, Dad," Briana said, and received a dark look from Jarrod, but she didn't want her father getting mixed up and inadvertently saying anything he shouldn't.

"Diamonds?"

"You know the ones, Dad," she continued. "I told you about them. Remember those four pink diamonds I found in my safe?"

Ray frowned. "Yes, but—"

"They belong to the Blackstone Rose necklace," Jarrod said, obviously deciding it was time to take control.

Ray blinked. "What?"

"Dad, those four pink diamonds Marise put in my safe belonged to the missing necklace," Briana said gently. She understood his confusion only too well. "Do you know why she would have had them in the first place?"

Ray shook his graying head. "No." Then he seemed to realize they were waiting for more information. "Honey, your sister was a law unto herself. She was my daughter but she did what she wanted, no matter who she hurt, may she rest in peace," he said, his voice choking a little on the last sentence.

Briana blinked back sudden tears as a moment crept by. Yes, that had been Marise.

"Ray," Jarrod began, his voice quiet but unwavering. "You and your wife used to work for Howard Blackstone, didn't you?"

"Yes. And I remember when the necklace went missing."

"It was never recovered."

"Not as far as I know." All at once her father's shoulders tensed. "What are you implying?"

"Ray, did you steal the necklace?"

"What the hell!"

"Jarrod," Briana warned at the same time. She didn't like Jarrod playing the lawyer with her father.

"Did you steal the Blackstone Rose necklace?" Jarrod demanded, ignoring her.

"No!"

"Then how did Marise come by it?"

Ray shot him a hostile glare. "Perhaps Howard gave it to her."

"If it had been recovered earlier, Howard wouldn't have been able to keep that to himself." He gave a cynical twist to his lips. "No, I don't think Howard gave it to Marise at all."

Ray shrugged his shoulders. "Then I'm afraid I can't help you."

"Barbara—"

"I can assure you my wife didn't steal it either." If her father's glare was hostile before, it was doubly hostile now.

Jarrod stood his ground. "Ray, look. Try and step back from this for a minute. It's a possibility, isn't it?"

"Anything's a possibility," her father snapped.

Briana had had enough. "Dad, what Jarrod is getting at is that you and Mum stole the necklace, then we moved here to get away with it, that you gave it to Marise as the elder daughter, and that I got the diamonds valued to put everyone off the scent."

"But—but—that's preposterous!" Ray exclaimed.

"Really?" Jarrod said. "Then the rumor Matt heard is obviously wrong."

Her father's forehead creased. "Rumor?"

"From the underground grapevine. They're saying there's a Davenport connection to the missing necklace."

"Good Lord!" Her father looked totally confused. "I don't understand. How can they say that?" He shook his head. "Why would someone jump to such a conclusion?"

"Just like *you're* doing now," Briana said pointedly to Jarrod.

Jarrod ignored her. "I could accept that was the case *if* it had been an open rumor, but for it to be an underground one it must be pretty well substantiated." He watched the older man carefully. "The interesting thing is that only four diamonds were recovered and there were five. One is still missing. Matt believes it's something to do with your family, and seeing that Briana and Marise weren't even born when the necklace was stolen, we can only assume you or your wife must have appropriated it."

"Jarrod, will you stop this!" Briana exclaimed. "Dad knows nothing about it."

Amazingly, Jarrod stood his ground. "I think he does."

"What gives you the right to come in here and—"

"I took it," Ray cut across her.

Briana gasped. "What?"

"I said I took the necklace."

"Dad, no!"

Jarrod's expression became thoughtful. "Then where is the other pink diamond?"

"I—um—sold it."

"To whom?"

"I—um—can't say. It's confidential."

"It was stolen. It can't be confidential." Jarrod stared

hard. "I don't think you're telling the truth, Ray. I think your wife stole the necklace." He paused. "Am I right?"

Ray held his gaze. Tension filled the air. Then he took two steps to the sofa and sank down on it. "Yes," he whispered.

Briana's mind spun. This wasn't true. It couldn't be. Her mother wouldn't do such a thing. "No, you're wrong. You're—"

Ray looked up. "Sweetheart, I'm sorry, but she *must* have stolen it."

Briana frowned. "How do you know that?"

"Because *I* didn't."

Tears pricked at her blue eyes. "Oh, Dad, don't be silly. Just because you didn't take it doesn't mean Mum *did*." She spun toward Jarrod. "This is all your fault. You're browbeating him into a confession so that he can keep my mother's good name."

"Briana, shhh," her father said. "Jarrod's just trying to get to the truth."

"For what?" she choked. "To prove some stupid rumor? There's no evidence, Dad. None at all. Jarrod is just—" All at once she noticed her father's dismayed expression. "Dad, are you all right? Dad, what is it?"

"Oh God. I've just remembered something. Your mother wanted you and your sister to go to a private school. We didn't have the money but then a spinster aunt left her a legacy—quite a substantial amount—and your mother put it into an account for your schooling."

Briana's heart jolted. "What are you saying? That there was no spinster aunt?"

"That's exactly what I'm saying."

"But Mum would never—"

"Honey, I loved your mother dearly, but she was never quite the same after Howard fired her. She rarely mentioned him but I always had the impression she had never forgiven him, and rightly so." His mouth turned grim. "I know she was upset at first when Marise went to work for him, but then she seemed to accept it. And the same thing happened when you were given the Blackstone contract, though I know she didn't let on to any of us."

Briana was trying to take all this in. Her mother...her beloved mother...

Jarrod's voice cut across her thoughts. "You realize that the police may well come around and investigate now that the diamonds have been discovered."

Briana pushed aside thoughts of her mother. "But we gave them back," she said somewhat stupidly.

"The police will still investigate."

Ray swallowed hard. "Then they're going to find out about the million dollars," he said, sending a jolt through Briana.

Jarrod seemed to go on full alert. "What million dollars?"

"The one I stole from Howard's secret account."

"What the hell!"

"Just ignore him," Briana said quickly. "He doesn't know what he's saying."

Ray shook his head. "Honey, the guilt's been getting to me, and this has just made me decide to turn myself in to the police." He turned to Jarrod. "Remember that million dollars you loaned Briana to buy more property?" he said, making her inwardly groan.

Jarrod darted a look at her, and her eyes pleaded with him to nod. "Er—yes."

Ray then went on to explain how he'd taken the money for his wife's medical expenses. "I'll hand myself in to the police tomorrow." He glanced around the room. "I just want to spend one more night in the home I shared with Barbara."

Briana's heart tilted with pain. "Oh Dad," she whispered. "I'll come with you tomorrow. You won't be alone."

"Thank you, honey."

Jarrod cleared his throat. "Ray, embezzlement is embezzlement but there *were* extenuating circumstances. I know a good criminal lawyer who'll take on your case and hopefully will get you a lesser jail term."

At the mention of jail, Briana gave a small sob, but Ray squeezed her hand. "Honey, I committed a crime. I have to go to jail." He gave a forced smile. "You know I love you, but without your mother it doesn't really matter where I am."

"Oh, Dad, that's grief speaking."

"Maybe, but by the time I'm out of jail I might be over the worst of it." He smiled. "Look, you two get out of here. I've got a few things to do now."

A thought occurred to Briana. "Dad, you're not going to do anything silly, are you?"

His face softened. "I promise you I'm not. I just want some time alone."

"Okay." She hugged him then kissed his cheek. "I'll be back first thing in the morning."

"Fine."

"I'll be here for you, too, Ray," Jarrod said, and her father thanked him.

Briana hated that Jarrod had forced the issue, but she had to admit it was a relief to get it all out in the open. If only she could do the same with her feelings for Jarrod. If she could just tell him she loved him.

But that was never going to happen. It couldn't. She had to stay cool and calm in front of him. Jarrod had only ever wanted to bed her, not marry her. He'd told her from the beginning not to ask for more, so there was no way she would go back on her word. Not even after she told him about Patrick and the blackmail.

Once they were in the car, Jarrod looked at Briana in concern. "Are you okay?" he asked, realizing only now how hard this had been for her. The money must have weighed so heavily on her mind all this time.

She looked straight ahead, as if she knew she'd fall apart if she didn't. "Please take me home, Jarrod."

He waited a moment, a distinct feeling of unease rolling through him. Then he started up the engine and drove off, his thoughts turning to what had just taken place back there at Ray Davenport's house. He felt bad about Briana, not for pushing her about the diamonds— no, that had to be done. But for thinking the worst about her all this time.

Dammit, she didn't deserve all the rotten things he'd

thought about her from the beginning. He knew now she was a woman who could be trusted, and a woman who put her family before herself.

Unlike Marise.

Unlike his biological mother.

He owed Briana one hell of an apology. And he would give her one, too, just as soon as they were inside her apartment. He intended to make up for it all somehow—if she let him.

Only, when they arrived at her apartment building, she tried her old trick of telling him to just drop her off out front, but he wasn't having it this time. They needed to talk. And he needed to apologize.

She didn't say another word until they were inside her apartment. Then she stood in the middle of the living room and faced him, a cool look in her eyes. "You were wrong to force my father into a confession, Jarrod."

He couldn't back down. "If I hadn't, the police would have. And they'd have been much less considerate." He paused, then said in his defense, "Hell, I had no idea he was going to confess to embezzlement."

She flinched, then, "Perhaps you should have listened to me when I said to leave things alone. But you never listen to me, do you, Jarrod? It's always about what *you* want."

He inclined his head. "That's a fair comment," he admitted, and caught the look of surprise in her eyes before honing in to further the discussion. "So, the million dollars was actually for your father."

"Yes." Then out of the blue, her mouth began to

tremble. "And now I'm…going to lose…him." Tears bubbled up and overflowed down her cheeks.

Jarrod was at her side in an instant, pulling her into his arms, hugging her tight as she cried it all out. "Shhh. I'll do what I can to help him," he murmured, slipping her his clean handkerchief. He wondered if she'd cried much these last few months, or if she'd stayed strong for her father. More likely the latter, and he admired her for it. But today had to have been an emotional day for her, and things always caught up eventually.

He continued to hug her. "Shhh, Briana. You won't be alone. There are people who…care about you." And he realized he did. He just couldn't bring himself to be personal about it right now. He had to stand back and keep some semblance of detachment.

After a few more moments, she sniffed and pulled back, dabbing at her tears with the hanky, still looking so very beautiful. "There's something else."

His gut clenched tight as he let her leave his arms. "I'm beginning to not like surprises."

She sniffed again. "This one's about Patrick," she said, slamming his heart against his ribs. "He's black-mailing me."

Jarrod's head went back. "Blackmailing you? For what?"

"About the money my father stole from Howard. He figured it out, you see." She took a shuddering breath before continuing. "That's why he came to see me at the airport and why I was forced into signing that agreement. He was insisting I take him back as my business manager so that he could come to Hong Kong with me."

"The bastard!"

"And he wants everyone to think we're lovers again, just until he signs up one of the other models as a client." She hesitated then met his gaze full-on. "I agreed to him coming with me, but I refused to become his lover again." She shook her head emphatically, her eyelashes still damp from her tears. "Never."

Just the thought of Patrick forcing Briana into bed made him want to do violent things to the other man. Physically forcing a woman was one thing he would never do. And it wasn't like Patrick really wanted Briana anyway. Not like *he* did.

He swallowed hard. "Were you going to tell me the truth?"

Wariness clouded her eyes. "No," she said, and he swore. "Not even when I returned in two weeks. I couldn't." She gave a shaky sigh. "Anyway, the end of the month is almost here. It wouldn't have made any difference to you what I do after that."

"It would have mattered, Briana," he growled, admitting the truth. And that was the whole truth. He didn't want to let her go.

He never wanted to let her go. He wanted to keep her in his arms, safe by his side. Always.

Suddenly that thought grabbed him by the throat and had him heading for the door.

"Jarrod, stop! Where are you going?"

Anywhere. Nowhere. Just as long he was somewhere other than here. He needed time to think this all through.

He made himself focus, and he turned to briefly face her. "To see your ex-business manager," he said, letting the anger come. "He's not forcing you into anything, Briana."

She sighed. "It's no use, Jarrod. I signed a contract. Please don't make a scene."

"You can't be serious. You signed that contract under duress," he pointed out. "It wouldn't stand up in court and you know it."

She raised her chin. "Whether it does or it doesn't, I won't renege on the deal, Jarrod, no matter what you say. I gave my word. And if it's good enough for you—"

"Then you're a fool," he snapped, finding it hard to believe that she could even consider going away with Patrick when she didn't have to. He stilled. Perhaps that was the problem. Perhaps she *did* want to go away with Patrick, despite her protestations.

Something shifted in her expression. "Yes, I'm a fool, Jarrod," she said, a sudden catch in her voice. "A fool in love."

Jarrod felt like he'd just been poleaxed. She was in love with Patrick. The thought staggered him, squeezed his heart. And suddenly he knew why.

He loved her.

But he had lost her. She wanted another man. She *loved* another man. God, did he really have the strength to walk away from her? He shuddered inwardly. He had to. He loved her, but when it came right down to it, her happiness was what counted. Not his own.

"Then I hope you two will be very happy," he said, turning away before she could see the anguish that must be in his eyes. In seconds he'd loved and lost the most beautiful woman in the world. Beautiful in more ways than one.

"Oh Jarrod, now *you're* the fool. It's *you* I love. Not Patrick."

He felt his world rock as he spun back toward her. "What did you say?"

She stood her ground like someone expecting to be reprimanded, but defiant all the same. "I said I love you."

He was back at her side in an instant. "Darling, I love you, too. I'm so sorry for what I've put you through."

Her heart stopped. "What?"

He put his hand under her chin and looked into her eyes. "I've only just realized I love you, Briana. Right now when I thought I'd lost you to Patrick."

Oh my. Was she dreaming?

"Then I have to be grateful to Patrick for giving you to me," she murmured, slipping her hands around his neck, enjoying the freedom of touching him with love.

Jarrod's hands slid down to her waist and pulled her lower half close against him. "No," he growled. "We don't owe him a thing. Patrick can go to hell for all I care."

"Jarrod!" Briana said, pretending to be shocked at his words, but more surprised by his arousal against her stomach. But she felt the same way about Patrick. He didn't deserve any consideration. He would have used her if he could and not given a damn.

"Forget Patrick," Jarrod said. "We'll deal with him tomorrow. Together. I'm sure the police will be very interested in his attempts at blackmail."

"Yes." She would report him, if only to stop him doing the same thing to someone else. Another woman may not have someone like Jarrod.

All at once the air softened with love. "And you're not going on assignment to Asia by yourself either," Jarrod said gruffly. "I'm rearranging my schedule so I can go with you."

For once she loved his high-handedness. "No argument from me," she agreed, just before he slid his mouth over hers and kissed her hard.

Eventually they came up for air. "But for now—" He swept her up in his arms and headed to the bedroom. "I think we need some practice."

"Practice?"

"For our honeymoon."

She gave a small gasp. "Are you asking me to marry you, Jarrod Hammond?"

He stopped to look down at her and she caught her breath at the sheer love in his eyes. "Darling, only special people get to come inside my heart and stay forever. And you're the most special person of all."

"Oh, Jarrod," she whispered, his words making her heart turn over and over until she thought it would never stop.

And then she realized she didn't want it to stop. Every beat of her heart would always be for him. Always and forever.

* * * * *

THE HAMMOND~BLACKSTONE FAMILY TREE

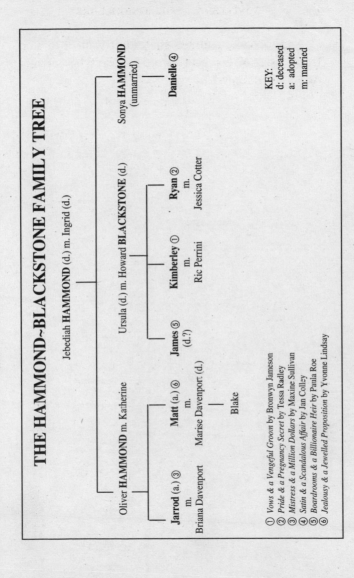

Jebediah **HAMMOND** (d.) m. Ingrid (d.)

Oliver **HAMMOND** m. Katherine

Ursula (d.) m. Howard **BLACKSTONE** (d.)

Sonya **HAMMOND** (unmarried)

Jarrod (a.) ③
m.
Briana Davenport

Matt (a.) ⑥
m.
Marise Davenport (d.)

James ⑤
(d.?)

Kimberley ①
m.
Ric Perrini

Ryan ②
m.
Jessica Cotter

Danielle ④

Blake

① *Vows & a Vengeful Groom* by Bronwyn Jameson
② *Pride & a Pregnancy Secret* by Tessa Radley
③ *Mistress & a Million Dollars* by Maxine Sullivan
④ *Satin & a Scandalous Affair* by Jan Colley
⑤ *Boardrooms & a Billionaire Heir* by Paula Roe
⑥ *Jealousy & a Jewelled Proposition* by Yvonne Lindsay

KEY:
d: deceased
a: adopted
m: married

SATIN & A
SCANDALOUS AFFAIR

by
Jan Colley

Dear Reader,

I love this job.

For this project, I revisited Port Douglas in northern Queensland, Australia. I again experienced the most beautiful stretch of beach, friendly people, a gorgeous winter climate and the superb restaurants in this small town that bats way above itself. Until we meet again, Port…

I have never been particularly enamoured with the "girl's best friend." I am now! Via books and the internet, I read about diamonds, from the mines to the perplexing world of the sightholders, and to the cutter's desk. I learned about the world's most famous diamonds – centuries old, desired by all, cursed for all time. I discovered big money, blood money and seductive marketing. I especially loved the beauty, diversity and astonishing prices of natural coloured diamonds. My heroine is a jewellery designer, so I checked out hundreds of incredibly talented designers' sites and drooled over the most beautiful jewellery. And I was lucky enough to see firsthand how a vision is created.

I am a convert. To me there is no gemstone more steeped in power, greed, beauty, love – and yes, curses – than the immodest diamond.

Best regards,

Jan Colley

JAN COLLEY

lives in Christchurch, New Zealand, with Les and a couple of cats. She has travelled extensively, is a jack of all trades and master of none and still doesn't know what she wants to be when she grows up – as long as it's a writer. She loves rugby, family and friends, writing, sunshine, talking about writing, and cats, although not necessarily in that order. E-mail her at vagabond232@yahoo.com or check out her website at www.jancolley.com.

Thanks to Richard Baird of Rohan Jewellery in Christchurch, New Zealand, who spent hours sharing his knowledge and passion for diamonds and let me peek over his craftsmen's shoulders, and to Max Rooney of Argosy Jewellery for the introduction.

To our intrepid editor, Melissa Jeglinski, who must have experienced a few conniptions with this project. And special thanks to a great bunch of girls: Bronwyn Jameson, Tessa Radley, Maxine Sullivan, Paula Roe and Yvonne Lindsay. Long live Desire Downunder!

One

"Danielle Hammond? I have a proposition for you."

Dani blinked, jolted out of a pleasant daydream, the Northern Queensland sun that had been warming her face at the outdoor café now hidden behind a wall of a man.

"May I join you?" The softly spoken deep brogue sounded more continental than Australian. She blinked again. It took a few seconds for her to understand that the subject of her daydream, the man she'd seen walk into her shop just minutes ago, had now crossed the road to the café and stood towering above her.

It took another few seconds to realise that she'd seen him before, and to swallow her jolt of dismay. It was him—what's his name—Quinn Everard!

The name exploded in her head as he tossed a

business card on the table and pulled out the flimsy white chair opposite her.

Dani eased her sunglasses down her nose and needlessly read the card. "Quinn Everard. Broker." Simple, classy, on a satiny-silver card. They'd never met personally, but she'd seen his face in many jewellery publications over the years.

His head turned toward the café door and immediately a waitress materialised. He ordered coffee while Dani's curiosity ran riot. What could the great Australian gem expert want with her? He'd made it very plain, very publicly, that she wasn't good enough to wipe his shoes on.

"Did you see anything you liked?" she asked, sipping on the straw of her thick shake.

Chocolate brown eyes under thick brows scanned her face.

"In the shop," she qualified, easing one hot foot out of her shoe under the table.

"I was looking for you. Your assistant pointed you out."

"You were checking out my window. I saw you."

He rested his elbow on the table and subjected her to a leisurely inspection. Just another nail in his coffin, as far as she was concerned. Dani stared boldly back, seeing in her mind's eye his tall broad form as he'd scrutinised her display window. How she'd admired what looked like an Armani suit—a rarity in the tropics—and his smooth, rolling gait as he'd straightened and disappeared inside. He moved like a fighter, and who's to say he wasn't? There was a definite break in his nose, the telltale bump high on the bridge, and a scar, smooth and pale, traced the corner of his mouth.

His inspection completed, he sat back in his seat. "I've been hearing your name around lately."

Thanks to Howard Blackstone, Dani's benefactor, who'd nominated her as his featured designer for the annual launch last February. "The Blackstone Jewellery launch, probably." Blackstone Jewellery was one retail division of Blackstone Diamonds, Howard's mining and manufacturing company. Dani pursed her lips sardonically. "Oh, I forgot. You weren't invited."

A flicker of amusement deepened the creases on both sides of his mouth, showing up an unexpected dimple. "I've never said I don't find your work interesting, Ms. Hammond. Which is why I'm here. As I said, I have a proposition for you."

She relished the sharp stab of triumph. This man had never made a pretence of liking her stuff, yet here he was. What on earth could he want to proposition her about?

Dani could think of some things…and they were all tied up with sizing him up as a hunk a few moments ago, before she'd realised who he was.

Hopeful that the lick of attraction she felt wasn't written all over her face, she cleared her throat. "A proposition for *me?* April Fools was a couple of days ago."

"I want you to design a setting for a large and very special diamond."

This was very satisfying. The great Quinn Everard wanted her, Dani Hammond, to make him a diamond necklace.

Oh, but there was that one small problem. They hated each other.

She raised her head. "No."

His eyes narrowed.

"Diamonds aren't really my specialty." His words, aimed at her four years ago at the prestigious Young Designer of the Year Award competition, the one everyone tipped her to win, came back to her. He'd said something along the lines of "A jewellery designer should stick to what she knows and is comfortable with. Ms. Hammond may have cut her teeth on diamonds, but she has little flair and understanding of the essence of the stones."

That wasn't the only public dressing-down Dani had received from Quinn Everard. She'd assumed it was because of the spat between he and Howard years ago.

"Remember?" she asked sweetly, and received a coolly assessing gaze in response. How could he sit there in his gazillion-thread suit and not melt?

"I am offering a generous commission."

Now, that was interesting… "How generous?" A little extra cash and she could make the final payment on her loan from Howard. Of course, she'd repay his estate, since he'd died earlier in the year. Generous enough to include some new display cabinets, maybe? A face-lift for the tired signage?

Quinn took out what looked to be a solid-gold pen, wrote something on the business card and turned it around so she could see.

A surprised cough escaped and she jerked her head up at the numbers on the business card. "You want to pay me that to make you a piece of jewellery?"

He nodded.

The amount was obscene. Damn the spruce-up. This could be the deposit for the bigger, more modern and vacant premises two doors down.

"That's way over the odds. You know that."

"Yes or no?"

She shook her head, positive she was the butt of someone's joke. "The answer's no."

Quinn leaned back, not attempting to cover his displeasure. "You and your family have endured quite a bit of unwelcome publicity lately, haven't you? Howard's death three months ago. Not to mention his companion on the plane."

Tell her something she didn't know. No one survived when the flight Howard Blackstone had chartered to take him to Auckland one night in January, plunged into the sea. When it turned out Marise Hammond was on board, the media were beside themselves. Marise was married to Howard's arch enemy, Matt Hammond, head of House of Hammond, an antique and fine jewellery company in New Zealand. Matt was also Dani's cousin, although they'd never met because of the feud between Howard and the Hammonds that spanned three decades.

The reading of Howard's will a month later rocked the family to its core. Marise was named as a substantial beneficiary and a trust fund was set up for her son, Blake, giving rise to the assumption that Marise and Howard were having an affair. Who was Blake's true father, everyone wanted to know, Howard Blackstone or Matt Hammond? All the old family history and hostility had been bandied around for months.

Despite a growing anxiety, Dani feigned nonchalance. "So?"

"And poor Ric and Kimberley," he continued. "They must have been bummed when the TV cameras crashed their wedding."

That was an understatement. Dani grew up in Howard Blackstone's mansion, along with her mother and cousins, Kimberley and Ryan. Kim had recently remarried her ex-husband, Ric Perrini. Their lavish wedding on a yacht in Sydney Harbour was nearly ruined when the media sent in helicopters.

What did Quinn Everard know about that?

"I haven't officially met Ryan," Quinn resumed, "but I do know Jessica slightly. I think she'll make a lovely bride, don't you?"

She opened her mouth to agree, then snapped it closed. Ryan and Jessica had recently announced their engagement, but the wedding details were a closely guarded family secret.

"I have no idea what you're talking about," she said warily.

Ryan was the most private of people. That's why he'd asked Dani to help arrange a secret ceremony up here, away from the Sydney gossip-mongers. Port Douglas was an excellent choice. Chances were, the family members wouldn't be recognised, and there were any number of world-class venues and caterers to choose from. With Dani's help, arrangements for the perfect intimate wedding in three weeks' time were well under way.

"Really?" Quinn mused. "There are some lovely beaches up here, aren't there? I hear Oak Hill is nice."

Dani's heart sank. He couldn't possibly have found out. Almost everything had been confirmed and all participants sworn to secrecy. "Your information is out of date, Mr. Everard," she lied. "There won't be a wedding in Port Douglas, after all. That was just a ploy to get everyone off the scent."

"A ploy? My source seems adamant that on the twentieth of April, the van Berhopt Resort is staging a very special event. It looks fantastic on the Web site, just the place for an intimate, discreet family wedding."

She heard the sound of her own teeth grinding. "How the hell did you know that?"

He tapped his nose. "The diamond world is surprisingly small."

Dani knew when her back was against the wall. "That's blackmail," she muttered.

He shrugged, all traces of amusement gone. "It's business, Ms. Hammond. Are you so successful you can afford to turn down a commission of this size?"

Intimidation really got her back up. "Do your worst." She pushed her glass away and picked up her purse. This was precisely why she had chosen to live up here, away from the city gossip. "The Blackstones and I are used to media attention." Howard's womanising and close-to-the-edge business dealings guaranteed that.

Quinn stroked his chin. "Poor Ryan and Jessica, their beautiful day ruined. And the rest of your family—especially your mother—will they be so blasé? All that distasteful speculation, old family wounds reopened, over and over…"

"Leave my mother out of this," Dani snapped. That

was the worst of it. The Blackstone-Hammond feud had ripped her mother's blood brother away from her thirty years ago, leaving a massive heartache. With Howard's death, Sonya Hammond's dearest wish was to bring the family factions together again.

"I can empathise, being a private person myself." His tone was sympathetic—reasonable, even.

Dani jutted her chin out defiantly, despite a sinking feeling that he was right. Did she have the right to expose those closest to her to more scandal and shame?

"You could spare them all that unwelcome attention. Ryan and Jessica will have the day of their dreams. And you, Danielle, will make a lot of money."

She glared at him. Only her family called her Danielle. Up here in Port, as it was affectionately known, she went by Dani Hammond, the brand name for her jewellery. Most of the locals had no idea she was connected to one of Australia's richest and most notorious families. Those who did, didn't care.

Quinn shifted impatiently. "Yes or no?"

Could she bear her anonymity here to be shattered by all the old gossip and innuendo she had lived with all her life? And worse, how could she let him ruin Ryan and Jessica's day and put that hunted look back in her mother's eyes? "Bring your damn diamond to the shop, then." Grasping her change purse in a white-knuckled grip, she stood abruptly and scowled down at him.

Quinn Everard tilted his head, peering up under his brows again. Then he rose, gesturing to the cars parked across the street. "My car is right over there. Take a ride with me."

Her internal alarm sounded. It wasn't that she thought a man with his reputation would try anything dangerous. It was her reaction—her attraction—that worried her. And how could she refuse a man who held such sway in her profession, especially one offering dream money?

"I don't carry this diamond around in my pocket." Quinn frowned at her hesitation. "I've rented a house in Four Mile Beach."

Four Mile was an outlying district in the shire of Port Douglas, and where her apartment was. "I'm working."

"Exactly. Time is money, Danielle."

She eyed him moodily, weighing her options. "Whereabouts in Four Mile?"

He impatiently motioned her to start crossing the road.

"You may be famous," Dani said tightly, "but you're a stranger to me. I'm going nowhere without telling my assistant."

He inclined his head. "Number 2 Beach Road." He stopped beside a sleek black BMW. "I'll wait."

Taut with indignation, she poked her head into the shop and told Steve, her assistant, and told him where she was going. Then she got into Quinn's car. They spoke little on the short drive, but her eyes widened in surprise when they pulled up outside his house. She'd walked past here nearly every day on her way to work. Never a morning person, she needed the fifty-minute walk along beautiful Four Mile Beach to improve her mood.

The house was right on the sand dunes, surrounded by high walls. A discreet plaque on the wall by the entrance said Luxury Executive Accommodation. Dani had always wondered what it was like inside.

She followed Quinn through the gate and entrance into a large multilevelled living and dining area. The house was a blend of Asian and Australian designs, the furnishings rattan, leather and teak. Striking floral arrangements with birds-of-paradise and heliconias seasoned the air with tropical scents, stirred by lazily rotating ceiling fans. This place was even better than she'd imagined.

"Shall we?"

Quinn stood at the door leading to the stairs. Dani hesitated for a second. She didn't trust Mr. Quinn Everard one inch, but it wasn't a threat of physical violence that made her pause. More his attitude, the impression that he got what he wanted so effortlessly. He smelled good, looked good, obviously lived well. She'd need her wits about her with a man prepared to resort to blackmail to get his own way.

He opened the first door and intense light flooded what was obviously a dream workroom. In one corner, under the perfect lighting, sat an easel. A workbench ran fully down one side, two stools at the end and tool organisers that held an array of implements, everything from tweezers to gauges to loupes. There was a waxing station, engraving blocks, micro torch, rollers and grinders—everything she had in her shop, except the equipment was new and top-of-the-range and must have cost a fortune.

It slowly dawned on her that he expected her to work on his diamond here. A laptop sat open on a desk, no doubt with the best CAD software available. The desk and bench were lit with magnified true-light lamps. He must have had all this brought in, she thought dimly, lights included.

Dani ran her hand over the workbench. "You were that sure I'd agree?"

"I've questioned your motivation in the past, Ms. Hammond, not your intelligence."

She glanced over to where he leaned casually against the doorjamb, arms folded. "Why?"

"The diamond does not leave the premises."

"So I come around here when I feel like it? When I have a spare minute?" She shook her head. "That would take months."

Quinn turned to the door and stretched his arm out, indicating she precede him. His steady gaze challenged her to refuse.

Cautiously Dani edged past him, down the hall away from the stairs. She paused at the next door. He leaned past her, pushing it open, and she took a couple of hesitant steps forward.

Long white curtains stirred at the open window, and she heard the sea lapping the sand beyond the trees. A huge bed, covered with shiny satin in bold red-and-gold stripes, took up most of one wall. Purple-shaded lamps on the bedside tables matched plump purple cushions scattered on the window seat. Dani felt the smile start; it was a dream of a bedroom, and to think she could hear the sea. She was still smiling when she turned around to see Quinn in a long-legged lean against the doorjamb, arms folded, a pose that was fast becoming disturbingly familiar.

Her smile faded as his intentions finally sank in. He expected her to stay here—alone—with him. "No," she said firmly, even though he hadn't asked the question yet.

His dark head tilted. "Those are my conditions. You stay here and work on the diamond in the room provided until the job is done."

Frowning, she shook her head slowly.

"It's not negotiable."

Dani thought he sounded bored. "I'm not staying here alone with you."

His eyes were scathing. "Don't be puerile, Ms. Hammond. Just what do you think is going to happen?"

If his intention was to make her feel gauche and stupid, it worked. "Wh-what possible reason…?" she stammered, her cheeks burning.

"Security and expediency. It is an extremely valuable diamond and I am a busy man. I don't have time to sit around up here in Nowhere-ville for a minute longer than necessary."

Dani shook her head again. "No deal. Bring the stone to the shop. I'll work on it between customers."

Quinn's brows raised. "I don't think so," he said softly, and, turning, left the room. But the certainty of his voice, his potent male presence remained.

Dani waited a couple of seconds, worried. There was sympathy in his face as he'd turned away. Her refusal had not even registered. A vision of being locked in, of pushing against him, pounding against his broad chest to get out, made her head swim.

She was being ridiculous. Quinn Everard was an internationally regarded man in the gem and fine arts world. He was not going to kidnap her. She started off after him. "Look, if you're worried about theft, don't be. There hasn't been a robbery in town for years."

"You don't understand, Ms. Hammond." He turned so sharply to face her that she almost bumped into his impressive chest. "This is a very special diamond."

"It will be perfectly safe in the shop, and, anyway, I'm insured."

His eyes bored into her, making her heart thump. She stepped back hurriedly, excruciatingly aware that he hadn't given an inch.

"Have you heard of the Distinction Diamond, Danielle?"

"The Dist...?" Air punched out from her lungs and her heart thudded. Either that or her chin hit the floor. The Distinction Diamond was nearly forty carats of fancy intense yellow, originating from the Kimberley mines in South Africa. No one had heard of it for years. "You've got the Distinction Diamond?" Her swallow was audible. "Here?"

Quinn Everard could do scathing very well. Was it the curve of his lips or the dangerous glint that lit up his eyes? "No, Ms. Hammond." He turned his back and continued on to the door next to "her" room. "I have her big sister."

Two

Quinn turned his back and walked into his bedroom, smiling when he felt her creeping presence at the door. Opening the panel in the wall that concealed the safe, he began keying the code into a digital keypad. The whole house was burglar and smoke alarmed, including this room and the workroom. The safe was dual combination and key, complete with trembler sensor. His company had the best security money could buy. After all, it was vital in his business.

He glanced to where she fidgeted at the door, chewing on her bottom lip. Quinn miskeyed and the thing beeped at him. He swore softly, ordering himself to stop thinking about whiskey eyes and plump bottom lips. She was on the hook. It was time to reel her in.

He went through the elaborate security measures

with exaggerated care, then took out a heavy steel box from which he lifted a hand-stitched leather case after a barrage of additional code numbers. A hydraulic mechanism raised a small velvet-covered platform on which the diamond sat. Reaching out, he flicked the desk lamp on. Then he faced her and tilted his head, giving her permission to come near.

She moved slowly into the room, her eyes on his face. The light from the lamp washed over her skin, and he thought again, as he had earlier on meeting her, that her face was all wrong, a contradiction. Wide-set, wild-honey eyes, a straight no-nonsense nose, and then rosebud lips, suggesting innocence and insecurity.

And just like earlier when he'd first looked at her, the impact jolted him. She'd attempted to tame her wildfire hair with a scarf, but still, dark red curls sprang up in interesting dimensions. Her colour sense was outrageous, combining a red-and-pink-striped top with a captivatingly short floral skirt. She was exotic, unconventional, bubbling over with life and energy. He knew more beautiful women, but none so colourful, so vibrantly original.

She looked down at the diamond on display for her, her eyes glowing. When she finally looked back at Quinn, the gratitude in her eyes stunned him. She would know well how few people had ever been given the opportunity to look upon this treasure.

Enjoy it, he thought grimly. If it were down to him, he wouldn't have Danielle Hammond within one hundred metres of this baby, no matter how interesting her face.

She put out her hand. It hovered over the glow and she hesitated. "May I?"

Half of him wondered what the diamond would look like against her skin, her hair. The other half protested, *Get the hell away from this diamond!* But he had his orders. He nodded tersely.

Her slim hand dipped and the middle finger stroked lightly, reverently over the crown of the perfect octahedron. Then she took her hands away, crossed them in front of her body and just looked down at the stone, as if giving thanks to a god. Her lashes made shadows on her cheek.

"Do we have a deal, Ms. Hammond?" he asked quietly, reluctant to interrupt what was obviously an awe-inspiring moment for her. As it had been for him when he had procured this very special diamond for his client six years ago.

"I have a choice?" she murmured.

He knew she didn't. No jeweller in her right mind would say no to this opportunity.

She continued, "Since you're blackmailing me…"

Quinn smiled at her nice recovery. "Of course I am." He knew that she would crawl over broken glass to get her hands on this stone, blackmail or not. Money or not.

He perched on the edge of the desk. "The conditions are these—you stay here in the house for the duration of the work. You work on it day and night if possible. You tell no one about this stone."

She sucked in a breath. "I have a life, you know."

"No, you don't." He shook his head decisively. "Not for the next few weeks."

"And my shop?"

Quinn had initiated a decent conversation with the

young hippie called Steve in her little shop this morning. "Your assistant needs more hours. His partner is pregnant. They're struggling financially."

Dani frowned. "You found all that out in a couple of minutes?"

"I did not draw your name out of a hat, Ms. Hammond," he said sharply. While he couldn't blame her for being surprised, his reputation alone should have swayed her. Put that together with one of the most incredible stones the world had ever seen and it was unfathomable that he was still trying to persuade her.

"What sort of setting?"

Quinn shrugged. "You're the designer."

"I mean," she sighed, "pendant? Brooch? What type of piece? I didn't see any cutting gear."

He drew himself up to full height. "You will not touch this stone with anything but your fingers, do you hear?"

Danielle Hammond rolled her eyes at him. "Of course not, but I may use other gems." She eyed him speculatively. "You are supplying findings? Platinum, diamonds, the whole deal?"

"As long as you keep the stone whole, you have carte blanche to design whatever you like. I will need to approve a model and a list of your requirements."

"This could take weeks…."

"You have three, less is preferable. The accommodation is acceptable?"

She nodded.

"I will feed you. Everything you need for the job is there. All you need to do is tap into your talent and work."

"Who's it for?"

Quinn opened his mouth, staring at her face. "A friend," he said shortly. "A special friend."

Dani nodded, and he could almost hear her mind ticking over. That was his brief; she was not to know who commissioned the piece. No harm letting her think there was a special lady friend. "Do we have a deal?"

She exhaled noisily and stared down at the diamond as if for reassurance.

Just to play with her longing, he closed the lid—slowly.

"I want half the money up front," she said, "and throw in Steve's wages."

He scowled. "How very Blackstone of you." Her family connections were his main objection to the deal. Quinn had no time for anyone bearing the Blackstone stamp and was sorely tempted to delegate this job to one of his staff. But it was a sensitive matter, one which he'd reluctantly agreed to handle personally.

He picked the box up off the desk, noting with pleasure the regret and loss in her eyes as she watched him put it away.

"This is going to be a barrel of laughs," Dani muttered from behind his back.

"The sooner you get on with it, the quicker we can go our separate ways." He banged the safe door closed. "I'll take you home to pack and make arrangements."

When he turned back to her, she was rubbing the side of her long pale neck, eyes closed, her head rolled back. Quinn teetered on the edge of a rogue wave of desire so intense that it stopped him dead in his tracks. Behind her, not two feet away, his king-size bed sprawled, inspiring all sorts of suggestive images.

Her eyes snapped open, finding his gaze immediately. "No need. My place is only a minute or two from here."

He gestured to the door. "I'll drive you," he said firmly, intent on getting her out of his bedroom.

Quinn prowled her living room while she packed and made arrangements to cover her absence from her shop. He was fond of his comforts, and the climate up here in Northern Queensland was not to his liking. Luckily, unlike Dani's tiny apartment in a dated resort complex, the beach house was equipped with an excellent air-conditioning system. He wiped the back of his neck while she scurried about packing with the phone plastered to her ear. The prospect of baby-sitting a spoiled girl with an artistic temperament and inflated opinion of her own talent, whilst sweltering in the suffocating humidity, was not a good one.

His internal temperature soared even higher when later that afternoon, after settling in at his rental, his house guest took a swim. Quinn's office window offered an unobstructed view of the pool. His work forgotten, he stood at the window, watching the long-legged, flame-haired beauty. She wore long shorts and an oversize T-shirt; perfectly respectable attire—until it got wet. Quinn turned the air-conditioning dial down a couple of notches and undid the top two buttons of his shirt.

For the first time in many years, he wanted, with a savage unrelenting intensity. He was certainly not celibate, but preferred older, cultured and financially independent women. Women with similar interests and social mores as he. Danielle Hammond looked to be mid-to-late twenties and certainly had the wealth of the Blackstones behind her, but they were light-years apart.

It was totally undignified to stand at a window, salivating over the sights of wet fabric clinging lovingly to a fine pair of breasts, and of water streaming down well-toned, lightly tanned legs. He was much too discriminating to crave the slide of her wet, spiralling curls on his burning skin. Wasn't he?

He returned to his desk, pushing aside the unwelcome intrusion. This wasn't supposed to be a holiday, he chided himself. The next Famous Paintings auction was only days away. It was frustrating to be stuck here for such an important date on his professional calendar, but at least he had a contact to inspect a very special lot number for one of his most important clients.

Clearing his head one final time, he refocussed his attention where it belonged. On his work. He remained at his desk until Danielle interrupted him, after the dinner hour. Apparently she was ready to work and wanted the diamond to be brought to the workroom.

Quinn set it up on the workbench and watched her circle the desk, her small digital camera clicking and whirring as she took snapshot after snapshot.

He was totally absorbed by her concentration, not to mention her lithe form bending and stretching, and the interesting strain of fabric across her rump and thighs as she crouched and circled. So when she suddenly straightened and looked at him, he was a few seconds behind the eight ball.

Her finely arched brows seemed to mock him. "What's she like?"

"I beg your pardon?"

"Your lady friend. The one you're giving the diamond to."

"Like?"

She looked at the ceiling briefly. "Her height and build. I don't want to design something dainty for a big strapping girl. Or vice versa."

Quinn hesitated. It wasn't an unreasonable request.

Tonight she wore flowing baggy summer pants of an indeterminate colour that fell between pewter and light brown. A purple lacy top accentuated her shape, which was, he conceded, a work of art. A strip of matching fabric tied bandanna-style kept her forehead free of springy curls, and lime-green beads circled her throat. "Five nine, five ten." He shrugged. "Slender but strong-looking."

Dani held the camera up, checking the images. Quinn noted with surprise that her nails were short and some of them jagged, as if she chewed them.

"Pale or tan?" she asked distractedly.

"Lightly tanned," he told her. "Freckles."

Click, click. "Okay. Hair?" When he didn't answer immediately, she lowered the camera and frowned at him. "What colour is her hair?"

Several superlative responses came to mind, but while he was deciding which best described her vibrant curls, her frown gave way to sarcasm. "You're a little unobservant, Mr. Everard. Do you have a photo, perhaps?"

His mouth quirked. "Red. Dark red." He pursed his lips, wondering when she would twig. "Curly."

Her brows arched up to kiss the edge of the bandanna.

"Rather multifaceted in style," Quinn went on, warming to his task. "Unconventional, definitely. Some would say bohemian, but that's not it… She's like no one else." And that was the truth. Her use of colour, breaking all the fashion rules, should have offended a conservative like himself, yet somehow, it charmed the hell out of him. Living with Danielle Hammond, he knew, would never be boring.

Dani pursed her lips sternly. "You have good taste in women, Mr. Everard," she told him smartly, and put the camera down with a sharp thud. "Contemporary bling, then, for the lady."

"Knock yourself out." Quinn pushed himself away from the doorjamb, trying not to be horrified about her terminology in reference to this diamond. He'd spent hours trying to talk his client out of this, citing Danielle's age and inexperience.

Surprisingly though, he smiled all the way down the hall, pleased with himself, and with her. Maybe the next few weeks wouldn't be so bad, after all. Dani Hammond had a bite to her. She seemed smart—almost street-smart—and Quinn knew all about that.

But how did she, with her luxurious upbringing?

Sightings of Dani were scarce the next couple of days as she immersed herself in her design. She worked late and rose late. Mid-morning she would request he bring the diamond to the workroom. He restored it to the safe on his way to bed. He kept the refrigerator stocked and was thankfully spared the ignominy of standing by the window like a Peeping Tom, because she didn't use the pool again. Most of the food he prepared went to waste as she said she was too busy to be hungry. Despite himself, and without seeing any tangible results yet, he was impressed by her dedication.

The third night, she joined him for dinner, an impressive meal catered by one of Port Douglas's surprisingly fine restaurants.

"Why me?" she asked over coffee. "You must know twenty world-class designers who would gnaw off their right hand to ingratiate themselves with you."

He tapped his teaspoon lightly on the cup, giving a brief smile. "But not you."

"Aren't you afraid I'll mess up your precious diamond out of spite since you're blackmailing me?"

"Then I would have to mess up your reputation."

"Haven't you already?" She raised and crooked her two index fingers in a parody of speech marks. "'Ms. Hammond has passable talent but chooses to use it working for chain stores....'"

Quinn rubbed his ear, amused. That was one of his missives in the *DiamondWorld Monthly* about a year ago. She'd had the cheek to respond in the next issue. He'd retaliated by saying she was "one step up from a Sunday-market vendor in a one-horse town, pandering to the tourist buses."

"A mere dent, which doesn't seem to have harmed

you at all. Although, why you would shut yourself away up here in the middle of nowhere is anyone's guess."

"Another snobby Sydney-sider," she sighed, giving him the impression this wasn't the first time she'd had this conversation. "I like the tropics."

"What's to like? A beach you can't swim in because of the stingers…"

"Only for a few months…"

"Insufferably hot and sticky weather…"

"I like it probably for all the reasons you don't. Especially now in cyclone season."

So the lady was into sultry, steamy nights. He sniffed and rubbed his jaw, clamping down on where that thought would take him. "Bugs and snakes…"

"You get those in Sydney," she countered.

"Not in *my* neighbourhood, you don't."

"They wouldn't dare," she muttered under her breath.

He ignored that. "No shopping to speak of. Is there actually any nightlife in town or does it shut down at five-thirty?"

"Remind me to take you cane toad racing while you're here," she said, then smiled wryly and leaned her elbows on the table edge. "Laid-back it might be, but there's an interesting dynamic of village charm and sophistication here. Port is famous for its restaurants and you never know which Hollywood stars or ex-American president you'll bump into around town or checking out the reef in their big chartered yachts."

His fingers tapped the tabletop, drawing her glance. "We know you like to play with the rich and famous, but you're limiting your opportunities here, Danielle. Why is that?"

"I do all right, and don't call me Danielle."

He inclined his head. "And 'all right' is enough?"

"For now." She sipped her coffee. "Tell me about you and Howard."

"You don't know?" he asked, surprised.

Dani shook her head. "I was at uni around that time. All I know is, he bristled every time your name came up."

That didn't surprise him. Back then, Howard Blackstone had thrown his whole vindictive weight against the young broker from the wrong side of the tracks. "I was just starting out," he began. Laura, his wife, was sick. His whole world was going to hell.

"Howard wanted to be nominated as the Australian representative to the new World Association of Diamonds. Everyone had finally woken up to the fact that our industry, the diamond trade, was subsidising wars in Africa."

"Conflict diamonds." Dani nodded. "What good could some worldwide association do against the one or two massive conglomerates who control the mines?"

Sharp, he thought, but then she had grown up in Australia's foremost mining family. "The association has definitely raised awareness. Even America, the largest bastion of consumerism, reports that a high percentage of people in the market ask for certification that their diamond is conflict-free."

"A certificate's only as good as the person who completes it," she stated, again rousing grudging admiration for her appraisal of a very grey area.

"So, the feud?" Dani prompted.

Quinn pushed his empty plate aside and leaned back. "Blackstone wined and dined me. He wanted my vote. I suppose he could have got the impression I was a solid bet, but in the end, a fellow broker asked and my vote went his way. To be honest, I expected Howard to romp in, with or without me."

"But he didn't." Dani nodded. "He likes—liked—getting his own way."

Quinn wondered about the relationship between her and Australia's King of Diamonds. "He lost the nomination by one vote, and took it a lot more personally than it warranted."

"Let me guess. You were off the Christmas card list."

Well and truly, Quinn thought grimly. Howard's wrath nearly sent him to the wall with his financiers. "He banned me from accessing the Blackstone mines. I had to borrow heavily to source the stones I needed offshore."

If it hadn't been for one or two friends in high places—notably Sir John Knowles, owner of the diamond upstairs—Quinn's fledgling business wouldn't have survived.

Dani whistled. "That must have hurt. The broker with no diamonds."

"It put me in a very bad situation," he agreed.

She glanced around the room, her eyes resting on a magenta orchid in the corner. "It doesn't seem to have had any long-term consequences."

"No thanks to the Blackstones."

"Have you approached Ric or Ryan? They may be willing to ease the ban now."

Now that Howard was dead, Quinn thought scathingly. His dislike of the former head of Blackstone Diamonds wasn't just business. Howard had made it personal. How ironic that he was sitting across an elegant table with his nemesis's protégée. "I can manage without the precious Blackstone mines, thanks."

Dani's gaze sharpened a little. "Forgive and forget, hey? The man's dead."

He couldn't forget. The slights in the papers. Door after door closing in his face. The old-boys banking networks, determined to pull him down. "It's hard enough starting out without the most influential man in the business doing a number on you."

And all while he was barely keeping his head above water to cope with his wife's terminal illness.

And that's where Howard's vindictiveness really came into its own. Quinn could overlook the loss of business, the tearing down of his reputation, the condescending snubs by former backers. He would never forgive the look in Laura's eyes when he couldn't give her the one thing she wanted above all else.

It never failed to surprise him how much it grated after all these years. "Howard Blackstone was a manipulative, vindictive bastard."

Dani blanched, and just for a moment, he felt a needle of sympathy. Was it possible that someone in this world mourned the man so many hated?

"You know all about being vindictive, don't you?" she asked tightly. "Wasn't that what marking me down at the awards was about? Or the slagging off you gave me in various industry papers?" She drained her cup and banged it down on the saucer. "Maybe you and Howard aren't so different after all."

"Maybe you just aren't that good," he suggested, eying her evenly.

"If that's so," she snapped, "why am I here?"

"I don't know, *Danielle*." He stressed the syllables of her name. "Haven't you got work to do?"

She glared, and in the candlelight, her hair and eyes crackled like embers. "Luckily, it's a big house, Mr. Everard. Why don't we keep our distance?"

She shoved herself to her feet and stalked from the room.

Three

"Fine by me!"

Dani slammed the door on his retort and stomped up the stairs, muttering to herself.

Granted, Howard Blackstone had been no angel. His abrasive nature combined with immense wealth was the perfect enemy magnet, but that aside, he had provided a good life for her and her mother. Sonya and Dani Hammond were two of the very few people in this world who truly mourned him.

She opened the workroom door and banged that, too. Bloody man!

Sonya had moved in with Howard and her sister, Ursula, when she was twelve years old. After their first-born was abducted, Ursula became depressed and took her own life. Howard was inconsolable so Sonya stayed

on to look after her niece Kimberley and nephew Ryan.
When she became pregnant, Howard persuaded her to
remain and bring up her child with all the advantages
his own children enjoyed. He paid for Dani's education,
and over the years, they'd forged quite an affectionate
bond. Sometimes she thought he liked her better than
he did his own children.

Her mother had refuted that. "He loves Kim and
Ryan fiercely. He enjoys your company because he has
hopes for you rather than expectations of you."

People didn't know the real Howard, Dani thought
belligerently, tearing off her latest mishmash of a
sketch. His faults were legion, but she and Sonya saw
a side of him he didn't show to many. They would
always be grateful.

By unspoken mutual consent, Dani and Quinn
avoided each other the next day. She needed to pinpoint
a design, but every time she looked at the diamond, her
ideas changed. She held it up to the light, admiring the
purity, depth and distribution of colour throughout.
There was a cynical old saying popular in her trade: a
polished diamond is only rough ruined. How she wished
to have seen this beauty before it was cut.

Dozens of pages littered the floor under the sketch
pad as she pared back the initial outpouring of inspiration into a few shapes vaguely resembling a setting she
might be able to work with. About the only thing she
knew for sure was that the setting would be platinum
because it complemented a diamond's finest qualities
so perfectly, especially fancy pinks and yellows. Dani
intended the stone to be the star, not the setting.

As the hours passed, ideas rushed through her mind, most disappearing a few seconds after their arrival. She played around on the software Quinn had provided, but the solution eluded her and the beautiful diamond taunted her on its velvet pillow. Finally she took it from the display box and slid down to the floor with it in her hand, loving the milky coolness of it in her palm.

Quinn walked into the room with a plate in one hand and utensils and a wineglass in the other. He stared at her incredulously for a moment, then turned to set his load on the desk. Dani pressed back against the leg of the workbench, suddenly wondering what her hair looked like. Had she showered today or not...?

She gazed at him, thinking how seriously appealing he was. He wore pleated charcoal chinos and a light polo shirt that accentuated the breadth of his shoulders and had her peeking at his strongly muscled arms. Boat shoes, no socks. His platinum Rolex flashed as he leaned forward to switch a lamp on.

"What are you doing?" he asked, staring down at her sternly.

"Thinking. What's it look like?"

After a pause, he nodded at the food he'd brought. "Eat."

"What time is it?" She raised her head to peer out the window. It was dark. Where had the day gone?

"Eight." He frowned at the sight of the uneaten sub he had brought up at lunch, the cold cup of coffee beside it.

Still holding the diamond, she uncrossed her legs and rose, drawn by the smell of the food. A twinge in her stomach reminded her she'd had little to eat today, if anything. She replaced the diamond in its box and reached for the wineglass first.

"How's it going?"

The wine was smooth. She swallowed and opened her mouth to answer but was hijacked by a huge yawn. "'Kay."

It wasn't okay yet, it was driving her nuts. Inspiration never came easy. She could spend hours or even days on an idea and toss it because of a niggling suspicion she had seen it somewhere. Originality was paramount.

His large shoe ventured out to drag a ball of screwed-up paper toward him. "What time did you work till last night?"

She shrugged, still smouldering a little from their altercation the night before. It would be better if he'd just leave her alone with her thoughts and her food.

"Eating and sleeping will be tolerated on an occasional basis."

Had he made a joke? Emboldened, she moved closer to the food he'd brought, suddenly ravenous. "Thanks." The wine had cleansed her palate and spiced her appetite, and she sniffed appreciatively.

"Is there a problem with your setting?" He bent to pick up the ball of paper by his shoe.

"No." Dani picked up the fork and stabbed at a floret of bright green broccoli. "I haven't nailed it yet, but don't worry. I will."

Quinn tossed the ball of paper into the trash bin. Then he moved to the easel and tilted his head at the latest sketch, one she hadn't torn off yet. "Have the graphics I supplied been any help?"

Dani shook her head and cut into tender lamb drizzled with a sauce that tasted of paprika. Software was great for learning on, but most designers she knew preferred to work freestyle.

He moved to the desk where she sat and laid his hand on her portfolio. "May I?"

Dani stilled mid-chew. His past comments about her work still rankled. Yet here she was, staying in luxury accommodations, being catered for to her heart's desire. Awaiting the payment of a colossal sum of money, and all for the privilege of working on an incredible diamond.

She shrugged. Whatever he thought of her stuff, he'd paid her an enormous compliment by commissioning her. Quinn Everard, the great Australian gem expert, wanted *her* to design for him. Not Cartier. Not JAR. Dani Hammond.

Quinn flicked the desk lamp on and stood, one hand in his pocket, the other leisurely turning the pages of the big black binder. He studied each page intently, unmoving except for his lashes dipping and rising as his eyes moved over the page. She watched under the guise of chewing and swallowing.

His shirt clung to the contours of his chest and hinted at an impressive-looking abdominal ridge or two. Fine dark hair sprinkled his forearms. The harsh light of the lamp picked out definite traces of silver in his side-burns. Mid-thirties, she guessed, with plenty of exercise to keep him toned and strong.

She tore her eyes away before he caught her, suddenly feeling way too warm. Quinn was too big for this room, too enticing and wickedly attractive.

His deep brown eyes were suddenly on her face. "These are good."

She hadn't realised she was holding her breath, but now it suddenly left her in a rush. "Oh. Thanks."

"You have improved, matured."

Improved? Matured? *Don't go overboard with the compliments, mate.* "Thanks," she sniffed, and turned back to her nearly empty plate.

"Maybe," he continued, "you chose the wrong piece for the awards."

"You were the only one who thought so."

That was a lie. She had thought that, worried about it. Her entry for the Young Designer Awards was a wide gold bangle featuring pink and white Blackstone diamonds. It was supposed to capture the sweep of the outback ranges and show the riches within. Although it was a stunning piece and created comment from whoever saw it, Dani had never felt peaceful about it, never felt that she actually got it.

Quinn Everard, the judge, was the only one who had seen past the "wow" factor and found it wanting.

"Now, this…"

He flipped the pages back to where his thumb had marked the spot. She stood up and moved beside him, inhaling a warm masculinity so clean and refreshing that the air in the room was revitalised. Dani nearly swayed with the pleasure of being close to him, her fatigue from the long day washing away.

She looked down at the book. "The Keishi!" This was one of her first pieces, and still a favourite. Nineteen millimetre champagne Keishi pearls strung on white gold interspersed with gold roses, each centre a small round blue sapphire.

"This would have won you the award, just for colour and lustre alone."

She thrummed with pleasure. "I wanted to enter it. People said it wasn't high value enough."

Quinn looked into her eyes and her heartbeat stuttered.

Heat bloomed inside and filled her. She couldn't look away for the life of her. This close she picked out the fine lines at the corner of his eyes; the scar by his mouth she wanted to trace with her finger to see if it was as smooth as it looked. His eyes were dark and a little perplexed, and then he looked down at her mouth.

"Trust your instincts," he said softly.

Oh, boy, if he only knew what her instincts were telling her now. He was so close, his breath wafted over her face. She felt her body tighten, sway slightly in his direction. The man was a magnet, her own personalised magnet. The back of her neck prickled and dampened under the rumpled hank of hair she had twisted and last looked at ten hours ago.

Ten hours ago? She stepped back hurriedly, thinking how dishevelled she must look. There was probably broccoli in her teeth, and she remembered now that she had not showered today….

Dani had her pride. She didn't even know if she liked this man, but if succumbing to an intense attraction was an option, she would at least be clean and fragrant.

"I—I think it's time for bed." She groaned inwardly, thinking, *You smooth talker, you.* Her embarrassment was heightened by how strangely husky her voice sounded.

"It's only eight."

She ran her tongue over her teeth. "It's been a long day."

Quinn nodded, and in the process, his eyes swept over her chest and lingered long enough to tell her what she already knew, that her nipples were tight and hard, visibly so.

She didn't dare look down. "You can take the diamond to bed," she said weakly, then wanted to clap her hands to her head. Verbal clumsiness didn't sneak up on her often, but she'd made the world team tonight.

Quinn's mouth twitched.

Her cheeks stung with heat. No doubt his "lady friend" would be so much more sophisticated, never a hair out of place or a word out of turn.

"You look hot, Dani," Quinn said smoothly, and there was no mistaking his amusement.

She cleared her throat. "You could check the air-con in here. These lights really raise the temperature."

"They do, don't they?"

She'd made enough of a fool of herself. "Good night." She escaped without waiting for his response.

Quinn let his head roll back and stared at the bright lights on the ceiling. "Control yourself," he muttered, his weakness taunting him. Had she noticed his arousal? He'd sure noticed hers! The sexual charge he got just from being in the same room was beyond a joke, and he was toast once he clapped eyes on her chest.

So despite her snippiness, the lady was interested.

That added a new dimension to the proceedings. He'd not so much as touched her, but he knew instinctively that they were sexually compatible, or more aptly, explosively combustible!

Interesting... He looked down at her empty plate, remembering why he'd come up here in the first place. Quinn was tired of his own company, bored eating alone—which was weird since he was used to it. Preferred it, in fact. His life was a never-ending roundabout of fancy dinners in up-market restaurants, with the added non-bonus of countless airline meals.

But his apartment in Sydney was ordered and peaceful. To his mind, a cheese sandwich in front of the wall-to-ceiling windows that showcased the most beautiful city in the world was far more enjoyable than any two-hundred-dollar meal he had ever eaten.

A throwback, he supposed, to the chaotic mealtimes at home when he was a kid.

Quinn grew up with loving but eccentric parents who filled their huge old Sydney home to overflowing with troubled foster kids. He shared everything as a boy: his parents' love and time, his room, toys, even his wife, who moved in while they were at university. She was studying to be a social worker and loved helping out with the kids. Quinn shared her right up to the day she died of a brain tumour, aged twenty-six.

These days, he didn't share so much anymore, but still loved his parents dearly. Although he wished they didn't keep asking him when he was going to get around to giving them grandkids. Quinn's response hadn't changed since he was twenty: "I learned growing up that there are too many unwanted kids in the world."

He picked up the boxed diamond and took it to his room to lock away. Then he collected her empty plate and the food he'd brought at lunch. His phone rang as he descended the stairs. Matt Hammond calling from New Zealand.

He'd met Matt before since they were both share-holders of several different companies, including Black-stone Diamonds.

"Can we meet up in the next week?" Matt asked. "Among other things, I'd like to thank you properly for bringing the pink diamonds home."

Last month, Quinn had authenticated four pink diamonds for Matt's former sister-in-law, Melbourne supermodel, Briana Davenport. Briana found them in her apartment safe after her sister Marise was killed in the plane crash. Quinn was astonished to find they were from the Blackstone Rose necklace, stolen from Howard nearly three decades ago. He told Briana they must be returned to their rightful owner. At her request, he'd de-livered the stones to Howard Blackstone's estate lawyers.

It was well publicised that Howard's will had been altered shortly before the crash to bestow his jewellery collection to Marise. Quinn was less clear on whether the stolen necklace would be included in the jewellery col-lection, since it was not specifically named and still listed as stolen. He had to be sure he was not acting illegally. It would pan out better for Briana, his client, that way.

After deliberation, the lawyers declared that the Blackstone Rose necklace *was* included in the jewellery collection. Since Marise hadn't changed her will before the accident, the pink diamonds now belonged to her spouse, Matt Hammond.

"I'm holidaying in Port Douglas for the next couple of weeks," Quinn told Matt now.

"You're kidding! I'm coming up there myself in the next couple of days. We can catch up then, if you're agreeable."

Quinn wondered if Matt was coming to Port Douglas to see Dani. They were cousins, but from what he'd heard, the rift between the Blackstones and the Hammonds included both Dani and her mother, Sonya.

"In the meantime," Matt continued, "I'd like you to put the word out. I'm willing to ask no questions and pay top dollar for the fifth Blackstone Rose diamond, the big one."

The centrepiece of the old necklace was a pear-shaped 9.7 carat diamond. The original Heart of the Outback stone was just over one hundred carats in the rough. Stones lost a lot of weight in the cutting, especially if the cutter wanted several diamonds from the one stone. Some cutters went for weight, which did not necessarily correlate to value; fire and brilliance came from the shape the cutter chose.

In this case, the cutter had done a masterful job, realising a creditable thirty-eight carats in total. This, along with the name and the legend, accorded the stones a massive price tag. The last big intense pink Quinn could recall coming up for auction several years ago— an unnamed twenty carat, pear-shaped beauty—fetched six million dollars. The Blackstone Rose diamonds could sell for as much as half a million dollars per carat, more if they were sold together.

Although laser identification wasn't around when the stones were cut, the Blackstone Rose's thief must have sold the big stone on the black market for it to have disappeared without a trace. Quinn had extensive connections, and there was always someone who could be persuaded to sell information about less-reputable art and gem collectors. A pink of this size would cause comment wherever it turned up.

Quinn hung up, thinking that his whole existence lately—professional and personal—seemed to be tied up with the Blackstone and Hammond families. First Matt and the pink diamonds, now his enforced cohabitation with Danielle Hammond. His very *personal* existence stirred again when he recalled the desire in her eyes a few minutes ago, heard the huskiness of her voice. He knew that he was destined to spend another night alone in his bed, dreaming about her intriguing face and lithe body.

He would have Dani Hammond, he decided. It would help while away the hours in this sauna until he could return to civilisation.

He grinned as he stripped and slid between the sheets, allowing himself the uncharitable thought that tupping Howard Blackstone's little girl would be like thumbing his nose at the old man, dead or not. That would be twice in a month he'd shafted the old goat. Howard must have turned in his freshly dug grave when the Blackstone Rose diamonds came full circle to a Hammond again.

Four

Soon after 6:00 a.m., an ungodly time for her, Dani crept out of the house to watch the sun rise over the beach. The tide was high and the temperature around twenty. Yawning widely, she stumbled through the ten-metre stretch of trees that fringed the beach, then slipped off her sandals and carried them down to test the water.

The physical response she'd had to Quinn in the workroom had played on her mind all night. Her fumbling efforts to gloss over it, knowing he'd noticed her tongue practically hanging out, made it ten times worse.

This man was not her friend. More than that, he already had a woman, a special woman, judging by the value of the gift he was having made for her. But why did he have to be so gorgeous? How was she to exist under the same roof for the next two to three weeks without succumbing to his charms?

She knew how. Remember Nick…remember the humiliation.

The water licked around her toes, a cool surprise, reminding her that winter was on its way. She remembered a cool winter's day two years ago. On cue, her cheeks burned for no one but her and the breeze as she walked on deserted Four Mile Beach. Nick had nearly finished her.

Dani should have known better, even back then. Twenty-five was hardly wet behind the ears. Nick had wined and dined her, swept her off her feet in an indecently short time. Promised love and marriage and forever. And even though she'd lived all her life in a fishbowl being targeted by the Sydney tabloids, she trusted him.

Until the day she'd left the house to go to a wedding dress fitting and found ten journalists camped outside the gate in the rain. To this day, Dani loathed large black umbrellas. They reminded her of vultures waiting for someone to die.

The journalists gleefully filled her in on the details. While she'd been sitting at home happily planning her wedding, Nick had been entertaining a well-known soap actress in an alleyway beside a nightclub. The photographs were pornographic. When confronted, the louse drunkenly accused Dani of misrepresenting her position in the Blackstone family. It had finally sunk in, despite her repeated insistence, that far from being an heiress, his fiancée was penniless and illegitimate.

Howard came to her rescue, just as he had for her mother years before. Dani wanted nothing more than to disappear. A few months backpacking around Asia eased her pain a little but caused her mother tremendous worry. Tired of the constant media scrutiny, she refused to return to Sydney, and Howard agreed to bankroll her business here in Port, where no one knew or cared that she was Danielle Hammond of Blackstone fame.

The sunrise was beautiful, reminding her of why she loved this place. She filled her lungs with sea air, knowing she had to resist Quinn, because if she didn't, there would be far worse heartache than Nick had inflicted. And that would spoil this beautiful place for her forever.

She turned around at the halfway point, feeling stronger and determined to finish this job quickly and eliminate the temptation. But her heart fluttered as a figure in blue shorts and a black sleeveless T-shirt jogged leisurely toward her. She had forgotten he liked to run in the early morning before the heat and humidity gained purchase.

Quinn slowed as she approached. "Too hot to sleep?"

Whether it was there or not, Dani imagined a sardonic twist to his mouth, and her hope that he would ignore her stammering reaction to him last night faded. He knew. And he wanted her to know he knew.

"Have a good run," she said as politely as she could muster, still walking steadily toward the turnoff through the trees.

But Quinn began jogging backward, facing her. "Did you know Matt Hammond is coming to town?"

That was unexpected. She slowed. "No, I didn't."

Dani had never met Matt in person. He'd attended Howard's funeral in February but kept an icy distance from the family. She'd wanted to introduce herself but decided, under the circumstances, to present a united front with the family of the man who had raised her.

She'd met Matt's brother Jarrod a couple of times and liked him immensely. But Matt was understandably bitter about Marise's presence on the ill-fated plane and her inclusion in the diamond magnate's will. Especially when a lot of the bad press zeroed in on the paternity of little Blake, Matt and Marise's son.

"How did you know that?" Dani asked.

"He called last night."

"Called you?" She frowned.

Quinn stopped jogging and propped his foot on a half-buried log to retie his laces. "We're both in the gem trade. That's not so odd, is it?"

Dani hovered nearby, curious.

"When I told him where I was, he said he was on his way here himself. I assumed, since you're his cousin, it was to see you."

She shook her head. "He wouldn't come here to see me."

Quinn utilised the log to stretch his calf muscles. Dani couldn't help but notice the dark hair salting his long strong legs.

She wrenched her mind back to Matt. Why would he seek her out? And what was his business with Quinn? A mutual dislike of Howard Blackstone was their only connection as far as she could see. "What exactly is your business with Matt?"

Quinn stilled, his hands on his thighs. "Is that anything to do with you?"

"Is it to do with the Blackstone Rose diamonds?"

"What do you know of the Blackstone Rose diamonds?"

Dani exhaled. "How they mysteriously turned up at Howard's lawyers a month ago and they had no choice but to send them to Hammonds." Suddenly it all fell into place. "*You* found them. *You* sent them back."

"I didn't find them. I was given them. A simple authentication job."

"Who from?"

"You'll have to ask Matt for the details, but they're his property, fair and square."

"I told you, I don't know him." She sighed. "He came to the funeral but wouldn't have anything to do with us."

"You should be more picky whom you fraternise with," Quinn said lightly. "Is there anyone in the world Howard Blackstone hasn't rubbed up the wrong way?"

"The feud wasn't all Howard's doing, you know."

"Tell me about it."

"Everyone knows. You must know."

"I know what the papers say." Quinn sat down on the log and patted the space beside him. "I want to hear it from an insider."

She sat tautly, aware of his big hot body just inches away, warming her side. A trickle of sweat crawled down his temple and she bet his back would be slick, too. Why didn't that turn her right off, instead of accelerating her pulse to alarming levels?

She bent and picked up a handful of white sand, letting it run slowly through her fingers. Since Howard's death, the Blackstone-Hammond feud origins had been printed and reprinted. Dani was sorry if her rendition was reminiscent of a bored teenage boy recounting his summer holiday to his class, but frankly, she was tired of the whole thing.

"Jeb, my granddad, and Howard were friends and partners after Howard married my auntie Ursula. Uncle Oliver, Mum and Ursula's brother, was left behind in New Zealand to run the family business. Anyway, when Granddad Jeb got sick, he signed over all his mining claims to Howard. Naturally, this didn't go down too well with Oliver."

That was an understatement. According to her cousin Jarrod, even after a stroke five years ago, the old man still got apoplectic at the mere mention of Howard Blackstone.

"He was particularly upset when Jeb gifted the Heart of the Outback stone, his most famous find, to Auntie Ursula." The massive pink diamond was part of Australian folklore, but as with many other exceptional diamonds, it brought its own share of bad luck with it.

"Howard had it cut and set into a fabulous necklace he called the Blackstone Rose."

"Rubbing salt into Hammond's wound," Quinn murmured.

She nodded. Oliver was incensed that the name Hammond was now completely usurped of its rightful place in the history of the famous Heart of the Outback.

"But after James, Howard's firstborn, was abducted,

Auntie Ursula became depressed. To cheer her up, Howard threw a huge thirtieth birthday party. Everyone was there, even the prime minister." Dani smiled, remembering her mother's awestruck tone as she'd described the finery, the dresses, the beautiful decorations. "But it all ended in tears."

"The night the necklace was stolen," Quinn murmured.

Everyone had their theories. Some thought it was a failed ransom attempt. No doubt Quinn thought Howard had hidden the necklace to collect the insurance money. "Howard accused Oliver and things got pretty heated," Dani continued. "Oliver denounced his sisters and said they were dead to him...." She turned to him, lowering the depth of her voice and adding some volume, "'So long as you have anything to do with a Blackstone!'" She wagged her index finger at him.

He smiled at her. Really smiled, and her insides melted.

"You missed a bit," Quinn admonished.

"What? Oh well, you obviously know about poor old Auntie Ursula toppling into the pool...."

"After drinking too much."

She put her finger to her lips. "We don't talk about it," she whispered dramatically. "In the melee, Howard accused Oliver of engineering the kidnapping of wee James, as well." That fact was probably not as well known as the rest.

Unfortunately, that accusation was the one thing Oliver could never forgive. He and his wife, Katherine, could not have children of their own. Jarrod and Matt were adopted.

"Nice bloke," Quinn said, an edge to his voice.

"You have to remember that he'd lost a son," Dani countered. "And whatever rumours you've heard about his womanising, Mum says he really loved Auntie Ursula. It can't have been much fun watching her struggle with depression."

Quinn didn't look impressed or moved. Whatever had gone down with him and Howard must have been spectacular. She sighed. "I don't get it, Quinn. Matt has a legitimate right to be angry, especially after the past few months. But your little spat was years ago. I wonder, why do you hate his guts still, even after his death?"

"Curiosity killed the cat." His tone was cool.

It had to be more than just the diamond-association vote, Dani reasoned. Quinn was a very successful broker, one of the most prominent in the world. She refused to believe that he still held a grudge because Howard had made life a little difficult for him years ago. "You know, your dislike of Howard borders on obsession."

He cocked a cynical brow. "That so?"

"It's too personal. What did he do? Take a woman from you?"

His bark of laughter rang out, startling her.

"Professional jealousy?" she guessed.

Or maybe she was needling, trying to pick a fight. Trying to find some external conflict to justify the internal conflict of wanting him. "He beat you to the deal of a lifetime?"

Quinn's brows knitted together. "Howard Blackstone never beat me at anything."

"Or maybe you've heard the stories and decided that you are the missing Blackstone heir." She was joking, of course, even knowing it was a terrible thing to joke about.

Howard alone always had faith that his firstborn, James, would walk through the door one day. He'd never closed the investigation and must have had a strong lead just before he died, because he changed his will. The new will effectively cut Kimberley out, favouring instead his oldest son, James should he be found within six months of Howard's death.

Naturally the press enjoyed this extra twist to the ever-changing, always-enthralling saga of the Blackstone family. Several candidates had been discussed and discarded over the past months, including Jarrod Hammond, Matt's brother. You had to hand it to Howard, she thought with a spark of admiration. He sure knew how to keep the paparazzi guessing.

Just like Quinn kept her guessing, mostly about how long it would be before she gave in to an unusually severe case of the hots… Reining in her errant thoughts, she returned to the topic of the missing heir. "Let's see, you'd be about the right age, mid-thirties. And I heard somewhere that you'd grown up in a foster home."

He spread out his fingers on his thigh, snagging her gaze for a moment. Tension curled his fingertips around his muscled leg, tension that radiated toward her in a hot cloud. Dani tore her eyes away and braved a look at his face, hearing the waves just a few metres away as if they were sloshing against her ribs.

Quinn gave no sign that he agreed or disagreed, but a rising sense of incomprehensible excitement pushed the next words from her mouth. "What, did you go to him with your theory and he laughed you out of the room?"

He stilled for a long moment, then slapped one hand on the log right beside her leg and heaved to his feet, turning to loom over her. The smell of him, sweat and soap and desire, swamped her. Then his other hand slammed down on the log on her other side.

She was trapped.

His face descended quickly to within an inch of hers, so close she could almost feel the scrape of his morning beard.

"You've got it very wrong, Danielle," he said, his soft voice at odds with the dangerous blaze of warning and desire in the espresso depths of his eyes.

Her stupid joke had pushed him too far.

"I'm not the missing Blackstone brother," he murmured, his chin dipping as he inched closer. His pupils were enlarged, the centres pinpoints of fire that hypnotised and immobilised.

"Because if I was," he continued in a low murmur that made the hairs on the back of her neck leap to attention, "I wouldn't do what I'm about to do."

Dani knew what he was about to do. She saw it coming like a train wreck—and she was chained to the tracks. It was inevitable that her head tilted back and her fingernails dug in to the rough surface of the log, bracing her. The cords on her neck stretched, rigid and tight. She watched, wide-eyed, as his face and mouth crossed the last millimetre, the point of no return.

If she'd been standing, her knees would have buckled at the first taste. They stared at each other until his salty mouth with its silky tongue started teasing hers, then she felt her eyelids flutter and close. He kissed firmly, not touching her except for his mouth, yet involving her senses totally. Every kiss she'd ever experienced was just window dressing; she'd been waiting for this, the real thing. Every man she had ever kissed before was a boy, and Quinn was here to show her how a man kissed.

Where were her cautionary affirmations? Where was her regard for that unknown woman, waiting some-where for her diamond? That woman, at least, would understand, would realise that to be kissed like this was impossible to resist.

Dani wouldn't have stopped it; he taught her that in just a few seconds. How beautiful and right it was that she sat on a log in her favourite place in the world at sunrise, and the door to perdition was open and inviting. With his tongue stroking hers, his lips commanding hers to give him more, desire pushed her to where the sunrise would claim her, consume her with pleasure.

Then he raised his head abruptly and she sagged back onto her log, gasping for breath. The young sun disappeared behind him as he straightened, and all she could think was "I've done it now."

Quinn looked down at her, his eyes a swirling brown storm of intent. "Did that feel like a cousin's kiss, Danielle?"

While she was still trying to collect coherence and dignity—and maybe some form of protest—he turned and jogged away, his strong legs pumping, his back bristling with tension.

She registered a sharp pain in the tip of her middle

finger and raised her hand to her mouth to nibble at the splinter.

She was so out of her depth.

Five

Thankfully Quinn left her alone for the rest of the day and she completed the first of several wax models she would make in these initial stages. Dani worked late, said her good-nights from his office door and went to bed, trying to dampen down the memory of the kiss. But even though she'd had little sleep the night before, it still eluded her tonight.

She tossed and turned, listening to the waves through the open window. She considered a walk along the beach, something she did sometimes when troubled or unable to sleep. But she discarded that idea, knowing all she'd see was his face, all she'd feel was his mouth on hers.

Finally at about 1:00 a.m. she rose and threw on her robe, hoping that chocolate milk might help.

Downstairs, Quinn's office light was on, the door ajar.

· She halted for a minute that seemed to stretch on forever, her heart thudding in her ears. All was quiet so she crept closer and pressed her ear carefully to the wooden door. Then his voice sounded and Dani nearly leapt into the air. She only let her breath out when she realised he was on the phone.

Who could he be talking to at one in the morning? A nasty combination of guilt and jealousy clawed at her as she wondered about the special woman in his life. Perhaps it was a long-distance love affair and that's why he was calling so late. *Hi, honey, I kissed someone today....*

But it was soon apparent this was a business call—exciting business. From what she could make out, he was in the middle of a live auction, bidding by phone. When she heard him murmur "Five million," her decorum abandoned her and she straightened and inched forward, snaking her head around the door.

Quinn sat at his desk, the phone to his ear. She felt the leap of interest as his eyes swivelled toward her, a palpable, inescapable sense of awareness, zeroing in on her. He'd rolled his shirtsleeves up to his elbows and undone his top buttons. One hand rested on a file in front of him, under a half-full glass of some amber liquid. The desk lamp was on, but otherwise the room was in darkness.

Dani lingered in the shadows, although he gave no sign that he was either displeased or happy with her presence. But he did not release her from his gaze. She leaned against the door, her heart thudding along in the silences that punctuated his infrequent responses.

After a couple of minutes, Quinn sipped his drink and then laid the receiver down and turned the speaker phone on, all without taking his eyes off her face. She took that as something of an invitation. Here was an opportunity to have a glimpse into his world, see the negotiator at work.

She moved a few steps farther into the room and rested her hands on the edge of a chair to keep that barrier between them.

The voice on the speaker was unmistakably English. She heard the name of a well-known auction house and the words *lot seven*. Presumably the auction was being conducted in London. Dani wondered if the man on the phone was a bid clerk from the auction house or an employee of Quinn's.

The item being bid for was a famous painting by a contemporary Irish artist who'd died in the sixties. She only knew that because Howard had one of his paintings. She wasn't sure how many bidders there were for this particular item. The bids were relayed to Quinn as they happened, although Dani heard nothing of the activity in the auction house, only the man's voice. The pauses in between bids seemed interminable. They probably weren't, but she guessed there was a lot of tension on the other side of the world. Lord knows there was enough in this office.

Would he smile if he won the bid? Celebrate with a drink? She held his gaze, and no doubt her face was alive with questions. His, however, was framed in intense concentration that held her captive.

The price was now up to eight million pounds. Dani

inched a little closer to the desk, marvelling at his calm.
It probably wasn't his money he was spending, but if
it'd been her, she would have buckled under the
pressure. The next million took only two or three
minutes to be disposed of. Still Quinn looked at her
face.

"Ten million pounds, sir?"

He didn't flinch, but she did. While she'd been
thinking about him, about his face and concentration and
possible means of celebration, she had waylaid a couple
of million.

Quinn quietly affirmed.

Ten million! That was *how* much in Australian
dollars? For a painting?

The next pause was a long one. Dani was halfway
across the room now, just a few more steps to the chair
in front of his desk.

"The other party has just bid eleven, Mr. Everard."

"You may proceed," Quinn said quietly, and flexed
the fingers of his right hand.

Dani covered her mouth with her hand and moved
to the desk. The tension was killing her, but how cool
he was. No sign of emotion crossed his features. He
might have been reading the paper.

The minutes crawled by. Twelve million came and
went. Her throat felt like sandpaper and she swallowed.
Quinn lifted the glass and moistened his lips, then held
it out to her.

Cognac. She would never smell it again without remembering this night. It slid down her throat and
washed her lungs with heat. Slowly she rolled the glass

over her forehead before setting it down on the desk. She had to lean well forward to get it within his reach, so she edged one hip onto the desk, twisting around to face him.

His eyes were inscrutable. A trickle of sweat began its journey down her spine, surprising her. She arched a little as the fabric of her silky robe slid over and cooled the moisture. A tiny flicker of that mahogany gaze told her he'd noticed, but not one muscle in his face twitched.

"Mr. Everard," the bid clerk's nasal voice intoned. "The other party has entered into a consultation with his client. Are you happy to hold?"

"Yes."

Dani's breath gushed out and she stretched her tense limbs and rubbed the back of her neck, thankful for the intermission.

"By the way, Quinn…" The man on the line lowered and warmed his voice. "That commodity you were interested in? A blank wall so far, I'm afraid. However…"

Quinn shifted but made no response to her raised brows. "Go on."

"A gentleman of my acquaintance has recently returned from visiting the big house on the other side of town. He owes me certain favours."

Quinn chuckled. "You run with the most appalling crowd, Maurice."

"I will let you know directly if I can be of any further assistance," There was a muffled crackle and muted voices. "I think we are ready to resume, sir."

"Thank you," Quinn murmured, his eyes back on Dani's face.

She lost the ability to judge time in the airless room. The performance may have lasted ten minutes or an hour. The last two million pounds advanced and Dani took another sip of liquor, her nipples prickling with the knowledge that he watched her every move. Rather than push the glass across the desk, she walked around to his side, placed it in front of him and leaned against the desk beside him. Quinn swivelled in his chair to face her, still holding her prisoner with his eyes.

Fourteen million pounds.

Dani swallowed.

Fourteen-point-two million. The other bidder had opted to chop the bid. Quinn offered no objection, neither did the auctioneer, apparently. Dani cleared her dry throat and helped herself to another sip of cognac while he watched.

Fourteen-point-five million. The room spun a little, which could have been the cognac. It was like a vacuum in here. Quinn Everard stared at her calmly, steadily, and the bid rose another massive increment. The tension was unbearable.

The skin of her throat and face tickled and she swiped at it, somehow agitated and afraid for him. She could not even contemplate him losing now, not after this. Not when she felt so sensitised, so aware of his gaze gripping her, holding her up.

Fourteen-point-seven million pounds for lot seven, going once. She chewed on her thumbnail, praying. Her chest rose and fell as each breath tortured her lungs.

Fourteen-point-seven million pounds for lot seven, going twice. Dani sucked in a massive breath, held it. This was it!

It was over! Quinn had won the bid.

Air gushed out from her lungs and she slumped momentarily, but then elation poured through her like the most illicit rush. She leapt in the air, her arms high above her head, her hands fisted in victory. For the first time in many minutes, maybe even an hour, Quinn was not looking at her. He stared at the file on the desk. His shoulders were rigid.

"Congratulations, Mr. Everard, and thank you for participating."

He exhaled slowly. "Thank you, Maurice." He paused, as if about to add something, but then looked up into Dani's face. "Thank you," he repeated, and she saw that his teeth were clenched. His hand shot out and hit the switch of the phone. Then he was standing in front of her, gripping her waist hard. He dragged her forward into him, his body like stone against her soft, yielding form.

She wrapped her arms around his neck and sagged against him, burying her face in his shoulder. Quinn moved so that her head tilted up, her throat exposed.

Bite me, she thought, her blood screaming in her ears. She was leaping out of her skin. Never had she reached this peak of excitement in her life, and she couldn't begin to think of consequences, other women, her heart, his hatred for Howard.

As if he'd heard her plea, Quinn lowered his head and nuzzled the hollow at the base of her throat briefly, then took her mouth hard. The taste of leather and almonds from aged cognac filled her mouth. His need for her came from farther down where his groin pushed into the silk-clad vee of her thighs. With a strangled gasp, she pushed back, feeling the distended ridge of his fly, every link of his zipper.

His tongue lashed hers, teeth knocked and scraped. She gasped breathlessly when his hand cupped and squeezed her buttock, forcing her forward. Then his hand ran down the short robe and to the sensitive back of her thigh, lifting it high and hard against him, so that her leg came up and wrapped around his hip. Her mind splintered with a desperate need of carnal contact.

She got it in spades, and the more she jerked against him, the higher she went. Grinding and straining, she became something—someone—she had no control over. She was on a collision course with a cyclone, building higher with every lash of his tongue deep in her mouth and every hard, fast thrust against her hot centre. And then he gripped the soft inside of her leg from behind and moved up, his seeking fingers sending a bolt of fiery energy searing through her. She lost the battle to be aware of her actions or his. All she knew was a wave of scalding pleasure that fisted and ebbed and fisted again and again, driving everything out of her mind.

She sagged against him, trying without success to halt the slide of her leg down his. Boneless, still swimming in pleasure, she trusted him to hold her up because her only tenuous grip was one hand around his neck. The other arm was behind her, palm pressed into the desk and trembling.

Quinn dragged her thong down her legs and made short work of the knot of her robe. While she still lagged, he plunged his hand into her hair and lifted her face to his.

His eyes snapped at her, fierce and hot. "Again."

"Yes." She sucked air into her lungs and pushed up off the desk and the madness started again.

Hands tore at clothing, mouths scraped over heated flesh, breath gushed from screaming lungs. When she got her hands inside his shirt, they slid on his slicked flesh. Cool, calm Quinn Everard was sweating, her mind crowed. She had reduced him to this, a wild animal desperate to copulate, so far removed from the suave, sophisticated businessman he was.

Where had she come from, this wanton, panting woman using her teeth and nails, taking his tongue into her mouth as if it was a drug she was addicted to? She was a nice girl about sex, only did it with someone she really cared about. One didn't do nasty sex when one had lived in a fishbowl all one's life, just like one didn't do drugs or drunken rampages, either.

"Do it!" the nice girl panted, desperate to have all of him now.

His hands tangled in her hair. "You think I have any control over this?" he gasped, holding her face up and scowling down into her eyes. "That went when you walked into the room."

The only answer she was capable of giving was to pull his torso against her and swipe her breasts back and forth, again and again. His crisp chest hair scraped and burned her nipples, spurring her into intensifying her efforts with his pants fastening. She finally got his pants down and at last he was naked, in all his pure, proud, masculine glory, roped with muscle, rough with hair, fierce with need.

There was a brief halt when he clapped a hand to his head. "Wallet?" Feverishly, he picked up his pants, slapping the pockets, then his face cleared and he reached behind her to the drawer and drew his wallet out.

Grateful for his foresight—protection hadn't even occurred to her—she took the pack from him and made it memorable, smoothing the condom over his hot, hard flesh with a dedication that had both of them holding their breaths for long seconds. He was built. Even her wildest daydreams hadn't done him justice. Then he groaned and grabbed her hands in a viselike grip. This agitated man before her, streaked with sweat and with rumpled hair, was a side of him she could come to like. But right now, her body was screaming for him, she needed more than *like*.

Then his palms were covering her breasts and his mouth was stealing her breath and the eye of the storm moved on, throwing them into a sexual frenzy again.

Quinn kept one arm firmly around her back for support while the other swept clear the surface of his desk. Then down she went, clutching at his shoulders and arms, dragging him down, too. Limbs tangled, teeth gnashed, her heart threatened to explode out of her chest. The storm overtook her, both of them. The air was filled with grunts and bumps and harshly drawn breaths. He dug his fingers into her hips and dragged her forward. She felt heat meeting heat and then the delicious, brimming slide of his total invasion. For a second, the absolute shock and pleasure of him deep inside immobilised her. Then she strained up, locked her legs around him and held on for the ride of her life. He kept one arm under her to shield her from the unforgiving desk. The other he plunged into her hair, pulling her head back to give him access to her mouth. Bodies and mouths locked together, she threw herself heart and soul into a coupling so intense, as full of the fire and brilliance of the diamond upstairs, that she wondered if they'd survive or just combust.

Her second orgasm slammed into her, making her falter and lose her rhythm. Her legs relaxed suddenly from around him, splaying wide as coils of sensation pumped and flowed to every extremity. She sobbed with delight and Quinn straightened a little, lifted her higher, changing the angle to drive new pleasure into her. She was assailed by so much sensation, she couldn't contain it and was swept away in another inferno of red-hot pleasure that never cooled, only soared higher. Somehow she held on, lifting her legs around his waist again, rising to meet him, until she felt the change in his grip intensify, his arms becoming so rigid, her hands lost purchase. But he gathered her whole body to him, right off the desk, threw his head back and in a groaning rush of breath that went on and on, he pumped, again and again, and then collapsed on top of her.

Minutes later sometime in the next millennium, Dani stirred and tried lifting her head. She was trapped with Quinn's face buried in her hair on one side. It was an interesting predicament, unable to move, the harsh light of the desk lamp only inches away, burning her face and revealing all her flaws, no doubt. Quinn's heartbeat, right on top of hers, rattled away at an impossible rate. She swivelled her eyes to the side, saw the devastation on the floor, clothes mixed with papers and with cognac.

Her hair scratched and whispered on the white blotter pad. She blew softly into his ear, repeating the gesture when there was no response. His lashes flickered and he turned his head and licked his lips. Slowly his eyes focussed on her.

"You okay?" he asked weakly.

Dani's dry lips stretched in a strained smile. Oh, man, was she ever!

He blinked apologetically, lifting his torso a couple of inches. "Sorry. I'm squashing you."

Quinn Everard was embarrassed, she thought. Like her, he probably didn't do nasty sex.

That made her smile wider. "I never took you for a desk man."

He blinked, looking appalled. "I'm not. I'm...sorry. Did I hurt you?"

She bit back a full-on smile. "Only if you call pleasure pain."

They shifted jerkily, which brought about an interesting sensation since he was still inside her. He lifted a little higher and ran his eyes down her body, making her squirm. Distracted by her belly button jewellery, he tugged lightly on the barbell she wore; a triangular knot of sterling silver, studded with deep red Swarovski Austrian crystals. "Did you make this? It's very pretty."

Dani made belly button jewellery only for herself. The precious stones she preferred working with were too expensive, since they were destined, for the most part, to be hidden under clothing.

His big hand, spread wide, covered her belly, then moved slowly up to pass lightly over the tips of her breasts. She squeezed around him, as tight as she could, pleasuring them both. Smiling, he bent his head and tongued a rapidly hardening nipple, even as she felt him harden inside her.

"I think I can dredge up some finesse, if you'd consider giving me a second chance."

"While I have nothing at all against the desk man—" she smiled and put her arms around his neck, arching up into him "—I wouldn't be averse to some finesse in the very near future."

Six

Quinn declared the next day a holiday to celebrate the results of the auction. He'd made all the arrangements by the time she'd showered, and within the hour, they were at Port Douglas Marina boarding a bareboat charter catamaran named *Seawind,* a ten-metre flared-hull beauty with mainsail.

They sailed out to the Low Isles and snorkelled around the breathtaking underwater garden of the Great Barrier Reef. But by late morning, the area was overrun by hordes of tourists on day trips, so they set sail for a small inlet to put into and enjoy the hamper the charter company provided.

The weather was perfect, calm and clear. Quinn was happy to find that on the water the humidity didn't bother him at all. Either that or he was becoming acclimatised.

"This is the life." Dani appeared from below deck with her lime-green sundress on again; he liked the bikini better but she'd burn easily with her skin. And at least he now knew exactly what was under that dress. It would give him something to do later, peeling it off her....

He offered her a plate and glass from the hamper and she stretched her legs out along the seat, sighing with pleasure.

"Ever sailed before?" he asked.

"No. Howard was never interested in boats."

Quinn popped a cheese-topped cracker in his mouth. "Did you get on?"

"With Howard?" She considered. "Most of the time. He wasn't averse to sharing his opinion on clothes, friends, music and so on, but I suppose that was his right since he paid the bills."

She unscrewed the cap of the chilled sauvignon blanc wine and held it up to him.

Quinn had his mouth full but shook his head, holding up a bottle of water instead.

Dani leaned back on the seat with her wine and a plate of nibbles. "He was kinder to me than to the others. I was never going to run his company, so I guess he went easier on me."

"He bought the shop for you, didn't he?"

"It was a loan, one I've nearly paid off."

"Why do you think they never married?" Quinn really wanted to know why the bastard never publicly acknowledged Dani as his daughter.

"Who?" She looked blank.

"Your mother and Howard."

She took a sip of wine, her brow wrinkling. "Why would they marry? He was her brother-in-law."

"They obviously liked each other well enough to stay together all those years," he mused aloud.

"They were a bit like an old married couple, I suppose, when he wasn't out putting it around…" She grinned.

"But she still stayed?" Don't tell him Sonya wasn't in for all she could get. Quinn had never met Sonya Hammond, but the Sydney press had long speculated on the relationship between the womanising Howard Blackstone and his sister-in-law. No matter how often the Blackstone publicity machine denied it, Dani's paternity was subject to debate on a regular basis. Most—Quinn included—assumed she was Howard's love child.

"I know everyone thought Mum was his mistress," Dani said moodily. "I've lived with the scandalised looks and whispers all my life. But my mum has more class in her little finger than all of them."

"But there was you." If Howard didn't want to acknowledge his love child, why did he flaunt them, keep them in his house?

Her gaze was unwavering, if a little cool. "Howard's not my father," she said tiredly. "Look, I know you hate him and I know he has—had—his faults. But he looked after us." She looked down, picking at the hem of her dress. "Which is a lot more than can be said for my real father."

"Who is…?"

"Who cares?" she shot back. "Not him, that's for sure."

Quinn held up his hands, remembering the cliché about redheads and temper. "Sorry. Touchy subject, huh?"

He sympathised but was still reeling a little to find she wasn't Blackstone's daughter. That was a turn up for the books.

"Not touchy, boring." Her voice dropped. "He didn't want us. End of story." She stared moodily out at nothing but sea, and the sun glinted off her copper curls. "I wouldn't have minded very much if Howard was my father. At least he was there."

Quinn supposed he should feel guilty. Sleeping with Dani wasn't a victory over the old man, after all. Regardless, it still felt damn good.

And then she smiled brilliantly, unfolded those glorious legs and came to stand close and rummage through the hamper. "Who taught you to sail?"

"My father." Quinn spent many a Saturday morning on the water as a kid until his parents decided the boat was a luxury and the money would be better spent elsewhere.

"Was it very rough, growing up in a foster home?"

"Rough?" He smiled. "Sometimes. Bloody noisy. It was more or less open house. I doubt even Mum and Dad knew how many kids were under the roof at any one time."

"You called them Mum and Dad?"

"They are my mum and dad," Quinn said, bemused.

"Well, yes, but how long were you with them?" She looked confused.

Quinn scratched his head. "All my life. I think you've got the wrong end of the stick. I wasn't a foster kid. All the other kids were."

Dani's face cleared. "Oh, I see. So you and your parents ran a foster home?"

"Something like that," Quinn agreed. "They have a big old villa in Newtown, off King Street. Lots of rooms, all in various states of disrepair, and a kitchen that's the size of a hotel dining room."

"Not at all what I imagined for you."

She moved back to her seat, but her enticing floral scent lingered and he sniffed carefully, keeping it for himself. "What did you imagine?"

Dani grinned. "A grand old mansion with a butler. Everybody dressed for dinner and speaking very *na-i-cely*." She gave an apologetic shrug. "Sorry but you're just so damned refined."

Quinn chuckled. "My parents would love that. They are the most unpretentious people I know. Old hippies, very socially aware. They don't care about money or nice things, only sharing what they have with the less fortunate." He paused. "I'm sure I embarrass them, successful capitalist that I am. Not that they don't hit me up every couple of months with some harebrained fund-raising scheme or other."

She crossed one shapely leg over the other, snagging his attention, holding it for seconds. What was this hold she had over him? She was younger than him by seven years, but that wasn't the allure. He'd found her his equal in maturity and intelligence.

"You must have seen some sad things, though."

"Kids are selfish." He opened his bottle of water. "I was too busy marking my territory."

"Is that how you broke your nose?"

Quinn gave her a resigned smile. "Yep. That was Jake Vance, actually."

"Jake?" She sat up.

"You know him?" Something in him bristled. He'd be surprised if she didn't know of Jake; he was one of the most talked-about entrepreneurs in Australia. But as he was his best friend and also quite the ladies' man, Quinn wasn't sure if he liked the idea of Jake and Dani being friendly.

"Not very well. I met him a couple of times. He was at Kim and Ric's wedding, with Briana Davenport, actually, pre-Jarrod."

Quinn nodded, relaxing. "I'd heard that."

"Tell me about the broken nose," Dani prompted.

"We didn't see eye to eye when he first came to stay." Quinn absently rubbed the bridge of his nose, recalling the mother of all his teenage fights.

"Jake Vance was a foster child?" She sounded disbelieving.

He supposed it was difficult to think of Jake like that when the whole country associated him with immense wealth.

"Not exactly. He had a mother, but there were some problems, mostly to do with his stepfather. He ran away from home, looking for work in the city and things didn't pan out the way he'd hoped. Ma and Pa got to talking to him on the streets one day so he turned up at home."

Quinn as a teenager was well used to sharing but liked to be asked nicely. Jake didn't ask nicely. Quinn wasn't about to lose his standing as top dog in his own house. The battle was epic, and at the end of it, neither boy could stand. And that was the start of a long and valued friendship.

"He's my closest friend now. He and Lucy my foster sister. She was abused from the start. Came to us when she was eight and just stayed." He caught her horrified look. "She and Jake had a thing a few years back, but now she lives in London. Corporate banker," he finished proudly.

"How awful." Dani shuddered. "What makes people such monsters?"

"I don't suppose people start out that way," Quinn said thoughtfully. "But it's not that hard to be careful if you don't want a baby."

Dani nodded sadly, and he realised that was probably close to the bone for her. "Not these days, anyway," he qualified, not meaning to suggest her mother and the mystery lover had been careless.

"So have the things you've seen and heard put you off having kids?" Her voice trailed off when a shadow passed over his face. "Oh, I'm sorry, Quinn." Dani looked very uncomfortable suddenly.

"That's okay. I was married, yes."

"I remembered as soon as I'd asked. Laura Hartley, wasn't it? I only know because she was at PLC around the same time as Kim. I was a couple of years after."

"Ah." He nodded. "I didn't know that." PLC— Pymble Ladies College, a private college on the North Shore—had an excellent academic reputation, but it was strictly for rich kids.

"I'm sorry," Dani repeated quietly. "I remember now hearing that she'd died."

Quinn stared out over the waves. "We married when we were still at university. Laura wanted to be a social worker, whereas her parents…" his voice hardened as he continued, "They had other ideas. Sure, they sent her to a nice school and tolerated her going to uni, but they didn't intend their daughter to get her hands dirty. She was only marking time till the right rich husband came along." He smiled bitterly. "When she moved in with me on the cheap side of town, her family disowned her."

"What was the family business again?" Dani's brow wrinkled. "I remember they had stores all over the country. I think they were friends with Howard."

"Soft furnishings." Quinn swallowed, but it didn't erase the familiar burn of anger that flared up at the mention of Howard's name. He may not have caused Laura's death, but he sure influenced how she felt in those last days.

"How old was she when she died?"

"Twenty-six. It was sudden, only a few months from the first symptoms till the end."

"I'm so sorry," she said again, her golden eyes pools of sympathy.

"Don't be. I wouldn't swap those few years for anything, not a bit of it." He leaned forward and poured a little wine into a glass, mindful that he was skippering the boat. "She loved our life, my parents. She loved that we took in the unwanted and the street kids." Some of the good times flooded in, making him smile. "Every time I turned around, she was sitting in a corner, talking to some snot-nosed kid. They confided in her, told her everything.

More than Mum and Dad, even." He looked down at the wine in his glass, swirled it around before tossing it down in one gulp. "That was the hell of it. She would have gone places, helped so many. Why she had to die is beyond me."

It was his one taste of true failure. He couldn't understand how it could happen, how she could be taken.

How could he not have saved her?

He rubbed his chin. Part of him would always love Laura, or more accurately, love that time of his life, when he was young and silly enough to believe in forever, believe he and Laura were invincible.

But Howard Blackstone had tainted the memories. He'd never forgive him for that.

And as he tried and failed to swallow the hard knot of bitterness, he found himself wanting to justify it to Dani. He called himself a swine for doing it, for doing what Howard had done to him. Tainting the memories.

But he wanted her to know. "You want to know why I hate Howard so much?"

Dani blinked at his harsh tone.

"The bastard ruined the last weeks of Laura's life."

She visibly paled. "I didn't know he knew her."

"He didn't. But you're right about him being friends with the Hartleys. After the World Association of Diamonds vote went against him, he did all he could to blacken my name. That was fine, I could take care of myself. Laura always had faith her folks would come around and accept our marriage. But with Blackstone whispering in their ears, filling them full of hate, they turned their backs, even knowing she was terminal."

Dani's mouth dropped open in dismay, and she looked away as if she couldn't bear to look at his face. Yes, it hurts, doesn't it, he thought bitterly. She'd thought Howard was some kind of saint. Well, now she knew differently.

"When everything went to hell and the tumour came back, I went to them, begged them to come. Not that we ever gave up hope…" Laura would not permit anyone to think for a minute she wouldn't beat the cancer. "But they tossed me out. They said Howard had told them all about me. How I couldn't be trusted, how I was after her money, how she was my meal ticket out of the slums." His head rolled back and he breathed deeply of the warm air. "They couldn't even give her peace at the end," he said with disgust.

"I—I didn't know."

How could she?

Now that the anger was out, as always, it quickly faded. Time did that. Blackstone had a black heart and that wasn't Dani's fault. It seemed even being six feet under was no barrier to hurting people.

"They didn't deserve her, Quinn," she said quietly. "You did."

He sighed, thinking that Dani had her own problems. At least he had great family support. He suspected she'd never felt part of a real family. He'd glimpsed a vulnerability in her, an insecurity. He remembered it from long ago, when he used to notice such things. Loneliness, a need to belong.

Somewhere along the way, he'd just plain stopped looking.

The hell with it. Today was a rare day, one that didn't come along very often. She was sexy, fun, talented. Available. Why was he wallowing in the bitter past? And in some ways, telling Dani was kind of cathartic. She knew the man, knew his faults. She gave him a slightly different perspective.

Quinn would never forgive or forget, but he could let go a little more. That's what time did. And the fact that she wasn't Howard's daughter had to be a good thing, right?

He set his glass down, sorry that he'd made her sad. He wanted the warmth of her brilliant smile back, and perhaps he wanted to warm her a little also. When he held out his hand to her, she smiled up at him and he saw understanding and empathy. When he bent to kiss the soft, fragrant flesh just under her earlobe, her skin steamed up quickly and her pulse quickened under his mouth.

This was about sex, he reminded himself. Unbelievable and uncomplicated sex. If it made them feel good and if no one expected anything more, where was the harm?

He lifted his head to see her mouth turned up in sultry understanding. Quinn resolved to give her as good as she gave.

He pulled her to her feet and downstairs to the cabin, peeling her clothing off on the way. The salt from her skin tingled on his tongue as he revealed and then tasted every delicious inch of her. He made her stand still, legs braced, and made love to her with his mouth. She rocked on her heels with the sway of the vessel under them, clutching his head. His bitterness and her insecurities melted away as he tipped her onto the bed, slid deep into her body and looked into her eyes, and they became one with the motion of the sea.

"How's it going?"

Dani looked up from her workbench, where, days later, she was once again engrossed. "Today I start on the chain."

She was working with platinum, always a challenge but one she enjoyed. Many jewellers found the metal too soft and dense to work with, but with practice, it got easier and the rewards were worth it.

"You chose diamond cut and not snake," he noted approvingly.

Dani nodded. "It's classic and doesn't kink so much." She picked up her torch again and resumed her work. Quinn pulled up a stool. It was becoming a habit of his to come in here and watch her work. He seemed fascinated by the whole process.

"It must be exciting to create something from start to finish and know it will outlive you." He was flicking through her portfolio again, he did that a lot. On every page, he found something that interested him and would ask her how she decided on that particular combination of texture or colour. She broke all the rules, he told her, and yet her jewellery worked beautifully.

Dani was buoyed by his interest. He really seemed to get her, to share her vision of the relationship between gemstones and precious metals. Being a designer was a solitary occupation. Most people were only interested in the end product, not the journey of creation. It was nice to have someone to share ideas with for once.

Several days had passed since the boat trip, each one slightly cooler and calmer as the fitful cyclone season waned and autumn woke up. Dani barely noticed the weather since she only left the workroom to finalise a few last-minute wedding arrangements for Ryan and Jessica or to make love with Quinn.

She glanced over to where he sat at the desk, flicking through her portfolio. So far she'd shied away from badgering him on the intended recipient of the yellow diamond. He was an honourable man, despite the coercion he'd used at the start. She had to believe that. A loyal man who wouldn't make promises and trifle with her feelings.

It wasn't her normal way of doing things, but she had to be grown-up about it. One disastrous relationship had only added to her lifelong feeling of not being good enough, firmly entrenched in second best. But that wasn't Quinn's problem. They were from different worlds. This wasn't a "relationship" so much as a "situation"—and as far as situations went, it wasn't a bad one to be in.

So long as she didn't try to make it into something else.

Her phone rang and she put her torch down. It was Steve from the shop to say Matt Hammond was there to see her. She gave him the beach house address and prepared to meet her cousin for the first time, face-to-face. Several minutes later, understandably nervous, she let Quinn answer the door while she hovered a few steps back.

"Danielle?" Matt Hammond looked from one to the other, a confused look on his handsome face. "I didn't realise you knew each other," he said, taking Quinn's proffered hand.

Quinn stepped back and motioned her forward with a reassuring smile. "Dani's doing a little designing job for me."

She looked up into Matt's face. He was nearly as tall as Quinn, leaner, with thick sandy hair and sharp grey eyes that reminded her of her mother's.

"Come in and sit down." Quinn led the way to the living area, offered refreshments and then discreetly withdrew.

Dani twisted her hands together, unsure of the reason for his visit, hoping it was a genuine overture to get to know the Australian side of his family. Her first tentative questions concerned Blake. It was a tricky subject after the months of speculation about his late wife's infidelity and his son's paternity. But when she asked if he had a photo, like any proud father, he produced several from his wallet.

The snapshots showed a dark, rather serious-looking little boy. "Three and a half," Matt responded to Dani's query about his age. She dredged up the courage to ask if she could have one to send to her mother and Matt readily handed over a couple.

"Are you here on holiday?"

"I thought it was time we met," he said simply. "I also wanted to talk to Quinn, but had no idea I'd find you together."

Dani felt her cheeks glow. "As he said," she quickly inserted, "I'm helping him with a designing project."

"Good for you." Matt smiled. "A recommendation

from Quinn Everard is a valuable thing in this business. I saw the catalogue for the February launch, by the way. Your pieces were impressive."

Dani beamed. She'd had a lot of work as a direct result of the Blackstone launch, proving that Howard, who'd talked her into being the featured designer, had known his stuff.

But best not to mention that name in this company, she thought.

"And that is another reason I'm here," Matt continued. "You've heard, I suppose, that four of the Heart of the Outback diamonds have been returned to me?"

Dani nodded cautiously, noting his use of the Heart of the Outback—the Hammond diamond—as opposed to the Blackstone Rose diamonds.

"I have an idea and I'd like you to be part of it."

Her response was measured. Was this a ploy to upset the Blackstones? "In what way?"

"I want to make an heirloom necklace from the Heart of the Outback diamonds, to be kept in the Hammond family and worn by future Hammond brides."

Dani's mouth dropped open. "Matt, that's a wonderful idea!"

"Hopefully my father will think so, too."

She nodded. Bringing the Heart of the Outback stones—Jeb's legacy—together again for the next generation of Hammonds would surely ease the old man's bitterness in his last years. "Matt, my mother would so love to restore some sort of relationship with Oliver and your mother, and you and Blake, too. Do you think there is any hope of that?"

Matt's silvery gaze was steady and open. "I have no problem with Sonya, Danielle. But there is a lot of water under that bridge and I can't speak for Dad." Then his voice softened. "Small steps? Starting with you designing the Bridal Rose necklace?"

The Bridal Rose. Emotion almost overwhelmed her. "It would be an honour," she mumbled, staring fixedly at Blake's photos to hide a sheen of tears.

Although she was close to her cousins Kim and Ryan, and had never doubted her mother's love, finding a place she felt she belonged had always eluded her. To have found a new family and have a part in reuniting its members was a privilege. She and Matt seemed to click, just as she and Jarrod had.

Then a more selfish elation sneaked up on her. First, the beautiful yellow diamond upstairs in the safe, and now the pink Blackstone Rose diamonds. What were the chances of being offered two commissions with stones of this calibre? And at only twenty-seven years old! "What a pity the fifth diamond hasn't come to light."

"I'm working on that," Matt said mysteriously. "In the meantime, I'd like you to design the necklace as if there *were* a fifth diamond—the centrepiece. Can you do that?"

"Of course. Can you give me a couple more weeks to finish what I'm doing here?"

He acquiesced. "I hadn't thought further ahead than getting an answer from you."

"Well, you have it." She smiled happily. "I would love to do it. And I'm rapt you thought of me."

Matt's smile was slow to start but it lit up his face.

"You are a very talented designer and a Hammond. The perfect choice."

They talked for an hour about the jewellery trade and little Blake, and ended on his brother Jarrod's recent engagement to Briana. Dani thought it must be strange for Matt to see his brother marry his late wife's sister, but Matt confided he'd always been fond of Briana. More relaxed now, she mentioned the rumours doing the rounds a few weeks ago, suggesting Jarrod Hammond was really the missing Blackstone heir. To her relief, Matt did not seem offended at hearing the Blackstone name.

"Jarrod's birth mother may have something to say about that," he retorted.

Dani was surprised. There had been no mention of Jarrod's birth mother in the newspaper stories.

Matt's mouth tightened. "I've met her. She taps Jarrod up for money every so often, then disappears under whatever rock she crawled out from."

Her heart went out to Jarrod. Impossibly handsome, a successful lawyer, a beautiful new fiancée, and yet that suave exterior hid its own personal pain.

But at least he knew who his mother was....

As if her cousin had recognised her momentary sadness, he turned it on its head by agreeing to talk to his brother about a family get-together soon. "Briana has dragged him along on one of her modelling assignments overseas. Poor beggar." He pulled an amused face. "But maybe when they get back, we can have a bit of a get-together."

It was tentative but, still, it was an overture. "And Blake?" she asked. "And my mother, too?"

"Why not?"

The three of them had a wonderful dinner at a famous outdoor restaurant in the middle of a copse of huge tropical palms. Quinn toasted her when he heard about the Bridal Rose commission, saying it would really put her on the map in the designing world.

He turned to Matt. "I thought I had a lead on the fifth diamond, but the trail has gone cold, I'm afraid. I'll keep you posted."

Matt was clearly disappointed but still raised his glass to both of them. "I appreciate it, Quinn. Someone must know something. And Danielle, I am looking forward to working with you on the necklace, hopefully with all five stones."

It was truly one of the best days she'd ever had. Her mother would be over the moon that Matt had made contact, and to have the opportunity to rewrite the history of the Heart of the Outback Diamond was such a buzz. To think Quinn might have a hand in locating the fifth stone… It was the perfect end to the perfect day.

Until she walked in on them talking business some time later on her way back from the bathroom. She wasn't eavesdropping, but one palm tree looked much like another and she came in from a different direction to find Matt had moved into her seat and they had their heads together. Something made her pause behind the nearest trunk when she heard the name Blackstone.

"I have already spoken to three of the minor share-holders," Matt said. "If you were to get behind us…"

She heard Quinn's voice. "If you're serious about

this, you need Jake Vance on board, not me. I only have a handful of shares."

"I'm meeting with Jake next week, but listen, they're on shaky ground. The Blackstone empire is crumbling with Howard gone. Perrini and Ryan snap and snarl at each other and Kim spends all her time calming them down. I just want to keep the pressure on."

Dani's rosy wine-glow faded fast, leaving a nasty feeling that her cousin wasn't playing fair.

She waited to hear how her lover responded.

"I'm not interested in a dogfight, Matt. My few shares are performing adequately."

Dani relaxed a little and peeked around the tree trunk.

Matt had leaned back and put his hands behind his head. "I thought you'd jump at the chance to shaft a Blackstone, given your history."

Quinn frowned. "My beef was with Howard, not Blackstone Diamonds."

"Or," Matt continued nonchalantly, "maybe you're mixing business with pleasure."

She saw Quinn's eyes glint dangerously and couldn't expel her next breath.

His voice was low and cool and she had to strain to hear him. "Dani is private business, all right?"

Though her heart was beating loud and fast, mostly for fear of discovery, she heard Matt apologise. "But if I can get Vance on side, you'll go with us?"

"If Jake says sell, I'll sell."

She stayed behind the tree for a few more seconds, trying to make sense of all the emotions. She felt strangely buoyant that Quinn hadn't denied there was something between them. Keenly disappointed that Matt Hammond clearly wasn't ready to embrace the reconciliation of the two family factions just yet. Would he ever be?

And somehow uneasy that she was consorting with the enemy. Perhaps two of them.

Seven

"Quinn, have you heard a rumour about a corporate takeover of Blackstone Diamonds?"

His eyes snapped open. That was out of left field.

Quinn had been lying in bed, idly thinking that his sporadic sexual encounters rarely involved morning sex, especially dreamy morning sex with the same woman. He was always rushing off to a meeting or a flight. Maybe he'd been missing out all these years.

Now he abandoned his reverie to answer Dani. "You stopped screaming your delight one minute ago and suddenly you want to talk business?"

She lay with her head on his chest, her hair a riot of curls against his skin.

Quinn turned his head to look at the clock. Seven-thirty. Time he was up. "Yes, I have heard something. You want coffee or are you staying in bed?"

But she was persistent. "Do you think Matt is involved?"

Had she heard something last night?

Matt's request to sell his shares or support a takeover bid had not surprised him; Quinn had heard he was polling all the Blackstone shareholders for support. He was getting it, too.

But not from him, at least not yet. His fingers rasped over his chin. "What is this inquisition before I've had my coffee?"

She kept her face down on his chest, a fact he found strangely worrying.

"I heard you," she said in a small voice. "Last night at the restaurant. Talking about selling your shares in Blackstone."

Quinn's eyes narrowed in the dim room. Scratch all those nice thoughts about waking up with the same woman. He didn't know whether to laugh or be offended. Who the hell did she think she was? "Eavesdropping, Danielle? If you heard us, you'd know I turned him down."

She lifted her head and looked him right in the face. And it hit him: she was serious.

The urge to laugh disappeared. "A company takeover," he said, twisting his finger around a springy red curl, "is very complicated. It needs the support of the board and the requisite number of shares. I'm Little League in Blackstones, Dani."

That was the truth. He had very few shares himself. But he knew Matt was in for more than the Blackstones knew about—and climbing. And Quinn knew who else had a substantial portfolio.

"But if Jake Vance asks you to sell…?"

Quinn stilled. She had heard everything. And she was right out of line. He was not in the habit of justifying himself to anyone, let alone a woman he'd known for a week or so, even if the sex was amazing.

He injected plenty of cool in his reply. "Yes, if he gave me a good enough reason, then I'd sell."

Disappointment darkened her eyes, and just the fact that he recognised that pissed him off. There was no room for emotion in business. That was the dictum that Jake Vance, corporate raider, believed in, and Quinn agreed wholeheartedly, damn it!

"Quinn, what hurts the Blackstones hurts me, you *do* get that, don't you?"

Time to remind both of them this was just a fling. "Just because we're sleeping together, Danielle," he said coldly, "doesn't give you the right to ask about my business dealings."

She flinched. He knew that because he felt it in his chest and stomach, which lay under her torso, in between his legs where she'd squeezed her thigh, over his shoulder where she'd draped one of her arms.

But he held her gaze. He wouldn't negotiate on overstepping boundaries. After a long moment, he nudged her, indicating he wanted to get up. She moved over to her side of the bed. When the hell did they get into his-and-her sides of the bed anyway?

His refection stared balefully back in the bathroom mirror while he wondered what had suddenly happened, what had changed. One minute, he was savouring the delights of a very sexy body. The next, he was wallowing in guilt, thinking about someone else, considering someone else's feelings. Just how deep was he getting here?

Somewhere out on that boat, she'd stirred up some long-buried need to protect. His parents, his childhood home had always been a port in a storm, a harbour for lost and needy souls. Quinn had forgotten what it felt like, until now. Was that what Danielle saw in him? Was she searching for such a port?

He ran the tap and splashed his face, making sure it was good and cold.

This was supposed to be a brief fling, a bit of fun to while away the heat of the day while he was stuck up here in the middle of nowhere. Wanting her every minute of the day in the limited time they had together was acceptable. Thinking about waking up to her every morning was probably teetering on the edge and would have to be addressed—and soon. It had been years since he'd considered relationships and he was perfectly happy with his life just as it was.

But justifying himself to her was definitely off limits.

Steve called at breakfast to ask if Dani could mind the shop for a few hours; he and his partner had an ultrasound to attend. Quinn went into town with her. She was quiet but not snippy, and he had some ideas for marketing he'd been thinking about. He pushed aside the feeling that giving her some decent advice may assuage his guilt somewhat.

"What are you doing here, Dani?" he asked, after a customer walked out with a very nice pair of pearl earrings that she'd gotten for a bargain, he noticed.

Dani looked up from locking the cabinet. "Making a living. Just."

Quinn paced out the tiny interior. The display was funky without being crafty; the quality of her jewellery was too high for that. But the premises were second-rate, security was inadequate and the whole place needed a complete overhaul. "Is it success or failure you're afraid of?"

Dani ran her eye slowly around the shop. "It could use some attention, I know."

"How did you end up here, anyway? Why Port?"

She scratched her neck and shrugged. "It's where I stopped." She picked up a cloth and bottle of glass cleaner and walked out from behind the counter. Today she was almost conservative in below-the-knee tights, high-heeled sandals, a mushroom-coloured tunic with voluminous sleeves and a huge orange silk rose pinned to her lapel.

Why he always noticed her attire was beyond him. He questioned her again. "What were you running from?"

Dani walked to the display cabinet on the other side of the shop and turned her back on him. He heard the hiss of the spray cleaner, saw the sleeves of her creamy shirt rippling as she rubbed and polished. "I was engaged."

As soon as she said it, he remembered a couple of sketchy details. Actually, what he remembered was watching it on a TV news programme and wondering how it qualified as news.

"I was engaged to someone who was convinced, even though I denied it repeatedly, that I was Howard's daughter and, therefore, a Blackstone heiress."

She moved around the cabinet, rubbing intently, but didn't look at him.

"I remember," Quinn murmured, noticing two distinct spots of colour on her cheeks.

"You remember the scandal."

She did look at him then and he saw that it wasn't so much pain setting her mouth into a thin line and colouring her cheeks. It was embarrassment.

"The media had a field day." She gave a tight laugh. "There were some really funny headlines. I would have laughed myself if…" Her eyes slid away and she moved to another glass-topped cabinet. "Do you know, he even demanded his ring back, until Ryan paid him a visit on Howard's orders."

Quinn exhaled. "I'd say you had a lucky escape."

She rolled her eyes and the smile she had forced disappeared. "I just got tired of it. I'm either the illegitimate love child, the scheming gold digger or the poor stupid fool whose fiancé got caught with his pants down. Just one more brush to tar me with."

She fell silent and continued to rub vigorously at some imaginary mark.

"Why here?"

She raised her shoulders. "I love the beach and the climate. It's far enough from Sydney that most people don't even know I'm related to the Blackstones." She glanced at him briefly and grinned. "And I'll admit to a bit of poetic license. The population is pretty transient here. I can be whoever and whatever I want."

Images of a wan face, tamed hair and indeterminate clothing flitted through his mind. He'd seen her featured several times in newspaper spreads or television reports. But he'd never noticed her beauty, her animated smile and sparkle, until he'd met her up here. Now he found himself consciously holding his breath when he heard her come downstairs in the mornings, wondering what jaw-dropping mishmash of colours and textures she would amaze him with today.

Quinn put his hand out. "Come here."

He led her outside and then turned her and gestured to the faded lettering above the door. "What does that say?"

"Dani Hammond. Fine Jeweller of Port Douglas."

"Fine Jeweller," he repeated. "We both know how much study and work experience it takes to be able to put those two words after your name."

He put his hands on her shoulders and turned her to face him. "Is this what you envisaged while you were putting in the work?"

Her head dropped a little. "Not really."

"What did you see?"

"What does anyone see just starting out? I wanted to be the best."

"Didn't you want important people to come to you, celebrities and royalty and private collectors?" he asked.

She pursed her lips. "I suppose…"

"Would Howard Blackstone have put his money up if he thought this was as far as you'd go?"

"Ouch!" Her eyes flashed and Quinn wondered if there might be a little residual anger from this morning.

"This," he said as he turned his palm up to indicate the shop front, "isn't good enough. Not the shop or the location."

He showed her back inside. "You have the connections, Dani. If the Blackstones won't help, invest in a marketing company. Maybe my people can point you in the right direction."

Dani frowned, not convinced. "Listen, I have so many orders from the February launch, I can barely keep up."

But Quinn was pacing again. "You need to move. Sydney…" He caught the negative set of her mouth. "Melbourne, then. Hell, why limit yourself? You're good, Dani, great, even. Why not New York or Europe?"

She put up a hand. "I was thinking of a couple of doors down, actually."

Quinn stopped and looked at her, put off his stride.

"The vacant shop two doors down," she repeated patiently. "It's nearly on the corner of the mall, so there's lots of foot traffic. It's twice the size and very modern."

His head went back and he stared down his nose at her. *Why* wasn't she getting this? "You want to be the best? The best in Port Douglas?"

"Yes, I do remember the one-horse-town comment," she said testily, her cheeks firing up.

"Hey, it's your career. But no one will ever know you if you don't give your profile a kick up the backside."

She stepped up to him, head thrown back, fingers curled into her palms, those golden eyes positively steaming. And Quinn realised, too late, that yes, she really was still sore about this morning.

"I can't be too bad," she said hotly, "since you practically *begged* me to design the necklace for you."

"Hey, it wasn't my idea," he retaliated. "In fact, I argued against you being allowed within ten feet of that diamond."

* * *

It was like a blow to her gut.

This morning he'd inflicted a neat cut, chosen his words carefully to put her in her place. She wasn't to question him, wasn't to expect anything from him.

This was punchier, without preamble or foresight. She realised from the stunned look on his face that he hadn't intended to tell her.

A deathly hush descended. So Quinn Everard wasn't here on the pretext that she was the best designer around. Crushed, she felt the blood drain from her face.

What did she expect? He had only just finished belabouring the point. The best—hah! Who was she kidding? He'd been right, again and again. This wasn't what she'd imagined for herself. Her shop was pathetic, and Howard had given her the loan but never stopped harping on her about moving back to Sydney and getting serious about her career.

Quinn inhaled and opened his mouth to speak, but she had to get in first, before she crumpled. "Who is your client?" she asked quickly.

"Dani, for what it's worth, I now have complete confidence in you."

Fine jeweller, indeed. Somehow she managed to keep her chin steady. "Am I not to know who hired me?"

He shook his head. "I'm sorry."

She should have learned by now never to get ideas above her station. She was second best. Always had been. The stigma of illegitimacy. Nick. Hell, even

Quinn Everard with his designer awards and chain-store quips.

She now felt justified to ask about the woman she was supposedly making the necklace for, a subject she had conveniently put to one side once he started blowing her mind in bed. "The diamond isn't for your girl-friend?"

Quinn looked away. "That was your assumption, one I chose not to correct."

She'd been feeling guilty for an imaginary girl-friend—not that the thought of wrecking someone's life had stopped her, or him. She was just some floozy to while away the hours with up here in the middle of nowhere. He was bored, he was hot. She was available.

Her mother always told her it was okay to make a mistake as long as you learned from it. Obviously Nick's betrayal was no deterrent for making huge lapses of judgement where men were concerned. She had known Quinn a bit over a week, a record time for her to sleep with someone. And that would reflect badly on her, she suspected.

But was she strong enough to keep away from his bed?

The next few days dragged by. The necklace pro-gressed well, even without Quinn's encouraging presence. It was as if all her frustrations poured out into the design. Without consulting him, she altered the model she'd supplied for his approval—that is, his client's approval—and worked fifteen-hour days. Ryan and Jessica's wedding arrangements were well in hand.

Quinn kept to himself and a kind of polite peace enveloped the house.

But by night, it was a different story. Dani was her own worst enemy, reliving their lovemaking over and over. He was a drug she was addicted to. To stop herself from marching into his bedroom, she began justifying his actions. After all, she was being paid an enormous amount of money and an enormous compliment to design a necklace for the most beautiful and valuable stone she was ever likely to see. What did it matter that it was for a client and not him?

And it wasn't like he had tricked her into bed, either. She'd practically ambushed him while he sat at his desk, conducting his business. She couldn't blame him for that.

Had she really expected that something more could come of this "situation" she had rushed headlong into? She was out of his league, not even in the same stratosphere.

One night he told her that Jake Vance's mother had passed away. "The funeral is Friday. Come to Sydney with me and catch up with your family."

She considered it dubiously. "It will put me back on the necklace. I wanted to finish it before the wedding on the twentieth."

"Relax. I'll put it in a bank vault here. I'll charter a flight for Thursday afternoon and we'll return Saturday."

It was the excuse she needed to keep away from him. She went all out for the next few days and made good progress, barely sleeping at all.

And that's probably why she fell asleep on the private plane.

She awoke slowly, fuzzily, dreaming of Quinn, so it was no surprise at all when she saw his face mere inches away. And when he leaned even closer and brushed her mouth with his, she closed her eyes again, didn't even *think* of resisting. After all, that was how the dream was supposed to go. Reliving their lovemaking was how she'd spent every night since the fight.

She stretched toward him, allowed the dream to part her lips, to feel the tip of his tongue seek and find hers. She combed her fingers through his thick hair and her heartbeat quickened and banged loudly in her ears. But she wouldn't open her eyes just yet. She didn't want this to stop, didn't want him to disappear.

His hand moved on her thigh, skimming her silk underskirt over her heated skin. Each stroke lengthened, higher and higher until she shifted restlessly, craving more. Another hand caressed her neck and face as they kissed. The seat belt dug into her hips, making her wriggle against it. Every part of her strained toward him, this faceless lover, this man with his tongue in her mouth, one hand moving down over her blouse to cup and stroke her breast, the other moving ever higher, scorching her thigh. Her arms were trapped against his chest, unable to move far with his weight leaning into her, but she moved toward him, trying to touch him, to inflict some of the same torture on him.

Breathing heavily, he grasped her wrists and stilled her. "Open your eyes, damn it!"

She did and almost quailed at the tortured desire in his. Desire and regret.

Regret for wanting her or for hurting her?

Wide awake now, she gave a shuddering breath, laid her head on the rest and just looked at his face. The heat of passion still smouldered sullenly in the pulse beat on her wrist where he gripped her, and in the aching tips of her breasts and deep inside her centre. But her breathing slowed and she searched his scowling, troubled face, trying to read what he was thinking and feeling.

His breathing had calmed. Gradually the grip on her wrists eased and became more of a caress. He, too, leaned back in his seat facing her, watching her.

Finally his eyes softened and he spoke. "You'll stay with me tonight."

It wasn't a question, or a demand. And—God help her—her heart leapt in her chest with welcome. She'd intended to take a cab to the Blackstone mansion in Vaucluse and surprise her mother. But Dani would take what she could get from Quinn.

Time with him was short and she knew there'd be less of her when their fling ended. The fight had torn them apart physically, and because it was unexpected, the end was hard to accept. Now she had the opportunity to say goodbye properly, make it special. Dani was going to make the most of the day or days she had left with him, and damn the consequences.

They spent the rest of the flight looking at each other. Not kissing now but touching, sweet touches to their hands, cheeks, throat, hair. His eyes burned for her, and that and his touch kept her at a simmer for the remainder of the flight to Sydney, the seemingly endless taxi ride to his building and equally interminable elevator ride to his penthouse apartment.

Giddy with desire, they barely made it inside before he was ripping her clothes off, pushing her up against the wall opposite a massive picture window that show-cased beautiful Darling Harbour, Sky Tower, the harbour bridge and the opera house. He took her there and Dani welcomed him into her body and came again and again as the lights of the city swirled behind her eyes like a kaleidoscope on drugs.

Eight

Dani survived the fierce hug and pulled back to survey her mother. "You look…different. Did you get highlights?"

Her mother patted her hair self-consciously while Marcie, the Blackstone housekeeper, bustled around the table.

Sonya Hammond usually wore her brown hair in a neat bun, but today she'd allowed several long spiralling tendrils to escape, giving her a completely different look. Was it her makeup or the unusually colourful teal blouse she'd teamed with smart-looking slacks? Her mother was the epitome of conservative elegance, but today, Dani thought she looked younger somehow, mature-chic. "Have you had a facial or something?"

Sonya ignored her question and instead tsked at

Dani's earrings. "Must your earrings always arrive before you do?"

"I thought these were quite demure." She touched one gold bar with a plaque of smoky quartz on the end. Since she had reinvented herself up in Port Douglas, some of her more bohemian creations stunned her mother, though Sonya was too nice and too fond of Dani's strong sense of individualism to criticise without humour.

"Sit. How is it you're here when we're seeing you in a few days?"

"I told you I was doing a little job for Quinn Everard." Dani leaned forward and sniffed appreciatively at the urn in the middle of the table. "Mmm. Pumpkin soup."

"Yes, I couldn't believe the cheek of the man, after all he's put you through."

The whole family had witnessed the deterioration of Dani's professional reputation at Quinn's hands. Dani tried to ignore the little pang of hurt at her mother's words. "Anyway, he has a funeral to attend today so I came down with him. I need some shoes for the wedding."

"What colour is the dress?" Sonya asked quickly. "No, don't tell me, I'll try to keep an open mind."

Marcie appeared with a soup bowl and a platter of warm Turkish bread and set them down. Her mother looked pointedly at the urn. "Eat up, I have an appointment. Ryan's picking me up any minute."

Dani ladled some soup into her bowl. "I thought you'd want to supervise," she said dryly, "but we can do dinner later and maybe I'll treat you to the movies or something."

Sonya looked uncomfortable. "I can't, dear. I have an engagement. The theatre, actually."

"Oh?" That was unusual. Sonya hardly ever went out in the evenings. She swallowed her soup, watching her mother. New clothes, new hairdo, appointments and engagements… "Who with?"

"Garth, actually."

"How is old Garth?" Dani was relieved. Garth Buick was the Blackstone company secretary and had been ever since Dani could remember. He was probably Howard's closest friend, a nice man, she recalled. A widower for a few years.

"He's not old," her mother said with an edge to her voice. "He's very young and fit."

Dani's spoon stopped halfway to her mouth and the two women locked gazes for a long moment.

Sonya reddened and looked away first. "Close your mouth, Danielle. It's just friendship. He's been teaching me to sail."

"Right," Dani said weakly. "That's great, really."

And it was, she told herself as she slathered butter onto the warm flatbread. Her mother had given her life over to raising her daughter and Howard's kids and then running his household and being his hostess. Whatever Dani's father had done to her, she'd completely withdrawn from relationships outside of the family.

Either that or she'd been walloped with a massive dose of unrequited love. Dani wondered what it would be like to love someone so completely that you never wanted to risk it again.

Was Quinn still in love with his wife? It must be six or seven years since Laura died. Did he still miss her, measure every other woman he met against her? Was Dani about to discover what her mother had all those years ago, that you couldn't compete with a dead woman?

Sonya's smile was resigned. "I can just see your mind ticking over, my girl. Poor old Mum, the dried-up old prune, wasting away for the love of Howard."

Dani shook her head admiringly. How did the woman do it?

"But no," her mother continued. "He was so devastated when Ursula died. I knew then that he would never risk giving his heart completely again. And I didn't intend to be one in a long line of his discarded women."

Clever woman, because that was exactly the way things had turned out. Howard was notorious for his womanising and had never committed to any of them.

Her mother sighed. "I may as well get it over with. My appointment this afternoon is with a real estate agent. I'm looking at a house over in Double Bay."

"But…" Dani was stunned. Her mother leave Miramare? "You have a permanent right to reside in this house." Howard's will stated that.

They both cast their eyes around the room and out to the vista beyond. The first-floor suite Dani had grown up in was much more informal than the rest of the house but still boasted spectacular views of Sydney Harbour and the Pacific Ocean. Sonya combined a love of antiques with a warm, comfortable style of her own. Miramare was a show home, she liked to say, but her suite of rooms was just a home.

Dani could not imagine her mother anywhere else.

"I rattle around here by myself now," Sonya said broodingly. "And what if James Blackstone comes forward? Howard was convinced he was alive or he wouldn't have left the mansion to him in the will."

"This is your home. You are legally entitled. James, if he exists, will just have to accept that." She pushed her plate away, suddenly not hungry. "Besides, what about Marcie?"

"There will always be a place for Marcie. She knows that."

"You've talked about it?" Dani frowned, a little indignant that her mother hadn't shared this with her first.

"I'm just looking, dear," her mother said airily. "When Garth suggested this place was up for sale, I decided to have a peek, that's all."

"Garth suggested... Wait a minute, doesn't Garth live in Double Bay?" Dani didn't know whether to be affronted or delighted, but in the end, delight won out. She couldn't help grinning as her mother fidgeted. It was about time Sonya thought of herself after a lifetime of looking after everyone else.

Sonya cleared her throat. "I'm not moving in with Garth, okay? I'm just looking at a smaller house that happens to be a few blocks from his."

Marcie passed by the table. "I've made up your bed, lovey."

"Oh, I'm not staying."

It was her turn to fidget as two sets of eyes swivelled toward her. "I'm twenty-seven, for crying out loud!"

Marcie scuttled out, grinning.

"Is he as nice-looking as his photo?" Sonya asked.

Dani shrugged. They'd be here all day if she was to outline the myriad ways Quinn Everard appealed to her.

"Do you like him, Danielle?" her mother insisted.

"Would I spend the night with him otherwise?"

Her mother's piercing gaze made her feel about ten years old, as usual. She reconsidered her defensive attitude. It had rarely worked in the past. "I suppose. But he's out of my league."

Sonya raised her aristocratic nose. "Must be hard to walk with that huge chip on your shoulder."

"You haven't met him. He's smooth." *And sometimes rough...* "He owns himself, very self-assured. Supremely comfortable with himself, his place, his ability. And he manages to convey all this without making the minions around him feel inferior." She rolled her eyes ruefully. "Even though it's painfully obvious that's exactly what they are."

Her mother rested her chin on her hand, a faraway look in her eyes. "You do like him," she said softly, and a silence descended as Dani tried and failed to think of a suitable rejoinder.

"Why don't you both come to dinner and the theatre with Garth and me tonight?" her mother asked.

Dani shook her head, somewhat relieved. "He won't be back until late."

"Oh." Sonya looked disappointed. "You, then."

"I'm not playing gooseberry." She was pleased her mother was stepping out but one tiny part of her wanted to think about this for a while. Dani had few enough absolutes in her life already. To think that she may never visit her mother at Miramare again was a sobering thought. "I have heaps to do on this flying visit, honestly," she lied, and decided to change the subject. "You'll never guess who came to visit last week. Matt Hammond."

Sonya's eyes lit up, just as she'd known they would. Dani rummaged through her bag for the photos of Blake that Matt had supplied. Her mother fell on them.

"What's more," Dani added, "he wants me to make him an heirloom necklace from the Blackstone Rose diamonds, though I'm not sure if that's for public consumption just yet."

"I can't believe it! What's he like? Tell me everything!"

"Nice." At least, she had thought so, thought they clicked, but that was now coloured by the conversation she'd overheard. "Really nice."

"You don't sound convinced," her mother said dubiously.

"Oh, I am, it's just that Quinn was there and they were talking business."

The doorbell rang downstairs and Sonya's face fell. "Not now." She grimaced at Dani, obviously wanting to hear more about her nephew. "That'll be Ryan."

"Don't tell him about Matt," Dani whispered.

Ryan looked pleased to see her and they spent a couple of minutes discussing the wedding plans. She was thrilled to see how utterly happy he looked. He and Jessica were expecting twins in a few months. Jessica was blooming, Ryan told her, but worried she'd already outgrown her wedding dress.

"What brings you to Sydney?" Ryan asked.

"I needed special shoes for my dress," she explained.

He rolled his eyes at Sonya. "God help us...."

Dani's fashion sense for these big occasions was legendary. "Don't be mean," she grumbled. "I've gone to a lot of trouble for this wedding. Keeping it quiet has been the hardest thing I've ever done." *Moving into Quinn's house, his bedroom, exploring his body, welcoming his touch...and all just to keep their wedding under wraps*.

Dani smiled, suddenly feeling quite kindly disposed to Ryan Blackstone. "Quinn was coming down for a funeral so I tagged along."

Ryan's brows rose. "Sonya told me you're doing a job for him. I was surprised, given your history."

She shrugged away a pang of hurt. "Client's request."

"Jessica knows Quinn slightly, likes him, I think." His face lapsed into a smile she had never seen on him before. "Still, she likes everyone these days."

Dani's eyes nearly misted over as she witnessed Ryan's happiness. He'd always been a troubled soul. His brother's abduction and mother's suicide were enough of a burden. Add to that the offhand way Howard treated both him and Kimberley, consistently choosing Ric Perrini over Ryan when it came to Blackstone Diamonds. She crossed her fingers under the table and silently wished Ryan all the happiness in the world.

"Who died?" Ryan selected an olive and a slice of cheese from the table. "Quinn's funeral?"

"Jake Vance's mother."

"I'd heard Everard and Vance were chummy. Has

Quinn said anything about Matt Hammond sniffing around?"

Dani shook her head, not looking at Sonya.

"Apparently Hammond was in town last week seeing Vance. The rumour doing the rounds is that Hammond and Vance are out to set up a corporate takeover of Blackstone. Seems Matt's been polling all the shareholders for support."

Sonya opened her mouth. Dani shot her foot out and connected with her mother's ankle. What good would it do for him to know Matt had been in Port talking business with Quinn, too? He'd turned him down.

Sonya prudently said nothing, and she and Ryan dropped Dani at the bus stop for the central city and headed off to their real estate appointment. But even the prospect of shoe shopping did little to quell a growing disquiet. Should she warn the Blackstones about the Jake-Matt-Quinn connection? Was she being disloyal to the family who had provided for her all her life?

She let herself in to Quinn's apartment using the key he had given her. Her feet ached and all she could think about was his large Japanese bath, so it was an unwelcome surprise when the sound of loud voices greeted her.

Four people stood around the island in Quinn's kitchen. A pretty woman with long, tied-back greying hair, looked up first. A tall, lean man stood beside her with one arm draped loosely around her shoulders. Quinn, too, had his arm around someone's shoulders. Someone beautiful, in a lilac suit, with a chic blond bob and striking eyes.

Dani couldn't really take in much more than that.

But then Quinn's eyes beat a path to her face and she felt the energy as if he'd shone an intense spotlight onto her.

"I—I'm sorry," she stammered. "I didn't mean to intrude." God, what must they think? She had his key. "I thought you'd still be out."

Then Quinn dropped his arm from the blonde's shoulders and walked toward her. His eyes shone as he drew her into the circle. There was no mistaking the warmth in his voice as he said, "*This* is Dani," as if he'd been waiting for her to come, dying to introduce her.

As it turned out, this was much better than her anticipated bath. She shook hands with his parents, Gwen and Joseph, and with Lucy, his foster sister, who had the most beautiful, sad violet eyes.

They were ribald and rowdy, and so close, they finished one another's sentences. It was incredible to see Quinn in this light. Outside of the bedroom, his reserve set him apart from everyone; he seemed untouchable. His parents were nothing like that, and when he was with them, neither was he. There was so much warmth, humour and concern for one another in this kitchen. She loved her mother dearly but she'd never stood around a kitchen counter with her family members, drinking, joking and sharing memories.

Yes, it was a sad day for the Everards, but as often happens with funerals, the relief of getting through it sometimes manifests itself in a need to drink. "Especially when you're Irish!" Joseph intoned, holding out his glass for a top-up, while Quinn shook his head at her, mouthing, "He's not Irish."

Dani thought back to the tensions that had accompanied Howard's funeral; the reserve, the constant media crush, everyone watching one another to make sure they didn't fall apart, or wondering who knew what about Howard's eventful life.

That all seemed a million miles away. Corporate takeovers, too, seemed a million miles away. She swapped blueberry muffin recipes with Gwen, had an eye-popping dance with Joseph to a Leonard Cohen song, and Lucy confided she had discovered Dani's knickers under the couch.

"Must be his other girlfriend," Dani told her. "I never wear them."

"I don't think so." Lucy laughed. "Quinn *never* invites a woman to stay over here."

Everyone left a couple of hours later and Quinn ordered in pasta, which they ate in his tub. She lay across from him as he struggled to keep his eyes open, and cautioned herself to guard her heart. Her expectations of people were too high. A throwaway remark by Lucy, the warmth in his eyes when she crashed their party…there was danger in allowing herself to hope she could ever be admitted to the circle of love she had just glimpsed.

Her fingers swirled the water in front of her, making a whirlpool, and Dani recognised she was in an uncontrolled spiral. She was falling in love, and not only with Quinn, but with the idea of his family, too.

Quinn came into his living room to see Dani standing in front of the window looking out at Sydney's skyline, her bag by her feet.

Yes, he thought. He'd wanted her here, to see what she looked like, see if she'd fit. And if that hadn't prompted him to take a swan dive off the balcony, then he was going to try her out on his parents. Only they had preempted that by inviting themselves over last night.

And hadn't that gone well?

The polite tension of the past few days in Port Douglas had made him miserable. Being relegated from lover to boss shouldn't have bothered a man who, since Laura's death, hadn't considered forever. At thirty-four years old, Quinn had never wondered till now whether he was missing out on anything.

He hadn't expected to enjoy her so much.

Dani turned and smiled at him and he gave himself a mental shake. "All packed?"

What the next step was, he couldn't be sure, but Quinn knew one thing. Where Dani Hammond was concerned, he was at least prepared to admit that there would be a next step.

She nodded and reached for her bag, just as Quinn's phone rang. It was Sir John Knowles, former prime minister, outgoing governor-general, and close friend and mentor of Quinn's. A call he had to take.

He walked into his office and after very little preamble, Sir John got to the point of his call. Incredulous, Quinn listened to the man's earth-shattering admission, and in seconds the feeling of peace Quinn had woken with was ground to dust.

"Taxi's here." Dani stood at the doorway to his office, holding her bag.

Quinn covered the mouthpiece of his phone. "I have to take this. You go on and I'll meet you at the airstrip."

She left and he returned to his phone call. Based on Sir John's admission, Quinn had no alternative.

"I want out, John."

The older man's quiet voice begged him. How could he turn him down?

"I've become personally involved. I won't lie about something like this."

"Please, Quinn, just another few days. I wouldn't ask this of you if it wasn't the last chance I have."

"Allow *me* to tell her, then."

"I can't risk her refusal, don't you see? And I haven't told Clare yet. Not about the prognosis or the other."

The old man sounded sick and alone. His last chance. Quinn had heard that before, had lived with his failure for seven years.

But still, it was a lousy thing to do. "You don't know what you're asking."

"I do, believe me. And I wouldn't ask it of anyone but you, because I know you won't let me down."

"Quinn, will you come to the wedding with me?"

He sat back in his chair and displayed the same careful expression he'd had since they got back from Sydney three days ago.

Dani was worried. The rumours Ryan spoke of in Sydney had now been aired on television. The shareholders of Blackstone Diamonds were restless, despite an assurance from Kimberley in the paper this morning that all was well.

Perhaps if he knew the Blackstones, was personally involved, he wouldn't be so hasty to offer his
support to Matt.

Quinn set his pen down. "That's not a good idea," he
said slowly.

"Why not?"

"It's a family occasion. With the events of the past
few months, everyone will be feeling a little nostalgic."
He looked at her steadily. "My history with Howard is
bound to raise comment. I don't want to rub everyone's
nose in it."

"I don't think anyone will—"

"I'll let you know if I change my mind, okay?" He
picked up his pen again, his eyes unreadable. "How's
the necklace coming along?"

"Okay." The client had imposed a deadline for com-
pletion—the twenty-fifth. She was on track, Dani
thought, assuming she kept her mind on the job instead
of wondering what Quinn Everard was up to.

Nine

"Look who I found on the doorstep." Dani was on her way out to collect various members of the Blackstone clan from the airport when Jake Vance's face appeared before her. She left the guest with Quinn, gave her apologies and rushed out to her task.

Quinn's smile faded at his friend's grim expression. What was up? Jake kept a brutal schedule. He didn't just show up on a whim.

Quinn waved Jake into a seat. "Coffee?"

"You have something stronger?"

Quinn narrowed his gaze but held up a bottle of cognac.

"My old mate Hennessey." Jake nodded gratefully.

Quinn poured two generous snifters.

"No wonder you're AWOL." Jake's head gestured to the door where Dani had just left. "Well, more AWOL than usual."

Quinn stayed silent and sipped his drink, waiting for Jake to come to the point.

The silence stretched, then Jake leaned forward and placed his glass on Quinn's desk. "Sounds important."

"I didn't say a word," Quinn retorted, exasperated.

"Exactly," Jake said smugly. "Not often you have a girl stay over at your apartment."

"How did you…?"

"Lucy."

"You and Lucy are talking?" Quinn leaned forward, arms folded on the desk.

"Don't get excited. She called the day after the funeral, before she headed off back to England. Just a friendly take-care-of-yourself call."

"She was worried you wouldn't want her at the funeral," Quinn mused. Jake was ripped to shreds when Lucy left him after several years together. Quinn tried not to take sides and loved both of them, but he never wanted to see that hurt inflicted on either of them again.

Jake shrugged. "I appreciated it."

"What brings you up here? Bottom fallen out of the market?" Quinn hoped it was nothing to do with Matt Hammond and his Blackstone Diamond shares. He didn't need any more secrets upsetting the applecart with Dani.

Jake took a healthy gulp of liquor, screwing up his face. "In a roundabout way, it concerns the little lady who just rushed out of here with her tail on fire." He fixed Quinn a stern look. "Drink up. This is going to come as a shock."

Quinn listened in disbelief as his closest friend related how his mother, shortly before she died, told him he was not her birth child. She'd found him as a two-year-old at the site of a fatal car accident. The car had been washed into a river and the two other occupants were dead.

Jake rubbed his eyes wearily. "I thought she was delirious. And when she insisted that I was Howard Blackstone's son, I was sure she was delirious."

Quinn's eyes felt like saucers. He raised his hand. "Back up. This was before she died?"

"I didn't mention it at the funeral because…well, I just didn't believe it. But I've been going through the house." He opened the briefcase he'd laid on the other chair and took out a large scrapbook. "It's all in there, Quinn." He patted the book. "God Almighty, I've never been so scared in my life."

Quinn rose with the bottle and walked around the desk to top up Jake's glass. He perched on the edge of the desk and put out his hand for the scrapbook.

Jake kept talking as Quinn flipped the pages.

"How I was kidnapped as a toddler by the house-keeper and her boyfriend. How they sent a ransom note and Howard did all he could to get me back, but on the way to pick up the money, the car crashed."

Quinn glanced at him periodically while reading the newspaper clippings. He tried to imagine the dark-haired little boy in the photos as a grown man, even as his rational mind rejected the notion. He glanced up at Jake's dark green eyes, coal-black hair and at the fully formed widow's peak—as opposed to just a hint of one in the baby photos.

"My mother happened on the accident and it all went a bit haywire. She'd lost a baby the year before to SIDS and was on the run from her deadbeat boyfriend. She was going somewhere where no one knew her. Anyway, she was probably a little crazy at the time—hormones, grief, whatever—so she picked me up and passed me off as her own."

Quinn got to the last page and snapped the book shut. The dates could work, though it would make Jake a year older. It must be true, or else a very elaborate hoax, but why would April, Jake's mother, lie at the end when she had nothing to lose?

"My God," he breathed. "You're a Blackstone."

"I'm *not* a Blackstone!" Jake countered, then he put his face in his hands. "What the hell am I going to do now?"

They talked and drank all afternoon. Quinn suggested a DNA test to eliminate April as his birth mother.

"Already done it," Jake said. "The results should be through in a few days."

They agreed he should talk to his lawyers and accountants. It was common knowledge that Howard Blackstone's amended will instructed a six-month delay of disbursements pertaining to James while his whereabouts were investigated. Jake thought April's ex-husband, Bill Kellerman, must have got wind of the investigation and threatened her, so she decided to forewarn him.

The living Blackstones were not likely to welcome him with open arms. Matt Hammond's intention to stir things up in the Blackstone boardroom was another complication. "You'll need Matt onside in case they turn on you," Quinn warned. "And watch your back. Ryan and Ric Perrini are chips off the old block. Don't trust anyone. The Blackstones have a leak somewhere in their organisation." That much he knew. Someone close to the Blackstones was providing little snippets of information to those in the industry. That was how Quinn had stumbled onto Ryan and Jessica's wedding plans.

When Dani arrived home a while later, she popped her head in the office to ask if they wanted coffee. Though they both probably needed coffee by this point, judging by the depleted brandy bottle, they declined.

"Don't worry," Quinn reassured his friend when he saw him staring after Dani. "I'll keep it quiet."

Jake turned his head to look at him. "You serious about her?"

The million-dollar question, Quinn thought, leaning back and folding his arms. "Define *serious*."

"I couldn't define squat at the moment."

Quinn had given considerable thought to the question but was little closer to an answer. At his mother's funeral, Jake had spoken of the importance of family, which made Quinn think of the relationships that were vital to him. He was as proud of Lucy, who'd dragged herself up from nothing, as if she were his real sister. Watching Jake grow into the confident, successful business baron he was had been one of Quinn's greatest pleasures in life, and he had no qualms that however upsetting the situation with the Blackstones became, Jake would face it squarely and prevail. Even his parents were constantly motivated to change things for the better. They were now busy fund-raising for a caravan to take to the inner-city streets as a drop-in centre for the street kids of Newtown.

Quinn loved them all and was proud to share in their successes, but sharing was nothing new for him. He'd grown up sharing everything until Laura died—and then he had nothing left. He'd closed himself off, kept his motor idling, but somehow had stalled here in Port Douglas.

He was passionate about his work, hugely successful, but he did have to question whether or not he was growing. Because from where he sat, he was doing the same things he was five years ago, while everyone else had moved on.

Quinn stared at a point somewhere above his friend's shoulder. "I've always felt it was unfair to ask a woman to sit around waiting while I'm off travelling the globe."

"Liar!" scoffed Jake. "You've never even *considered* asking a woman to sit around waiting for you."

Quinn grinned and picked up his glass. He made a thoughtful study of his friend through the amber liquid. "There's this woman I know in Milan. I see her every three or four months for one or two nights. I like her, but we both know that's all it is, a one-night stand every so often. I remember her birthday, I buy her nice things, take her out somewhere nice…." He emptied his glass in one swallow, grimacing at the burn. "But that's all there is. I was happy with that, damn it!"

"About time." Jake stood and approached the desk, tipping the bottle up to empty the last drops into Quinn's glass.

"You can talk!" he retorted. His grin faded. "She's like no one else. Every minute with her is a keeper. Suddenly, my life, which I've always thoroughly enjoyed—"

"Stinks!" Jake nodded sympathetically.

"No!" Quinn drained his glass and his eyes watered. "It just seems a bit lame, that's all."

After he poured Jake into a cab and sent him off to the airport, Quinn went to find Dani, nursing a moderate headache from the effects of the brandy. She lay mostly submerged in a bath full of fragrant bubbles, chewing her nails. He tapped her hand away, admonishing her. "You going out, I suppose?"

She nodded. "I didn't think you would want to come."

Quinn sat on the edge of the bath, the steam and the brandy fuzzing his brain. He most certainly didn't want to spend the evening with the Blackstones.

Then again, maybe it would help Jake to know something of the family dynamics. Who was top dog, who was most likely to oppose his appearance, and who—if anyone—might offer the hand of friendship.

An idea was forming….

"Quinn, have you told anyone about the wedding?"

He squinted at her. Her hair was mostly piled up on top of her head, a long coiled strand clinging to her damp shoulder. "Nope." He reached out and tugged the curl gently, straightening it. It bounced back when he let it go.

"It's just, I know Port Douglas, and there's something going on. I can smell a press photographer a mile off."

He blinked as her words sunk into his brain. "You think *I* tipped off the press?"

She reached out and touched his knee, leaving a wet

patch, but Quinn's indignation faded fast when her movement stirred up the bubbles and a very pink and pert nipple peeped out of the froth.

"No," she answered. "I just think there's something going on, something not quite right."

He bit back the words before they tumbled from his mouth. *"With us, you mean?"* Where the hell had that thought come from? Whatever he did, he could not get into a deep and meaningful conversation after half a bottle of cognac. He dipped his hand into the steaming water and rubbed his face. "I probably deserve suspicion." After all, he had blackmailed her about the wedding in the first place.

When you thought about it, he deserved to be hung, drawn and quartered for all the lies he'd told, all the secrets he withheld. Layer upon layer of secrets. Just when he'd decided he might take a chance on her, look ahead a little—*kapow!* And then *kapow* again. First Sir John, and now Jake. What next? And however could he justify it to her?

She looked up at him thoughtfully. "I didn't think you would contact the media. I just...," She sighed and reached to the side for a sponge, her knee bending up out of the water. "I just so want this day to be perfect for Ryan and Jessica."

Perfect? Quinn knew what was perfect. A smooth pink knee foaming with bubbles. He felt hard as a rock suddenly and licked his dry lips. "Jake," he croaked. "The press will be after Jake."

She looked up at him, a relieved smile forming on her delectable mouth. "You think?"

"He attracts attention wherever he goes. You planning on finishing that?" He nodded at the sponge resting on her knee. The thought of it was attracting all sorts of attention in all sorts of places.

"What was he doing here, anyway?"

Quinn reached out and took the sponge from her hand, his fingers digging into its soft porous depths. "Business. Lift your leg."

"My leg?" Dani hesitated, probably expecting a more expansive reply to her question about Jake's unexpected visit.

Quinn's eyes shifted to hers, challenging her. He had business in mind, all right. Funny business.

And he didn't want any more questions—or any more guilt.

Holding her gaze, he moved his hand into the water and soaked the sponge. Sultry understanding glowed in her eyes. Forget Jake. A trickle of steamy sweat slid down his temple. Forget Blackstone and the press and the shares. Forget life-altering secrets. The swish of streaming water filled his ears as her shapely, heat-flushed thigh rose up from the foam, and then her calf and foot flexed prettily. Quinn caught hold of her foot, washing it while she squirmed.

He cleared his throat. "I've been thinking, may I change my mind and come to the wedding, after all?"

The little smile that curved her lips warmed him. "I'd like that," she said slowly, watching as he dipped the sponge and stretched her leg out. "I'll set it up tonight," she promised.

Quinn stroked the back of her calf and thigh with the

sponge. Water dripped down his forearms and onto his thighs and he thought he must be one sick unit because the warmth and wetness of it only fuelled his desire more.

"Exactly how long do I have to get you clean before you go out?"

Ten

The day of the wedding had finally arrived.

Quinn knocked on her door to say the car was here. Dani was on edge, swimming in questions. Would he like her dress? Would her family like him, and vice versa? What was Jake doing up here? Why were the media swarming all over town, sipping coffee in the cafés, propping up the bars everywhere she turned?

And Quinn's sudden turnaround about accompanying her to the wedding. What was that about?

She made a final adjustment to the chiffon scarf she had cleverly twisted into her long French knot, picked up her purse and joined Quinn downstairs, loving the light in his eyes as he watched her descend.

And would he leave for good once she finished the necklace? Dani worried about that most of all.

They were driven to a helicopter port and, minutes later, were lifted up and over the rain forest to a beach just a few miles south. Dani had inspected the premises previously but was unprepared for the beauty of the place from the air.

The entire van Berhopt Resort hovered above an unsurpassed vista of rain forest and sea. Built on a raised knoll, the lodge appeared to be suspended over the secluded beach below, like a bird about to launch into the air. With a body of glass and steel, somehow it merged with the surroundings, complementing the bird's-eye view. For one breathless moment, Dani thought they were going to land on the massive curved roof that arced above the building, its eaves on all sides overhanging and imposing.

"Spectacular!" Quinn breathed in her ear as the helicopter thankfully set down a couple of hundred metres away from the lodge.

Dani could imagine the reaction of the wedding guests as they were flown in pairs to this incredible secluded paradise. Golf carts took them up to the house. The reception was to start at four-thirty with cocktails and nibbles, then the marriage ceremony. Afterward, there was a sumptuous buffet, featuring the best the tropical north could offer. Only the bride and groom would stay the night here, with the guests being ferried back to their hotels in Port by limousines. It was a small gathering of only twenty family and friends.

In his platinum tux and mahogany-and-silver-striped tie, Quinn Everard was the perfect escort for a tropical, late-afternoon wedding, sophisticated and breathtakingly handsome. His cool against her flamboyance. Dani proudly took his arm and walked through the lobby out to the pool area where the guests were already gathered. Ryan and Jessica had arrived first to settle into their suite. Several other couples lounged around the pool, being served by white-jacketed waiters with silver trays that glinted off the blue water. Dani waved at Sonya and Garth on the other side of the pool and prepared to present Quinn to Ryan Blackstone.

"Well, well," said Ryan as they approached. "Quinn Everard, I presume." He held out his hand. "Welcome to the lion's den."

Quinn smiled and took the proffered hand. "Congratulations, Ryan. It's a pleasure to be here."

Jessica offered Quinn her cheek. "How lovely to see you, Quinn."

"Jessica, you look stunning."

And she did. The bride glowed in a jewel-encrusted champagne gown, a stunning clasp of rose-gold and pink diamonds in between her breasts. "A gift from Ryan," she whispered to Dani, who was so taken with the brooch, she instinctively reached out and touched her fingertips to it. The lovely gown flattered her rounded belly and no amount of sparkle could eclipse the proud smile on Jessica's face or the warmth in her beautiful brown eyes.

While Quinn and Ryan chose drinks from a tray, Jessica turned to Dani and hugged her. "I can't thank you enough for all you've done. This place just takes my breath away."

"I thought you'd like it."

"Everything is just perfect, Danielle. The setting, the weather, the menu you chose and, oh my God, the suite! I don't intend moving out of there for a week!"

The bride took Dani's arm and walked a few steps away. "You look positively beautiful. That colour has no right looking so sensational with your hair…"

Dani expected a few raised brows about her dress, especially from her mother. Strapless and backless, the fabric was hummer orange but the chiffon overskirt was made up of thousands of tiny overlapping patches of deep pink blush and vivid orange. When she moved, the patches rippled with the richness of the sunset.

"You and Quinn look cosy together."

Dani smiled. "I appreciate his invitation at such short notice."

Jessica nodded and sipped her orange juice. "I've met him socially a few times at launches and jewellery expos. He's charming and knows his stuff. And more handsome than any man has a right to be."

Dani helped herself to a delicious morsel from a platter offered her by a server, thinking she wasn't going to argue with Jessica's assessment.

Her soon-to-be cousin-in-law eyed her speculatively. "Is this part of the job description or likely to grow into a more permanent position?"

"I think I'll keep our positions to myself for the moment, Bridezilla." She stopped, her smile fading, and stared across the pool. "Would you look at that?"

Her mother and Garth were putting on a display for Kim and another couple she didn't know. Dani realised it was quite a well-rehearsed tango.

"Did Sonya tell you they were taking lessons together?"

"No. She mentioned sailing." Dani sipped her champagne. "They look good together."

"They *are* good together," Jessica murmured.

Dani felt a twinge of regret that she wasn't in the loop when it looked like this relationship was already quite advanced. But she shook it off. Her mother had never looked better and Dani was thrilled for her. It would just take a bit of getting used to. "Only last week she fobbed me off with the 'just friends' bulldust."

Dani moved to Quinn's side and slid her arm through his. "Let's go say hi to my mother before she dances into the pool and is swept out to sea."

Quinn and Sonya hit it off immediately, and Garth, the Blackstone company secretary and long-time friend and confidant of Howard's, showed no sign of any residual prejudice toward Quinn. Kimberley also greeted him warmly and Dani learned that they had met before in the diamond houses of Europe.

She sensed a slightly cooler dynamic from Ric Perrini toward her escort throughout the evening. She couldn't put her finger on it so decided not to worry about it, wanting nothing to spoil the beautiful wedding she'd helped arrange.

Ryan and Jessica became man and wife as the sun slid beneath the rain forest behind them, setting the sea in front ablaze with light. As if on cue, cockatoo and fruit bats set up their dusk chorus. It was a beautiful ceremony with a stunning backdrop, and there was barely a dry female eye in the place.

Afterward, everyone filled their plates from an amazing buffet of mud crab, ostrich, the local barramundi fish, and many other delicacies popular in this part of the country. The long table accommodated everyone and sat above the pool and the terraced grounds leading to the white sand beach. Jessica announced that the guests should sit next to someone different with each course. Dani knew everyone except a couple of school friends of the bride and her parents. Jessica's father was in a wheelchair but he didn't let it slow him down at all, and his wife and daughter were very attentive.

Sonya whispered that she was seriously considering making an offer on the house she and Ryan had viewed. Her mother living elsewhere than Miramare meant the end of an era was under way. Dani may not have known her father, but at least she'd had a family home, of sorts.

But there was a freshness and vitality to Sonya that Dani couldn't remember seeing before. Her life had been mapped out so young with a child of her own and the responsibility of Kim and Ryan. It gladdened Dani to think her mother was finally going to live a little.

At the next switch, she chatted to Jarrod Hammond and his beautiful fiancée, Briana. The handsome lawyer seemed very much at ease given the bad blood between the two families. Over dessert, she told him how pleased she was to see Matt in Port Douglas a couple of weeks ago. "He hinted that we might all get together soon, Blake, too."

"Great news." Jarrod sounded enthusiastic and

turned to Briana. "We'd be happy to host some sort of gathering in Melbourne, if that suits everyone."

Briana nodded enthusiastically and then responded to the bride's summons at the other end of the table.

Dani looked to where Sonya was deep in conversation with Garth. "Mum can't wait to meet him."

"Meet who?" Ric Perrini, resplendent in white, sat down in Briana's seat.

Dani liked Ric immensely. No one was more thrilled than she when he and Kimberley remarried last month. Despite their long separation, and the fact that relations were not always warm between Ric and Ryan, he was as much a part of the family as she was, in her mind. He'd stuck up for her over moving up here after the humiliation of her broken engagement. She was especially grateful for the support he'd been to Sonya in the past difficult months, and for bringing Kimberley home where she belonged.

"Matt Hammond," she answered. "He came to see me last week."

Ric's eyes shot to her face. "Here?"

She nodded, suddenly unwilling to mention her latest commission. Matt hadn't asked her to keep the Bridal Rose necklace a secret, but the Blackstones could not be expected to applaud the stripping of Howard's legacy and name from the famous pink diamonds. Dani wanted nothing to spoil this night.

"And what," Ric asked, glancing at Jarrod, "would Matt want to see you about, little one?"

Dani often felt like Ric's little sister. "Business of course, old man."

Ric's blue eyes sparkled. "You being such a hot businesswoman, Danielle," he quipped, "Hammond better watch out he doesn't lose his shirt."

Dani was distracted by a slight tension to Jarrod's jaw. Would this stupid feud ever disappear? Sure, it was decades in the making, but why did the younger generation continue to suffer? She turned back to Ric. "Not me, silly. Quinn."

"You called?"

Quinn's sleeve brushed her bare shoulder as he leaned over her to set his dessert plate down.

"Ryan wants a word," he said quietly. His breath trickled into her ear, reminding her of how she loved his voice and how much she had missed hearing it for the past hour. Closing her eyes, she leaned slightly back into him and inhaled, familiarising herself with his warmth and bulk and the unique scent of him that made her feel most like a woman. His woman.

Reluctantly she looked up the table to where the bridegroom stood talking to the manager of the lodge. Ryan's grim expression told her something was wrong. "Problem?" she whispered to Quinn, rising.

"Could be." Quinn put his hand on the small of her back and they walked up the length of the table.

"There's a reporter at the reception desk wanting confirmation of our wedding," Ryan said tightly. "I really don't want this to become a circus." He glanced to where his bride sat with her parents and Kimberley, looking for all the world like she didn't have a care.

"I'll go and talk to him," Dani began.

"I'll go," Quinn said quickly. "If he's from Sydney,

he'll know your face and that you're connected to the Blackstones. The vultures won't think for a minute I would be invited to a Blackstone wedding."

Ryan and Dani nodded, seeing the sense in that. "What will you say?"

"That I'm entertaining important clients from overseas. We're staying the night and will be leaving first thing in the morning. That way, hopefully your honeymoon will go undetected."

"Do you trust him, Danielle?" Ryan asked as they watched him follow the manager out to the reception desk.

She nodded, but unbidden, his threat to reveal the wedding plans to the media on the day they met pressed down on her like a grey cloud. "Don't worry." She squeezed Ryan's arm, swallowing her concerns. "Quinn is the soul of discretion. Nothing is going to spoil the night."

Two hours later, it seemed she was right. The champagne flowed and the party had become quite lively. Finally the bride and groom announced they were retiring to get started on their wedding night. One by one, white stretch limos pulled up to the lobby and the guests piled in and were treated to more champagne they didn't need on the way back to Port Douglas.

Dani and Quinn joined Ric and Kimberley in the back of the last car. Ric, still smarting from the media scrum at his Sydney harbour wedding six weeks before, thanked Quinn for getting rid of the press. "How the hell did they find out? I swear, when I discover who is keeping tabs on our family…"

"I'm starting to think it's someone in the office,"

Kimberley said thoughtfully. "There have been too many coincidences lately."

Dani felt pleasantly tired and snuggled into Quinn's side. "Quinn thinks the press are in town because Jake was here yesterday."

"Jake Vance?" Ric lifted his head. "What was he doing here?"

"He came to see Quinn," she replied. "They're friends."

The atmosphere in the limo chilled. In the dim interior, she saw Ric's nostrils flare and Kim's forehead crease with consternation.

Ric exchanged glances with his wife. "You've had a busy week, Quinn. First Matt Hammond, now Jake Vance." His fingers rasped over his chin. "Somebody is buying up a whole lot of Blackstone shares. You know anything about that?"

There was a long silence while Dani kicked herself for making the inadvertent comment.

"I might," Quinn said eventually. "What of it?"

"I knew it!" Ric said through gritted teeth. "I knew Matt Hammond was involved."

Kimberley put a hand on his arm, but Ric leaned forward and fixed Quinn with a piercing stare. "Hammond's called on both you and Vance in the past week or so. Do you expect me to believe you didn't discuss your Blackstone shareholding?"

"You can believe what you like. You know we're all shareholders. And for the moment, I'm happy with the status quo." Then Quinn, too, leaned forward, bringing his face close to Ric's. "And that's all I'm going to say about that."

His tone was dangerously low and loaded with warning. The two men eyeballed each other while Dani and Kim exchanged worried glances.

"I don't trust you, Everard," Ric said softly.

"Why should you?"

"Are you using Danielle to get an in with the family?"

"Ric!" Dani and Kimberley protested together.

"Watch your mouth," Quinn murmured.

The hairs on the back of Dani's neck rose. Danger throbbed in the air between the two men. Quinn pressed forward and slightly into her side, as if to shield her.

"Can you honestly tell me that you three are not plotting a takeover of Blackstone Diamonds?" Ric's voice was equally low, equally full of threat. "It's a reasonable request, Quinn."

"It's an unreasonable request," Quinn said evenly. "And I'm not privy to Matt's business dealings. But I'm happy with my minor shareholding." His chin rose. "At the moment."

Ric's eyes narrowed but he sat fractionally back, a little of the tension leaving his face. "And Vance?"

"What of him?"

"What's he been meeting with Matt about in Sydney?"

"Jake's business is his own…but I think he has other things on his mind right now."

"Jake's mother just passed away," Dani supplied in a small voice.

"But if he asked for your support?" Ric wasn't letting it go just yet.

Quinn paused while Dani held her breath.

"If he asked," Quinn said heavily, "I would support him."

Ric inhaled, glaring, but Kim beat him to it. She dipped her dark head between them and fixed both men with a formidable look. "That's enough! It's a happy day, damn it!"

Eleven

The car dropped Kim and Ric off at their hotel in town and set off for Four Mile. The tension remained, waves of it, and Dani and Quinn barely spoke. At least the actual wedding had gone off without a hitch, but the argument in the car had raised a barrage of questions that only Quinn could answer. Maybe because of the way they met, she would always have these reservations about him. That was a sobering thought.

They got out of the car and she stopped him from going inside. "We need to talk. Let's go out on the beach."

"You'll ruin your dress."

She shrugged and walked to the end of the road and the copse of trees that led out onto the sand. "I think better out here." She looked back at him. "And you have to tell the truth on my beach. It's my special place."

She was glad he didn't argue. The cover of darkness and the sound of the waves eased her nerves, which would help her ask the questions she needed to. Right now, she was more afraid than she had ever been in her life.

They walked slowly, aimlessly, onto the soft, thick sand. Dani slipped her sandals off, picked them up and turned to face him, her heart in her mouth. "Quinn, I want to know that you're not plotting to bring down Blackstone Diamonds."

He stood very still, looking at her for such a long time that she thought he wasn't going to answer. Would he cut her down again, tell her she had no right to question him? In the darkness, his eyes were unreadable.

Finally he spoke. "To tell you would be to betray a confidence."

She licked her dry lips. "I won't betray your confidence, but I need to know I mean more to you than a few shares."

Quinn inhaled deeply, his chest rising, his eyes boring into her. The silence stretched between them, and again she almost lost hope that he would speak.

She began to turn away, burning with humiliation.

Quinn reached out and caught her hand. "It's Jake. It's about Jake."

Her heart sank further. So Jake Vance *was* planning a corporate takeover, and Quinn had decided to be involved. Ric's words in the car—*Are you using Danielle to get an in with the family?*—returned to taunt her.

When was someone ever going to want her for her?

A full moon broke through the heavy cloud above, bathing everything in an eerie bluish-grey light.

"He…" Quinn's head rolled back and he sighed heavily. "There's no easy way to say this. Jake has reason to believe he is James Hammond Blackstone."

Dani jerked, staring at him stupidly. "Sorry?"

Quinn repeated himself.

Her reservations fled. That was the last thing she'd expected. "Doesn't he know who he is?"

"He thought he did."

"I don't believe it."

"He doesn't, either. That's why he's getting a DNA test done to prove that April—his mother—is his birth mother."

Her hand slid out of his. "He told you this yesterday? That's why he came?"

"It was the first I'd heard of it." Quinn nodded. He proceeded to give her the rundown on Jake's version of events.

"Jake didn't believe her. She was on morphine at that stage, and he thought her mind was going. But when he was packing up the house, he found a scrapbook and it's all there, Dani. Dozens of news clippings about the kidnapping and the housekeeper and her partner who took him. Toys and a blanket from the car that matched what was taken from James Blackstone's bedroom."

Dani's shoulder rose and fell in a helpless movement. "You're telling me this woman, this April, goes to the store one day and comes home with a baby and no one thinks anything of it?" She laughed disbelievingly. "That was big news back then, Quinn, all over Australia. She'd never have gotten away with it."

"He's still looking into it, but it appears that April had a baby who died the year before. At the time she found

Jake—James—she was running away from an abusive boyfriend. She moved around a lot and ended up in South Australia, where no one knew her." He exhaled and looked down, moving his shoe over a sandy mound of crab balls. "I knew April. She had her faults, mostly due to the men she hooked up with, but she was a decent woman. And she loved Jake. There was never any doubt about that."

Dani clasped her hands in front of her and rocked on her heels, sinking into the cool sand. "Oh Lord, this is really going to… So he's not trying to destroy Blackstone Diamonds, after all?" She gave another short sharp laugh. "In fact, that would be counter-productive since he is now the heir."

"Maybe," he warned. "Not confirmed yet."

In a tiny way, although this was earth-shattering news, Dani was a bit relieved. At least he wasn't plotting to bring about the downfall of her cousins. "So why did you suddenly change your mind about coming to the wedding?"

"I wanted to see everyone together, how they all get on, and who Jake's greatest opponent might be when—if—it all comes out." He exhaled. "I think we've established that."

She realised he meant Ric. "If Jake really is family, Ric'll accept it. If he does anything to hurt the company, that's a different matter. It's Kimberley and Ryan—especially Ryan—I'm worried about." Dani turned, rubbing her arms. Quinn slipped off his jacket and placed it around her shoulders and they began to walk slowly back the way they'd come. "I have to tell them."

Quinn inhaled sharply. "No!"

"Quinn, this is too—"

He grasped her arm firmly, turning her. "He won't get the results of April's DNA till next week. If that confirms that April is not his birth mother, then he is going to have to persuade Kim or Ryan, or both, to take a DNA test to prove Howard and your aunt were his parents."

Good luck with that, she thought, imagining Ryan's response to that request. "Quinn, I can't keep something like this from them. It's not fair."

Quinn smiled tightly. "Who said life is fair? Dani, there is a leak in the Blackstone offices. Kimberley said as much tonight. Do you realise the media frenzy something like this will generate? You have to keep it quiet until it's proved that April is not his birth mother." His eyes were grim. "Don't even tell your mother. Garth could be the leak, for all we know."

"Garth? He wouldn't!"

"Probably not. But there is no sense upsetting everyone till we know for sure."

Dani pulled the sides of his jacket closer, chilled by the realisation that on top of all this upset, there would be publicity. Lots of publicity. "God, I hate secrets. I can't even imagine what this is going to do to the family, after the year we've had."

"If it turns out that he really is part of the family, then that's a good thing for everyone, right?"

"Possibly." Possibly not. "Families aren't my strong point. Perhaps I have a jaundiced view." She raised her hand, nibbling on a fingernail. "How would you feel if it was your long-lost brother?"

Quinn considered. "Family's family to me," he said thoughtfully, pulling her hand away from her mouth. "But I suppose if a complete stranger suddenly appeared and wanted to take over the reins of all I'd worked for…" He held his palm up when she began to speak. "And just remember, it was Howard who changed his will to include James, it wasn't Jake's idea."

"Poor old Howard," Dani murmured with genuine sympathy for the man who had never given up hope. "He died before seeing his dream come true."

Quinn nodded. "It must be tough to lose a child."

Dani had her own views on that. "Not for everybody." Her own father had never looked back. She put a hand on his shoulder and raised a foot to slide her sandal back on.

Quinn took the remaining shoe from her hand and bent to put it on her foot. He remained squatting, peering up at her. His face was in shadow, the moon behind him. "Aren't you the least bit curious about your own father? Don't you want to know who and why?"

She looked at him sharply, wondering how the heck he'd known what was going through her mind. "Why should I? He's never been curious about me."

Even as the words left her mouth, she knew she was lying. She'd begged and cajoled, but her mother wouldn't be moved on that subject. *"Forget him, Danielle. He didn't want us and we're better off without him."* She wouldn't even confirm or deny if he was actually still alive.

Quinn slowly rose to his feet. "What if you found out that it wasn't his fault, wasn't his idea to stay away?"

"Then he is a lame excuse for a man," she declared.

What kind of a man made no phone calls, sent no birthday cards—not even once. Even if her mother hated him, it was no excuse to ignore his child. "He never gave a damn, end of story."

She cringed at the tight, self-pitying tone of her voice and turned and walked toward the house.

"You know, there is something my parents and Laura did with some of the kids at home," Quinn said from behind her, and she slowed to let him catch up. "Many of them hadn't seen or spoken to their parents in years. Many had been abused or beaten or just ignored. They used to say, 'If you had the chance, if your mother or father was standing here right now, what would you say to them?'"

Dani hesitated. "I wouldn't say anything. He means nothing to me."

Quinn caught her hand and turned her to face him. "If he was here, right now, Dani, and prepared to listen…?"

With a moody sigh, Dani looked past him, down to the waves lapping the sand. What would she say, indeed? She stared into nothing and tried to imagine what he looked like, this make-believe father. Would he be tall, have red hair like hers? A kindly face?

She could stare into nothing all she liked. There were no answers there. She'd already looked, many, many times.

"I'd say 'you're late.'" She looked into Quinn's face. "I'd say 'you're too bloody late!'"

The next day, they met Sonya for brunch at her hotel before the Blackstones took off for Sydney in the company jet. Her mother knew nothing of the argument in the car the night before with Ric, and Dani did not intend to enlighten her. Besides, the bombshell about Jake was the overriding topic in her mind.

During the meal, a reporter stopped by the table to ask for confirmation of Ryan's wedding. They did not confirm or deny; Ryan and Jessica deserved privacy on their honeymoon. After he'd gone, Quinn suggested that the exaggerated media presence in town was due to the imminent arrival of the governor-general, who'd been invited to officiate at the annual ANZAC Day festivities. Dani peered at the article in the morning newspaper detailing the commemoration of Australian and New Zealand military action in WW1. "Every year they drag some poor old dignitary out at five in the morning." She grinned. "Not that I'm complaining since it's a public holiday."

"You don't admire Sir John?" Quinn asked.

Dani shrugged. "I don't particularly admire any politician."

"He's not a politician," Quinn pointed out. "He is the governor-general, the Queen's representative in this colony of ours."

"But he was prime minister once." Dani rolled her eyes. "What a lot of fuss. The mayor is putting on a posh reception at the Sea Temple. VIPs only. Three TV stations, local and national celebrities—and all for some boring old—"

Sonya sighed heavily and put her hand on her purse. Dani looked up from her paper.

"I'm going back to the hotel," her mother said,

pushing her chair out from the table. "I think I have one of my headaches coming on."

"I thought you wanted to see the shop." Dani had been looking forward to showing off her new spring pieces. She also had a surprise for her mother and for Quinn. Yesterday, she'd secured a lease for the bigger shop a few doors down from hers. Whatever Quinn thought about the location, Dani Hammond was on the way up.

But Sonya got to her feet, looking pale. "I'd rather see if we could leave a little earlier and get the flight over with as quickly as possible," she said apologetically.

"You were perfectly fine a minute ago," Dani pouted in the flurry of activity as everyone rose from the table. "We'll see you upstairs."

"No, it's fine. Take care, darling." She hugged her daughter tightly, whispering "I *do* like him" into Dani's ear. When she pulled back, Sonya's eyes were suspiciously brilliant. "But I love you," she whispered, touching her cheek, then was gone.

What was that about? Dani wondered, feeling a little uneasy. Her mother wasn't given to emotional goodbyes. Perhaps she was sick. That wasn't the first time she'd had a migraine when they'd been out.

Maybe she and Garth had had an argument....

"Perhaps she just had a little too much champagne last night," Quinn commented, practicing that weird way he had of seeming to see inside her head.

"Probably. I'll call her later."

They drove back to the beach house and Dani's mind

turned to other matters. "Now that the wedding is over, I'd better get busy on the necklace."

"Yes. And if you finish it on time," Quinn murmured, "I have a surprise for you. How would you like to strut the red carpet wearing something fabulous, be the envy of all your friends?"

Her eyes shone as he told her he had an invite to the governor-general's reception—"The one to honour some boring old—"

"True?" VIPs liked jewellery. What a showcase! "How did you get an invite?"

"He's a friend."

"Sir John is a friend?" Dani unfolded the paper on her lap and peered at the photo of an old guy in an old suit that boasted a row of medals.

Somehow she couldn't see him and Quinn out on the golf course together. "He's too old and too frail to be your friend."

"Not at all," Quinn demurred. "He's an avid collector. I trust his recommendations and judgement above any man I know. I've dealt with him for years."

This was a chance to meet someone close to Quinn.

A chance to show off some of her pieces.

She sat back in her seat, already thinking that her lilac organza dress would be perfect for the occasion.

"*If* you get the necklace finished on time," Quinn warned.

The next two days, she closeted herself in her workroom, forbidding him to disturb her until she'd finished. Platinum was a fascinating metal, though it required a great deal of attention. As it was extremely pliable when heated, just one gram could be drawn to produce a fine wire more than two kilometres long. Luckily she didn't require quite that much. The cage she was making to encase the diamond was very delicate, but the density of platinum ensured its durability.

Finally it was done. Dani emerged, bleary-eyed, from the workroom to find Quinn sitting at breakfast, reading the paper. She glanced at the date on the paper, the twenty-fourth of April. The deadline was safe.

Quinn rose and picked up a cup from the tray on the table, concern in his eyes.

Dani stopped him as he picked up the coffeepot. "No, I'm going to bed."

"How's it coming?"

She hesitated, feeling almost nauseated with all the emotions raging inside. She was exhausted, relieved, cautiously optimistic that he'd like it. But mostly she wondered if this would be the end for them. "It's finished."

A small, slow smile appeared on his face. "Show me."

Dani backed away. "No, I'm too tired. And too nervous. You go look at it and formulate your hopefully complimentary comments later."

Quinn eased back into his chair. "All right. Get some sleep. I'll take you out somewhere nice tonight, just the two of us, to celebrate."

Dani nodded and climbed the stairs to bed.

Quinn walked into the workroom and immediately noticed that she'd tidied up. The workbench was swept clean, the tools stacked in their place. He thought how tired she'd looked and wondered if she had slept at all.

The necklace was up on its bust on the desk. Quinn switched the desk lamp on, pulled the chair well back and sat.

He was still there an hour later.

He looked first for impact, and got it in spades. A diamond inside a diamond. Mere filaments of platinum, like the gossamer wings of a dragonfly, held the huge trilliant-cut stone suspended inside a web cage. Platinum was the perfect setting for the intense yellow stone. It contained no alloys to tinge a diamond's brilliance and its reflective qualities enhanced the colour without distracting from it.

Quinn moved the bust from side to side to see every angle and put his judge's cap on. Innovative design, effective use of the gem, quality of workmanship, wearability. Ten out of ten in all categories. It was beautifully finished, totally professional, fresh and original.

And more conservative than he had originally feared, given her propensity for large, striking jewellery. The essence and personality of the diamond shone through, as a stone of this beauty and importance deserved.

Had she chosen this design, he wondered, as symbolic of herself, hiding in a cage of her own making? Was she brave enough to step into the limelight and let herself shine?

Quinn really was going to have to talk to her about moving to Sydney and marketing herself properly. His broker's brain started ticking. If this piece went to auction it would cause a stir. Just off the top of his head, he could think of three collectors who would pay a king's ransom for it.

But then he remembered. It wasn't going to auction. The owner of this necklace had quite a different purpose in mind.

That night, on their way out for dinner, Quinn placed the necklace around her neck and showed her what it looked like.

"Quinn, I can't," she protested, but her eyes were bright with excitement. "I'd be too nervous. What if someone sees?"

"Everyone should see, just for tonight." He tugged gently at her dangly angel earrings. "I think these are superfluous, don't you?"

She smiled at him in the mirror, her hand already reaching to dispatch the earrings. "You really like it?"

Quinn had spent the past couple of hours in bed with her showing her how much he liked it, but she deserved every indulgence. He nuzzled her bare shoulder, keeping his eyes on her reflection. "It is truly outstanding. *You* are truly outstanding."

He meant every word. It had come to him earlier in the workroom that he wanted to be the key to unlocking Dani's self-imposed cage. Throughout the day, waiting for her to wake up, he'd nurtured the idea, considered it, like the necklace, from every angle. More than that, he allowed himself to expand on practicalities, like geography, career, family. All the things he'd thought about in his apartment in Sydney.

Guilt had forced him to step back since then, but

Quinn was tired of denying it. He wanted to share in her life and wanted her to share in his. But there were still so many secrets and lies between them. Breaking Jake's confidence the other night had been about reassuring her, giving her something, because he knew he was about to inflict the most monstrous betrayal of all.

Over dinner, looking across the table at a masterpiece of design and the work of art wearing it, Quinn sought to be the perfect dinner companion, attentive and charming, as he knew she expected. But the food and wine were ashes in his mouth. He prayed her generous nature would forgive him.

Later he took her to his room and commanded her to strip until she wore only her high-heeled sandals and the necklace. He took the clip from her hair, letting it flow like a river of fire. Standing behind her as she peered into a mirror, he watched her face and saw that she, too, was struck by the beauty of her creation, and by the way her own beauty enhanced it.

He'd known she would look like this, but he drank the image in, in case it was all he'd have in the years to come. Her eyes mirrored the fire and sparkle of the intense yellow diamond, her irises ringed with gold. She moved her shoulders, a tiny repetitive sway from side to side, watching the diamond leap to life between her breasts. The perfect setting.

Quinn's large dark hands moved over her lush body, down the length of her torso, over the soft feminine curves of her bejewelled belly. He'd pulled the bed stool over in front of the mirror and now eased them down, bringing her slowly down onto him. Her legs parted and her eyes locked on his while he moved his hands over her, cupping her breasts, teasing her inside thighs, stroking her intimately. He made love to her tenderly, watching her hair ripple like firelight. The stone between her breasts changed the colour of her eyes to sheer, shimmering pleasure. When she shuddered and smiled her love and satisfaction back at him, he closed his eyes and allowed his release to engulf him in a wash of colourful ecstasy. And he knew he'd done the unthinkable. He had fallen in love with Dani Hammond.

Twelve

Sir John Knowles was tall and thin with drawn cheeks and a pallor of fatigue. She'd read somewhere he was in his early sixties, but from where she stood, Australia's most beloved statesman looked a lot older. To his right stood a birdlike woman, elegantly attired, her hands clasped tightly in front of her.

"Is that his wife?" Dani whispered to Quinn.

"Clare." Quinn volunteered nothing else.

Dani rolled her eyes and hoped he would loosen up a little once the formalities were out of the way. He'd barely spoken all day, except to reiterate how talented she was. She only hoped his client, whoever he or she was, thought so, too.

Quinn's approbation thrilled her except for an inexplicable feeling she could not define. It was nothing more noteworthy than his eyes sliding off hers just a fraction too soon, a watchfulness throughout the day, a hint of regret, even.

But then she remembered their lovemaking last night. Dani had never associated tenderness with this man, but last night she'd drowned in it, had truly felt special and cherished. Oh, there were logistical problems—the fact that he lived in Sydney, that he travelled constantly. But how could he make love to her so tenderly if he intended to leave her?

She rubbed her arms, pleased with her decision not to go with the summery organza dress. Her belted floral tunic, master-and-commander jacket and ankle boots might be a touch unconventional for a stuffy reception of this kind, but this was about exposure. The keishi-pearl-and-sapphire necklace was far too feminine to be trumped by lilac. It needed to rise above the bold, and triumph.

She fingered the necklace absently, looking down at the red carpet they inched forward on. As she did, she recalled the light in Quinn's eyes as she'd emerged from her bedroom earlier tonight.

"You always keep me guessing and you never disappoint," he'd said, giving her a little twirl.

Now Quinn's grip on her arm tightened and she realised they were at the front of the queue at last. He placed his hand over hers, staring resolutely ahead. The dignitary seemed to lose a little of his stoop when he saw them.

"Quinn," Sir John said simply, reaching out with both hands and clasping his.

"May I introduce—" she heard Quinn say as he tugged her forward "—Danielle Hammond."

Sir John took Dani's proffered hand and enclosed it with both of his. He stared down into her face for such a long time that she felt her smile stretch and become stale.

Quinn shook hands with Sir John's wife, then reached into his inside pocket and took out a long rectangular box. Ignoring Dani's wide-eyed comprehension, he offered it to the governor-general. With one last bony squeeze of her hand, Sir John released her and took the box from Quinn. Without opening it, he passed it to his wife.

Dani's smile froze. So the necklace—her necklace—was for Sir John, or at least his wife. The woman who smiled tentatively at her now.

Loss hit hard, followed by dread. It wasn't unusual to feel emotional when she sold a favourite piece, but right now she was just plain worried. Quinn had inferred she should make the necklace as if she were going to wear it. Somehow she couldn't imagine that necklace, that bold diamond, around this woman's neck.

Sir John turned back to her, and if he noticed her stricken expression, his calm smile didn't waver. "Thank you, my dear." He tilted his head at the jewellery box his wife held.

It's too young for you, Dani thought.

"Would you do me the honour," Sir John said, "of joining my wife and me for a drink in our suite in a little while?"

Quinn answered for both of them. "Of course, Sir John."

Dani could barely contain herself until they were out of earshot. "I don't believe it! He's your client?"

Quinn nodded, directing her over to a waiter with a tray of drinks.

"Oh, Quinn," she whispered loudly. "You encouraged me to make something contemporary. Something I would wear myself." She shook her head, very worried. "It's too young for her."

He handed her a glass of wine. "Dani, the necklace is perfect."

"But…" If only he'd told her, given her a picture of the woman or something. "She'd prefer brilliants all over it, possibly other gems, or pearls… Damn it, I should have gone for pearls."

Quinn took a long sip of wine, then tipped her chin up with his finger. "Sir John knows jewellery. He will see exactly what I see. You're world class, Dani Hammond, in every way."

Her nerves calmed somewhat. She trusted him. Quinn had too much integrity to let her fall flat on her face. His own professional reputation was at stake, too.

It was still a tense hour and a half until the mayor appeared and requested they follow him. And she still crossed her fingers on the way.

The mayor waved them into a luxurious suite and then left. Sir John and his wife sat on one of two settees. Behind them, French doors opened out onto a large balcony. Dani caught a glimpse of twinkling blue water from the lighted pool below.

On a coffee table between the settees sat the open blue velvet box.

Sir John rose and came to greet them, his smile born of real warmth rather than the restrained politeness of the reception. He seemed a little younger than before, more sprightly, and hugged Quinn, who warmly reciprocated. Then he led Dani to the settee.

She felt too nervous to accept a drink. Mrs. Knowles sat staring at the necklace while the two men made a little small talk. Then they sat, too.

An awkward silence descended. Everyone's eyes seemed to gravitate toward the open jewellery box. Quinn sat beside her, his shoulders back, as tense as Dani had ever seen him. He didn't look at her once.

Her eyes moved restlessly from one to the other, wishing someone would speak. After at least a minute of this, she began to pray for the floor to open up and swallow her. Finally she couldn't take the tension a moment longer. "Is something wrong with the necklace?" she blurted out.

Quinn grasped her hand, still without looking at her. She heard Mrs. Knowles clear her throat and murmur something that sounded ominously like "Poor child."

Sir John lifted his head wearily, fixed his wife and then Quinn with a stern look and said quietly, "Would you leave us?"

Mrs. Knowles rose quickly, looking at Quinn. With a last squeeze of her hand, Quinn rose. Bemused, Dani, too, started to rise.

But Quinn laid a heavy hand on her shoulder, pushing her gently back down. "Stay," he murmured, giving her shoulder a firm squeeze.

She subsided, completely confused now. Quinn and Mrs. Knowles left the room together and closed the door quietly.

What the hell is going on?

An ominous foreboding swamped her. If he didn't like the necklace, why couldn't he just say? She could change it, fix it; he was paying enough. She'd be happy to consult with his wife on the design.

Dani looked longingly at the closed door, wishing she was on the other side. With Quinn.

"He's a good man," Sir John said quietly, following her gaze.

She settled back in the seat, calling on all her composure. "Is your wife unhappy with the necklace?"

Kindly hazel eyes searched her face. He was very tall, as tall as Quinn, but his clothes and his skin looked like he'd lost weight in a hurry. "Clare thinks, as I do, that you're very gifted. But—" he cleared his throat and leaned forward "—the necklace is not for Clare." He picked up the open box and held it out to her. "It's for you."

She must have misheard. "Sorry?"

The box shook quite markedly in the old man's hands so she sat forward and put her hands on it to steady it.

"Quinn found the diamond for me six years ago, you know." His voice became a little less thready, a little warmer. "I always intended you to have it."

They sat there both holding the box in midair until he pushed it gently into her hands and she had no choice but to take it.

"You're starting to scare me, Sir John."

The man took a deep breath, looking earnestly into her face. "This is my apology and my legacy to you, Danielle, for I am your father."

I am your father.

Dani lowered the box slowly to her lap, her lips moving soundlessly. *Her father.* The two words chased each other around her head. Of all the things she might have expected at this glittering occasion, this was not one of them. And why didn't Quinn tell her? Did he know?

A piercing pain in her chest confirmed his betrayal. Of course he knew. He'd set her up.

Her father. She searched his face, thinking there must be some kind of connection, some kind of familiarity, surely. A proud nose, pockmarked with age and infirmity. A still-strong chin but sunken cheeks that whispered of pain. His bow tie seemed too tight around his scrawny neck, wormed with loose flesh. A plain white shirt covered what looked to be a wasted chest.

Dani stopped searching. There was nothing of her in this old man. She'd walk past him on the street and not feel the slightest hint of recognition. She wouldn't look at him twice.

A lump of anger slowly formed, not just toward him but Quinn as well. And her mother. She must have known this was coming. Dani let it burn just under the surface, wondering if he could see it on her staring face.

Sir John must have realised he wasn't going to get any help from her. He picked up his glass and sipped.

"I was the leader of the opposition. Your mother, Sonya," he said, his voice caressing the word, causing Dani to suck in air, "was helping out in the campaign office."

She swallowed heavily but managed to keep quiet.

"I was recently married to Clare, whom I'd known all my life. I noticed Sonya, I own to it. We were friends but nothing would have happened, for we were not bad people. I took my marriage vows seriously, and your mother was not the type of woman to wreck a marriage."

Don't tell me what my mother is, she wanted to snarl. *Don't even speak her name.* But she held her tongue.

"But then your aunt Ursula died. Your mother was inconsolable. I'd tried so hard to keep away from her. We'd both tried. The consequences were much more serious than my marriage, my career. I would have risked that happily for Sonya. But it was the party, the one that was going to take the country into the new decade...."

Dani had a sudden and savage insight into why she hated politicians, the way they tried to justify everything.

Sir John closed his eyes. "I intended only to offer comfort, but one thing led to another. She fell pregnant almost immediately."

In the dead silence that followed, a million questions and accusations swamped her. She knew she had to consider those different times, her mother's unenviable situation, the lure of a powerful, charismatic man. Heck, she was no angel herself. But her anger seemed to suck up her compassion for now. She'd get to it later, away from here.

"I loved her very much," the old man said plaintively. "Please never doubt that."

Her heartbeat sounded in her ears, loud, slow,

ominous. "Sure you did," she said softly, feeling the hot breath of her anger like fire in her throat. "That's why you kept in such close contact."

He closed his eyes briefly, his thin lips drawn in a slash of anguish. "I don't expect you to understand, but I am more sorry than you will ever know."

Dani clenched her teeth and looked down at the necklace. So sorry he was buying her off. Didn't he know she came cheap? A cup of coffee would have done, a bunch of flowers on her birthday or graduation. A simple phone call.

"I've thought about you every day." His voice was high and thin.

But not enough to get in touch. Her hand seemed to jerk up of its own accord, jabbing toward the balcony. "How fortuitous the ANZAC Day commemoration was up here this year. After twenty-seven years, you could kill two birds with one stone."

Sir John took a long time answering. "I'm so sorry, my dear. I wanted very much to be part of your life, but it wasn't possible. You see, Howard blackmailed me to keep away."

No. He wouldn't. A huge fist closed around her chest. Please say it's not true…. "Wh-why, what possible reason…?"

"The miners had been on strike for two years. The government was making a bad fist of it." His pallor became even more washed out and he inhaled deeply. "Industry was being crippled. My party promised to crush the strikers. Howard—all industry leaders—could not afford for us to fail."

And an affair outside marriage, a teenage pregnancy in those days would have been the death knell for the party.

How could Howard do it? She wanted to moan and scream with rage and betrayal. What right did he have? She wrapped her arms around her middle, still holding the jewellery box.

"I'm so sorry," the old man—her father—whispered, and she tried, she really did, to dredge up some compassion. But the rage was hot and hard and impossible to swallow.

"I'm dying, Danielle. Lung cancer."

The words hung in the air between them while she clutched herself, rocking. His eyes beseeched her.

Her brain was going into overload. He was dying. He wasn't here because he wanted to meet her, to get to know the bastard daughter. He was here to assuage his guilt before the end.

She couldn't breathe. The keishi necklace dug into her throat and the anger coursing through her wasn't hot and hard anymore. It was stone-cold fury.

Dani stood abruptly, holding the jewellery box. "How dare you!" And without any rational thought at all, just a need to rage, she threw the box at the wall behind him. It hit with a dull *thwack*, bounced off the cabinet and fell to the floor. The platinum cage holding the diamond glittered, the chain spilled out onto the white tiles.

"You selfish old…" Some kind of insane respect stopped her from saying the word *bastard*. He was after all, the governor-general of Australia.

Sir John remained seated, his head bowed, his sunken cheeks even more pronounced and impossibly pale. But she didn't care. She jerked into action, heard the quick, sharp click of her heels, and then she wrenched the door open and ran smack into Quinn's chest.

How dare he as well?

Dani reeled away, putting her hands up in front of her like a shield.

He spoke her name, took her wrists gently, and it required a superhuman effort not to slap him away, or slap his face.

Clare Knowles slipped past them and into the suite, looking very upset.

"How could you?" Dani demanded in a strangled moan. "How could you do this to me?"

"Dani, I'm so sorry."

"Let me go."

He tugged her toward a chair. "I had to. He's dying." She resisted his efforts to sit her down. "How long have you known?"

Quinn swallowed and looked away. "Since the day we left Sydney."

Dani bit down on the inside of her mouth. She remembered the phone call, his polite excuse "I have to take this…" She had gone on to the airstrip without him.

She tasted blood. "You bastard," she said quietly.

He jerked his head toward the suite where presumably Sir John was being comforted by his wife. "Howard Blackstone was blackmailing him to keep away."

"Don't!" Her voice cracked. "Don't even speak his name. Howard was twice the man you will ever be."

He rolled his head back and sighed. "Dani, he's dying. He's my friend and he begged me and he's dying." He kneaded her hands between his.

"I told you the other night my father meant nothing to me. God, Quinn, we *talked* about it. You had a golden opportunity to tell me."

"Would you have come if I'd told you?"

She shook her head, trying to pull out of his grasp. "You set me up. I don't know how you could do that, take me in there and leave me." The tears started in earnest now and she was ashamed. Ashamed of crying, of upsetting an old man.

Of believing in Quinn Everard.

"I thought I loved you, but I couldn't love someone who could do that," she sobbed, her hands still imprisoned in his grasp. "I hate you."

"Quinn?" Clare Knowles stood in the doorway.

Dani turned her head away, not wanting to see or be seen by the woman, even as she registered the worry in her voice. But it was the slide of Quinn's stricken eyes from her face to the other woman's that gave her the will, the strength to push away from him.

Once again, she was second in line, never number one. Not good enough to be a daughter. Not good enough to be a Blackstone. Not good enough to be a fiancée.

Not good enough to be his...

Thirteen

Late on a public holiday Friday, the streets thronged with inebriated activity. Shortly after storming out on Quinn and her father, Dani stood outside her shop, looking in, drowning in self-pity and hating herself for it. How could Quinn do it to her, allow her to walk into the most important moment of her life unprepared?

And her mother—she had a lot to answer for. With a flash of anger, Dani pulled her phone from her purse and dialed. Sonya cried, saying she had dreaded this moment since learning of the official visit a few weeks ago.

"John called me a couple of weeks after Howard's funeral, wanting to contact you. I said no, you were happy, I begged him." She knew nothing of Howard's blackmail, but admitted that it was Howard who told her the leader of the opposition wanted nothing to do with her or her baby. "He gave me a choice: the stigma and scandal of bringing down the next government, or security. He said he would always take care of us. I had to do the right thing for you."

"Did you love him?" Dani asked tremulously. "My father?"

"I thought I did." Her mother sighed. "You have to understand, I was just nineteen. Overnight my life changed from being a carefree teen to suddenly being responsible for two kids, because Howard was so devastated by Ursula's death, he wasn't coping. John was kind, attractive, important."

Her mother begged to come up first thing in the morning, but Dani knew she was far too low to resist the coddling and entreaties to bring her home to Sydney. She asked for a few days' grace and hung up.

A group of people came out of a bar, weaving across the road, then scattering to let a screaming ambulance pass. Her reflection in the window fractured, just like her heart, and she knew she needed the sanctuary of the beach. At this time of night, it would be deserted.

She walked aimlessly onto the dunes toward Four Mile. There was no hurry; self-pity was a leisurely activity. The events of her day, her life, flashed through her mind, keeping her company.

An unworthy man had asked her at the ripe old age of twenty-five to marry him, and she'd accepted because he'd asked. All she wanted was to be the apple of someone's eye, the centrepiece. That episode had dented her heart, and now it had happened again. And what she'd felt for Nick was pathetic compared to her love for Quinn Everard. It was the difference between being strapped into a wheelchair in the rain or walking on the beach on a sunny day.

It was a bad night for the men in her life, she thought bitterly. A long-lost father who'd never acknowledged or contacted her had finally appeared, only to tell her he was dying. Her cherished benefactor had cruelly betrayed her and her memories of him would be tarnished forever. And the man she'd fallen heart and soul in love with had not uttered a single truth since the day they'd met.

The waves soothed her, as always. The beach was her friend. She knew every palm, every half-buried log, every crevice in the iron-grey sand.

Pushing Quinn from her thoughts, she cajoled her brain to accept and get used to two words. My father. My father, the governor-general. My father who is dying. The man whose nonexistence had shaped the way she felt about herself.

Which was, for the most part, not good enough.

But her feelings of inadequacy weren't his fault. Had she not had every advantage in life? She hadn't grown up on the streets like the kids that Quinn and his parents took in. She'd enjoyed a luxurious home, the best schools. Hell, she hadn't even had to raise the money to start her own business. Howard had handed it to her on a plate.

A pretty stone winked up at her in the moonlight. With her booted foot, she kicked it and watched as it skittered away in a satisfying arc. Okay, she had reason to be angry and hurt that everyone had lied. Her mother.

Howard. Her father. Quinn. But she could snack on self-pity till the cows came home. It was still a meager meal.

Her father's sad face swam in front of her eyes. How could she not even have given him a chance to explain? How long did he have left? Twenty-seven years and it all came down to this, compressed into a bitter pill of recrimination.

Oh God, what if the upset tonight had triggered a turn for the worse? Dani quickened her step, suddenly not aimless anymore. She couldn't turn her back on him, not when she didn't know him. Not when he was the one person she had missed all her life.

She was at the halfway point between town and Four Mile, another twenty minutes to either, if she ran. What if she was too late? Her breath came in gasps as she broke into a jog. She was so immersed in her prayers and panic, she didn't even hear the motorbike until it was nearly on top of her.

"Dani! Get on!"

What on earth? Quinn, tux and all on a filthy, mud-streaked dirt bike.

"Stop, damn you!"

Dani stopped, her chest heaving with exertion and amazement. He ripped off his helmet and thrust it out to her, his mouth a grim line.

She hadn't even begun thinking about Quinn, where he fit in her life now.

"Get on," he repeated urgently. "He's been rushed to Cairns Base Hospital."

With a cry of dismay, she shoved the helmet over her

curls and clambered awkwardly onto the back of the bike. She wrapped her arms around him as they gathered speed, squeezed her eyes shut and prayed for all she was worth.

Less than an hour later, they screeched to a halt at the entrance to the hospital.

"Go. I'll meet you in there."

Chilled to the bone by cold and worry, she rushed to find her father.

To her intense relief, Sir John had suffered a mild respiratory attack due to excess fluid on his lungs, a common symptom of advanced lung cancer, she learned. He was awake and fairly comfortable and would be kept overnight for observation, but would be discharged in the morning.

Dani spent the next hour sitting beside him, her hand covering his. He gazed at her, unable to speak because of the oxygen mask, but he turned his hand up and squeezed hers and even smiled once. His wife sat opposite and told them both that he must take the next few days away from official duties to spend some time with his daughter.

It was after 3:00 a.m. when Dani left the emergency unit. She was exhausted, rumpled and grimy and had no idea where she was going to spend the night. She certainly didn't expect Quinn to be sitting in the waiting room.

Despite everything, her heart warmed at the sight of him, his tuxedo crumpled, black hair standing on end. A far cry from the sophisticate who'd escorted her up the red carpet earlier in the evening.

That seemed a lifetime ago, so much had happened. So much had changed.

"How is he?" His eyes were rimmed with weariness and worry.

"Resting. They're keeping him in overnight, but he can go back to the hotel tomorrow."

"To the hotel?" He looked surprised. "Not home?"

"They've decided to stick around Port for a few days." She sat down, leaving a couple of seats between them.

"I see." He looked glad for her. "Is that good?" His head lowered and tilted, his eyes turned up under his brows.

Dani gave a tired smile and nodded. "That's good."

She took a deep breath and repeated the words in her mind. It was good. She had a lot of lost time to make up for. So did her father, and she was going to make sure he did.

"Can you explain how you came to be riding a motorbike on Four Mile Beach in the middle of the night?"

Quinn scrubbed at the dark shadow chasing his jaw line. "I initially thought you'd be at the shop, but then I remembered the beach."

He'd remembered. Her special place. "And the bike?"

His hand moved to his hair as he tried to repair the damage an hour of speeding on a motorbike in cool, damp air had inflicted. "An interesting sequence of events involving four boys messing about on the beach, my Rolex, a few bucks and a few choice threats." His mouth quirked. "Not to mention the possibility of being arrested at any minute."

Dani laughed shakily. "My hero."

My hero, the liar. Her smile faded.

So did his. "I thought you'd never forgive yourself if…" He nodded toward the emergency unit.

"That's why I started running," she murmured. "On the beach." She paused. "Thank you." It sounded wholly inadequate, but Dani didn't know what else to say.

There was an awkward silence. She rubbed her arms briskly, grateful again for her jacket and boots. Imagine the bike ride in her organza dress.

"Dani," he said softly, his eyes tormented. "I'm so sorry I hurt you like that."

She looked away. Did she want to hear it? Could she trust him, after all the lies he'd told? His were pretty big lies, after all. Not "You look lovely" or "Of course I didn't forget your birthday…" His lies involved blackmail, enticement, shady business goings-on, concealing a father.

But after all the crying and all the emotions of the evening, her anger had drained away.

Her sadness had not. "I know why you did it," she began. "You couldn't give your wife her dying wish. This was another chance."

"A chance to even the score," he mused. "You might be right. I figured I had the time to make it up to you. Your father is nearly out of time."

To make it up to her? He was asking a lot. "We've established that you're a loyal friend, then. Maybe not such a loyal lover."

Pain darkened his eyes even more. "I think I can be. It's not love for Laura that has stopped me falling in love these past few years. I didn't need it and I didn't miss it. I lived well, travelled incessantly, made a lot of money." He shifted forward in his seat, exhaling noisily. "I thought I was happy. Being alone, pleasing myself. I thought I had it all together. But you…"

"I what?" Her pulse skipped, but then, being in the same country as Quinn Everard made her pulse skip. Was he saying he wanted her, that it wasn't over?

"I won't lose you," he said fiercely, grasping her hands, "not when you've turned my life upside down."

She gently pried her hands loose and twisted them in her lap. A great wave of emotion and exhaustion blocked her ability to make sense of anything. Lord, it had been a long day, but she needed to focus. Did he mean he wanted to change his life for her? That he was interested in a relationship?

There was movement in the corner of her eye. Quinn Everard sat two feet away, fidgeting. The great negotiator who had calmly tossed away fifteen million English pounds on a painting, without so much as a muscle twitch, was fidgeting.

"You said you loved me," he muttered through clenched teeth.

"Did I?" Yes, she remembered, at the reception before storming out. "I also said I hated you."

"I wasn't looking for this, but then I found you." He turned to face her and grasped her wrists again before she could snatch them away. "You found me. I love you, Dani. I didn't want to, I tried not to, but I do."

Her head jerked up, but somehow she kept her hands calmly, quietly in his. "You—you love me?" She searched his face for guilt or pity.

Quinn sighed gustily. "Dani, you're smart, funny, vibrant. You're bloody frustrating and incredibly talented. I think about you every second, and when I'm not with you, I miss you, your smile and your colour." He spoke quickly, urgently. "You're the only person in more years than I care to think about who's made me feel this way." He lifted and shook her hands gently. "The only person who's *ever* made me feel this way."

"Oh." Her tongue seemed to be stuck to the roof of her mouth. Light-headed with surprise and excitement and love, she swayed drunkenly, hoping she wasn't about to pass out. The light in his eyes made her dizzy with hope but still afraid to believe what she saw in them. Afraid to trust in the love that shone out.

Quinn leaned forward and brushed her cheek with his thumb, and she realised she was crying. "Can you forgive me, sweetheart? I'll gladly spend the rest of my life making it up to you."

She dug her nails into his palms as joy swelled inside. Could it be true that everything she'd ever wanted was within her grasp?

And he was everything she'd ever wanted. Sexy as hell and well-respected everywhere. Loyal and warm toward those he loved. Encouraging and motivated about her work. She'd loved him, probably since the moment she set eyes on him, but definitely since Sydney. "I fell in love with you in Sydney," she blurted, finishing on a big sniff.

"I wanted you to come to my place, meet my people and see where we went from there. But I don't think I actually accepted it as love until the other night when I broke a promise to Jake. And then, when I saw the necklace…"

He shifted over to the seat between them and enfolded her in his arms. "You're dead on your feet."

Dani sniffed again, rubbing her wet face on his lapel. "How are we going to do this?" she whimpered. "You live down there. You travel all the time…."

His mouth moved on her hair and he tightened his grip. "I have a plan. Half the year up here—the cooler half, if you don't mind—and the other in Sydney. Steve runs the shop and when we're up here in Port, you design." He pulled back and tipped her face up, looking down at her sternly. "Then we go all out to promote you in Sydney, Dani. The whole works, launches, publicity, celebrity photo shoots. It's time to stop running, to show everyone what you're made of."

"Okay," she said cautiously. "But what about your business?"

Quinn shrugged. "That's what staff are for. I'll cut back on the travel, except for those trips where you can come, too, and tout your stuff in the big centres."

She closed her eyes, leaning into his warmth, so tired yet awash with exhilaration.

With Quinn beside her, she would never be afraid of success or failure again. She would reach for the stars, stamp number one on everything she touched. He would continually push her to be the best, and that's what she wanted, more than anything else.

Dani's heart burst with joy, even as she felt her eyes drifting closed. She came first for him; she was his precious jewel. Her father wanted her around for the limited time he had left. Her cousins would hopefully forge new bonds through the younger generation. Love and family, and all in such a short time.

She belonged.

* * * * *